# THE YEAR'S BEST

## MYSTERY AND SUSPENSE STORIES

### 1990

## Other Books by Edward D. Hoch

# THE YEAR'S BEST
# MYSTERY AND SUSPENSE STORIES

## 1990

### Edited by Edward D. Hoch

## WALKER AND COMPANY
### NEW YORK

*Again for Patricia,*
*as we start a new decade*

First published in the United States of America in 1990
by Walker Publishing Company, Inc.

Published simultaneously in Canada by Thomas Allen & Son
Canada, Limited, Markham, Ontario

Library of Congress Cataloging-in-Publication Card Number
83-646567

Printed in the United States of America

2 4 6 8 10 9 7 5 3 1

# CONTENTS

# Acknowledgments

# Introduction

The wonder of 1989 was that mystery short stories continued to flourish, despite the presence of only two nationally distributed magazines to publish them. *Ellery Queen's Mystery Magazine* and *Alfred Hitchcock's Mystery Magazine,* publishing between them about twenty new stories each month, appeared on the surface to be just about the only markets remaining for writers. True, there were still weekly short-shorts in *Woman's World,* and magazines like *Playboy* and *Woman's Day* were still willing to publish name writers like Donald E. Westlake and Mary Higgins Clark. But more and more writers found themselves seeking publication in anthologies of original stories.

These anthologies, published on a one-time basis or as part of an annual series, became increasingly important to both mystery readers and writers during 1989. A look at the list of forty anthologies, which appears in the bibliography at the back of this book, shows that no fewer than ten titles contained all new stories while another six had a majority of new stories. A very rough count would indicate that the mystery magazines published about 255 new stories in 1989 while anthologies here and in England published about 225 new stories.

The main benefactors from the rise of the original mystery anthology have been women writers. While a mystery magazine could not be expected to devote an entire issue to women, 1989 saw the publication of no fewer than five anthologies devoted solely to women writers, most of them with new stories. Chief among these was *Sisters in Crime,* edited by Marilyn Wallace. With its second volume already scheduled for early 1990, this could well turn into an annual event. (Let it be noted that the first mystery anthology devoted entirely to women writers was the 1959 Mystery Writers of America volume, *The Lethal Sex,* published by Dell. It was edited by a male, John D. MacDonald.) Further evidence of the new vigor of women writers may be found in the present volume where, for the first time, half of the fourteen contributors are women.

With so many fine stories from which to choose this year, I

was unable to find space for one of my own contributions. I can only hope the trend toward better stories continues into the new decade.

As always I wish to thank all those who helped with various aspects of this book, especially Joan Hess, Douglas G. Greene, Bill Pronzini, Eleanor Sullivan, and my wife Patricia, to whom this volume is dedicated.

*Edward D. Hoch*

# JACK ADRIAN

# THE PHANTOM PISTOL

*The British writer Jack Adrian has come to be recognized as an authority on the lengthy series of "Sexton Blake" and Edgar Wallace books, as well as on such thriller heroes as Sapper's Bulldog Drummond and Dornford Yates's Barry & Company. Happily for us, he's also an expert on impossible crime stories and is currently editing an anthology, which will be appearing soon. This story, set in the atmospheric London of 1912, deals with the murder of a famous magician in full view of his theater audience. One may read it for its humor (and for mention of one or two familiar names along the way), or for the baffling puzzle and its satisfactory solution, or even for the presence of a master sleuth referred to only as Mr. H. For any and all of these reasons, it's an enjoyable tale.*

On this chill November night fog rolled up from the River Thames, a shifting, eddying blanket that insinuated itself inexorably through the grimy streets of central London. It pulsed like a living thing, moved by its own remorseless momentum—for there was no wind—great banks of it surging across the metropolis, soot and smoke from a hundred thousand chimneys adding to its murk. Within an hour from the moment the faint tendrils of a river mist had heralded its approach, the fog, like a dirty-ochre shroud, had entombed the city.

Here, in the heart of the metropolis, in High Holborn, the rattle of hansom cab wheels, the raucous coughs of the newfangled petrol-driven taxis, were muffled, the rumble of the crawling traffic stifled as it edged and lurched its way along, the dim yellow light of street lamps serving to obscure rather than illuminate. On the pavements, slick with slimy dew, hunched figures, only dimly discerned, almost wraithlike, groped and shuffled along through the gloom, an army of the newly blind, snuffling and hawking at the harsh, choking reek of soot and coalsmoke.

Yet only fifty yards away from the main thoroughfare, down a narrow side street that had not changed appreciably since Dr. Johnson's day, sodium flares fizzed and roared, powerful electric globes thrust back the muddy haze. For only a few feet, to be sure, yet enough to reveal the tarnished gilt portico of the Empire Palace of Varieties, a large poster outside announcing in bold scarlet lettering, two inches high, that here, and only here, were to be witnessed the dazzling deeds of the Great Golconda—illusionist *extraordinaire!*

Inside the theatre the atmosphere was just as miasmal, but here the fog was a blend of pungent penny cigars and the richer reeks of Larangas, Partagas, Corona-Coronas, and Hoyos de Monterrey, for the astonishing variety and ingenuity of the Great Golconda's baffling feats of prestidigitation fascinated the rich as well as the poor.

The Great Golconda was something of a democrat. He had consistently refused to perform in the gilded palaces that lined the Haymarket and Shaftesbury Avenue, preferring the smaller halls of the outer circuit. Thus whenever and wherever he appeared, rich men, dukes, earls, high-born ladies, and even (it was whispered) members of the Royal Family were forced to make the unaccustomed trek away from the gilt and glitter of London's West End to less salubrious haunts, there to mix with the lower orders—not to mention enjoy the unusual experience of paying half the price for twice the amount of entertainment. For certainly the Great Golconda was a magician and illusionist of quite extraordinary ability. It was even rumored that emissaries of Maskelyne and Devant—whose fame as illusionists was spread worldwide—had endeavored to lure his secrets away with fabulous amounts of money and, when these offers were spurned, had even gone so far as to try for them by less scrupulous methods.

Whether or not this was true, the Great Golconda stubbornly performed on the stages of the tattier music halls, and all kinds and conditions and classes of men and women flocked to see him, and to cheer him.

But tonight was a special night. The Great Golconda was retiring from the stage. This was to be positively his final performance.

Unusually, the act started the show. Normally, the Great Golconda and his assistant Mephisto came on for the last half hour of the first house and the last half hour of the second. As an act, nothing could follow it.

Tonight, however, the audience—restless at the thought of having to sit through the somewhat dubious hors d'oeuvres of jugglers, low comedians, soubrettes, and "Come-into-the-garden-Maud" baritones before getting down to the main course—sat up in eager anticipation as the curtain rose at last to reveal a totally bare stage with a black backcloth, from the center of which stared two enormous eyes woven in green and gold.

For several seconds there was utter silence, a total absence of movement—on the stage and off. Then the lights dimmed and the glowing figure of the Great Golconda himself could be seen—in black silk hat, long flowing cloak, arms folded across his chest—descending slowly from the darkness above the stage, apparently floating on air. Simultaneously, two more Golcondas, dressed exactly alike, marched towards the center of the stage from both left and right wings. Just before they met, there was a flash of white light, a loud bang, a puff of red smoke, and all three figures seemed to merge.

And there, standing alone, smiling a mite maliciously, stood the Great Golconda. The audience roared.

From then on, for the next twenty minutes, wonders did not cease.

White horses cantered across the boards, to disappear in a dazzling firework display; doves, peacocks, birds-of-paradise soared and strutted, all, seemingly, appearing from a small Chinese lacquered cabinet on a rostrum; a girl in sequinned tights pirouetted in midair, had her head sawn off by the Great Golconda's assistant Mephisto, then, carrying her head beneath her arm, climbed a length of rope and slowly vanished, like the smile of the Cheshire Cat, about thirty feet above the ground.

Part of the performance was what appeared to be a running battle between the Great Golconda and his assistant Mephisto. Mephisto made it plain he wanted to do things his way but invariably, like the sorcerer's apprentice, failed, the Great Golconda smoothly but sensationally saving the trick—whatever trick it happened to be—at the very last moment. Penultimately, Mephisto became so incensed at the Great Golconda's successes that he knocked him down, crammed and locked him into a four-foot-high oak sherry cask, and then proceeded to batter and smash it to pieces with a long-handled axe.

Triumphantly, he turned to the audience, his chalk-white, clownlike face (its pallor accentuated by the skin-tight black costume he wore, leaving only his face, neck, and arms below the elbows bare) leering malevolently—to be greeted by gales of laughter as the Great Golconda himself suddenly appeared from the wings behind him to tap him on the shoulder.

At last the stage was cleared for the final act. Mephisto was to fire a revolver at the Great Golconda, who would catch the bullet between his teeth.

Members of the audience were invited up to the front of the stage to examine the .45 service revolver and six bullets and vouch for their authenticity. Among them was a stocky, moustachioed man in his late forties, in frock coat and bowler hat, who clearly, from the professional way he handled the gun—flicking open the chamber, extracting the bullets, testing them between his teeth—had more than a little knowledge of firearms. The Great Golconda noticed this.

"You sir!"

The stocky figure acknowledged this with an abrupt nod.

"You seem to know your way about a pistol, sir."

"I should do," admitted the man.

"May I enquire of your profession, sir?"

"You may. I'm a superintendent at Scotland Yard."

The Great Golconda was clearly delighted. Seen close up he was younger than the Scotland Yard man had supposed—perhaps in his mid-thirties. Something else he noted was the distinct resemblance between the Great Golconda and his assistant Mephisto, now standing to one side, his pasty white face impassive.

"And your name, sir?"

"Hopkins. Stanley Hopkins."

The Great Golconda bowed.

"A name that is not unknown to me from the newssheets, sir. Indeed, a name to be—ha-ha!—*conjured* with! And what is your professional opinion of the revolver, Superintendent?"

Still holding the bullets, Hopkins dry-fired the gun. The hammer fell with a loud 'click,' the chamber snapped round.

"Perfectly genuine."

"Pree-*cisely!*"

With a flourish of his cape, the Great Golconda handed the revolver to his assistant Mephisto and ushered the half dozen or so members of the audience off the stage.

The lights dimmed. Twin spots bathed the two men in two separate cones of light. They stood at the rear of the stage, against the black backcloth, about ten yards apart. All around them was utter darkness. From his seat Hopkins watched intently.

Mephisto, wearing black gloves now and holding the gun two-handed, raised his arms slowly into the air, high above his head. Hopkins, following the movement could only just see the revolver, which was now above the circle of radiance surrounding Mephisto—then light glittered along the barrel as the assistant brought his hands back into the spotlight's glare and down, his arms held straight out. The revolver pointed directly at the Great Golconda.

It seemed to Hopkins that the Great Golconda's expression—up until then one of supercilious amusement—suddenly slipped. A look of mild puzzlement appeared on his face.

Hopkins glanced at the right-hand side of the stage but could see nothing but darkness. At that moment there was the oddly muted crack of a shot, and Hopkins, his eyes already turning back to the Great Golconda, saw the illusionist cry out and throw up his arms, then fall to the floor.

There was a stunned silence.

Even from where he was sitting, the Scotland Yard man could see plainly that around the Great Golconda's mouth were scarlet splashes, where none had been before.

Then the screaming started.

Mr. Robert Adey, the manager of the Empire Music Hall, looked as though he was on the verge of an apoplexy. His face was red, his mouth gaped, his mutton-chop whiskers quivered with emotion.

He stuttered, "It . . . it *couldn't* have happened!"

"But it did," Superintendent Stanley Hopkins said bluntly.

They were on the stage of the now-empty theatre. Even with all the stagelights up and the crystal chandeliers blazing over the auditorium, there was a desolate air about the place; shadows still gathered thickly in the wings, and above, beams and struts and spars could only just be glimpsed.

Since the shocking death of the Great Golconda—whose body now lay under a rug where it had fallen—nearly an hour had elapsed. During that time an extraordinary fact had emerged: although the Great Golconda had been shot, his assistant Mephisto (now detained in his dressing room) could not have shot him. Of that, there seemed not a doubt.

And yet neither could anyone else.

Adey—with a slight West Midlands twang to his voice—gabbled, "It . . . it's utterly inexplicable!"

"This is 1912," said a sharp voice beind him. "*Nothing* is inexplicable."

Adey turned. The man who had spoken—a tall, thin, almost gaunt individual of sixty or so, with a high forehead, dark hair shot with gray, an aquiline nose, and eyes that seemed to pierce and probe and dissect all that they looked upon—had accompanied Hopkins up to the stage when the theatre had been cleared. Adey had no idea who he was.

"A colleague?" he muttered to the Scotland Yard man.

"Just a friend," said Hopkins, "a very old friend. We're both interested in the impossible—why we're here tonight. The Great Golconda's illusions had certain . . ." he glanced at his friend ". . . points of interest."

"Although many, I fancy, were accomplished with the aid of certain kinematic devices," said the older man. "The girl in the sequinned tights, for example—a lifelike image only, I take it."

Adey nodded uneasily.

"Of course, I know very little about how he managed his tricks. Magicians are a close-mouthed bunch. This one in particular. He was adamant that during his act both wings should be blocked off, so no one—not even the stagehands—could see what he was doing. Always worried people were trying to pinch his tricks. Of course, he had to have some assistance in erecting certain items on stage, but all the preliminary construction work was done by him and his brother."

"Mephisto," said Hopkins.

"Yes. Their real name was Forbes-Sempill. Golconda was Rupert, Mephisto Ernest. They were twins—not identical. Rupert was the elder by fifteen minutes. . . ." Adey's voice sank to a worried mumble. "That was half the trouble."

"The reason why the Great Golconda was retiring from the stage?" said the gaunt man. "The baronetcy, and the 200,000 pounds?"

Adey stared at him, open-mouthed.

"How the devil did you know that?"

"Ah," Hopkins said waggishly, "my friend here keeps his finger on the pulse of great events—don't you, Mr. H?"

The older man permitted himself a thin smile.

"Now *you* tell us about the baronetcy, and all them sovs," said the Scotland Yard detective.

Adey shrugged his shoulders.

"Both Rupert and Ernest had a row with their family years ago. Left the ancestral home—somewhere in Scotland, I believe—never," he smiled faintly, "to darken its doors again. But their father's recently died, and Rupert succeeded to the title, estates, and money. It's as simple as that, although it wasn't generally known."

"I take it," said the gaunt old man, "that Ernest disliked his brother?"

"Ernest *hated* Rupert. Made no secret of the fact. One of the reasons their act went down so well—Ernest communicated that hatred to the audience. Rupert didn't object. Said it added spice to the performance. I don't see it myself, but it seemed to work."

"Doubtless the new Viennese school of mind analysis could explain that," said the older man dryly, "but for the time being I am far more interested in why Mephisto should for no apparent reason have donned black gloves to fire his revolver tonight."

"So he did," said Adey, in a surprised tone. "But how . . . ?"

"This is not the first time we have seen the Great Golconda perform. As Mr. Hopkins implied, his act was an unusual one, and I have always had an interest in the more sensational aspects of popular culture." The gaunt old man's eyes took on a faraway, introspective look. "On previous occasions Mephisto fired his revolver bare-handed. That he did not this time seems to me to be a matter of some significance."

"But the *weapon,* Mr. H.!" said Hopkins, almost violently. "We now know what ought to have happened. The real revolver is shown to the audience. It's stone-cold genuine. But when Golconda hands the gun to Mephisto—flourishing his cloak and all—he's already substituted it for another gun—one that only fires blank shots. The real gun is now hidden in his cloak. Mephisto fires the fake gun at him and he pretends to catch the bullet, which is already in his mouth, between his teeth. Simple!"

"Except that this time he falls dead with a bullet in his head."

"*From a phantom pistol!*" exploded Hopkins. "The gun Mephisto held in his hands didn't fire that bullet—*couldn't* fire that bullet! The real gun was still in the folds of the Great Golconda's cloak—so that's out, too! He wasn't killed by someone firing from the wings, because the wings were blocked off! Nor through the backcloth, because there ain't no hole! Nor from above or from the audience, because the bullet went into his head in a straight line through his mouth!"

Here Adey broke in excitedly.

"It's as I said—inexplicable! Indeed, downright *impossible!*"

The gaunt old man shot him a darkly amused look.

"In my experience, Mr. Adey, the more bizarre and impossible the occurrence, the less mysterious it will in the end prove to be."

"That's all very well, sir," said the manager a mite snappishly, "but facts are facts! The entire audience was watching Mephisto. When Golconda fell dead, all Mephisto did was drop the revolver he was holding and stand there gaping. Let's say for the sake of argument he had another weapon. What did he do with it? Damm it, sir, he didn't move an inch from where he was standing, nor did he make any violent gesture, as though to throw it away from him. We've searched the entire stage. We've even searched him—not that that was at all necessary because his costume's so skin-tight you couldn't hide a button on him without it bulging."

"Perhaps," said the older man slowly, "he didn't need to throw it away."

"Didn't need?" Adey's voice rose to an outraged squeak. "You'll be telling me next he popped it into his mouth and ate it!"

"By no means as outrageous a suggestion as you might imagine," said the gaunt old man sternly. He turned to the Scotland Yard detective. "You will recall, Hopkins, the case of the abominable Italian vendettist, Pronzini, who did just that."

Hopkins nodded sagely. The older man began to pace up and down the stage, gazing at the sable backcloth.

"Notice how black it is," he murmured, gesturing at the curtain. "How very black . . ." He swung around on Adey again. "Apart from the incident of the gloves, is there anything else to which you might wish to draw our attention?"

"Anything else?"

"Anything unusual."

Adey's honest face assumed a perplexed expression.

"Well . . . no, I don't believe so."

"The placing of the Great Golconda's act, for example?"

"Oh. Why, yes! Right at the beginning, you mean? That was unusual. They did have a bit of a barney about that. It was Mephisto's idea—begin the show and end it, he said. Golconda finally agreed."

"Nothing else?"

"Not that I can . . ."

"I noticed that tonight they both stood at the rear of the stage. Did they not normally stand at the front?"

"Well, yes. Now you come to . . ."

"You will forgive my saying so, Mr. Adey," there was a touch of asperity in the old man's voice, "but your powers of observation are somewhat limited."

"You believe Mephisto killed Golconda?" said Hopkins.

"I am convinced of it."

"Then we'd better have a chat with him."

The older man smiled frostily.

"That will not be necessary. You have a stepladder?" he enquired of Adey. "Bring it on."

"Stepladder?" muttered Hopkins. "You think there's something up top?"

"Of course, There has to be. A second gun. Golconda was killed by a bullet. Bullets, for the most part, are shot from guns. Golconda's revolver was incapable of shooting anything, only of making a noise. Thus . . ."

The Scotland Yard man interrupted. "Ah. But. Wait on, Mr. H. These two were masters of illusion, am I correct?"

"Certainly."

"But when you get right down to it, their illusions, like all illusions, are fake. Created. Constructed."

"To be sure."

"So this here Mephisto needn't have used a gun at all. He was a clever fellow. Could've built some kind of weapon that fired a bullet, and . . ." He stopped as a thought struck him. "Here, remember the to-do you once had with that tiger-potting colonel. Now *he* had a special shooter."

"Indeed, an air-gun constructed by a German mechanic, who, though blind, had a genius for invention." The old man smiled a skeletal smile. "But you miss the point entirely, my dear Hopkins. It matters not *what* the weapon is, but *where* it is. That is the nub of the problem. We have searched everywhere, eliminated everything, on this level. As we must inevitably strike out from our enquiry any suggestion of magic, the inexorable conclusion we must come to is that the weapon— whatever it is—must be above us."

Hopkins struck the palm of his hand with a clenched fist. "But it can't be! Mephisto stood stock-still the whole time. We *know* he didn't chuck anything into the air."

"As I remarked before, perhaps he did not need to. . . ."

By this time the heavy wheeled ladder had been trundled on and heaved to the center of the stage. A stagehand climbed into the darkness above.

"Merely look for anything that seems out of the ordinary," the old man directed.

In less than a minute the stagehand was calling out excitedly.

"Something here . . . wound round one of the spars on—why, it's elasticated cord!"

"Unwind it. Let it drop."

Seconds later a small object fell through the air, then bounced upwards again as the cord reached its nadir. The old man stretched up and caught it before it could fly out of reach. He turned to the watchers.

"What do you see?"

Hopkins frowned.

"Not a thing."

The old man opened his fingers.

"Come closer."

The Scotland Yard detective stepped forward, his expression turning to one of amazement. Gripped in the gaunt old man's hand—clearly seen against the white of his skin—was a miniature chamberless pistol, perhaps five inches long from grip to muzzle, painted entirely matt-black. The old man pressed at the bottom of the stock and the barrel slid forward, revealing a two-inch cavity.

"A Williamson derringer pistol, capable of firing one shot only—quite enough to kill a man," said the old man dryly. "Hand me the false pistol."

He held the blank-firing pistol in his left hand with the derringer gripped in his right, leveling both at an imaginary target. From the side all that could be seen was the massive bulk of the service revolver. Then he clicked the triggers of both guns and opened his right hand. The derringer, at the end of the taunt elasticated cord—totally invisible against the black backcloth—flew upwards into the darkness above, whipping round and round the high spar to which it was attached.

Adey looked utterly at sea.

"But how did you . . . what made you . . . ?" he babbled.

"When three singular variations in a set routine—the black gloves, the change of position not only of the act itself but of the two principals on the stage in that act—take place," said the old man a trifle testily, "one is tempted, to use the vernacular, to smell a rat. After that, it is a matter of simple deduction. The gift of observation—sadly lacking in the general populace—allied to intuition. Believe me, there is really no combination of events—however inexplicable on the surface—for which the wit of man cannot conceive an elucidation."

He began to pace up and down the stage again, his hands clasped firmly behind his back.

"Mephisto tied the derringer to the spar, letting it hang down just within reach of his outstretched arm. It could not be seen because he had painted it black and hung it close to the black curtain. In any case, the lighting was subdued. Even so, there was the risk of someone spotting it, so he persuaded his brother that their act should start the show. Came the climax of the performance. The two spotlights only lit up the area within their twin beams. Mephisto raised his arms, holding the false revolver, until his hands were just above the spotlight's glare. He has positioned himself perfectly—no doubt he rehearsed the entire sequence thoroughly—and the hanging derringer was now within inches of his right hand. If his hands had been bare, one might possibly have noticed that he was holding something else, but he took the precaution of wearing black gloves, thereby making assurance double sure. Grasping the derringer, he pulled it down on its elasticated thread, pressing it to the side of the much larger weapon, as his arms dropped to the leveled-off position. He was now holding not one, but *two* guns—one hidden from the audience's view and in any case virtually invisible. Except to the man at whom he was pointing them."

"Yes!" snapped Hopkins. "That's what made Golconda look surprised. I thought he'd seen something *behind* Mephisto."

"Mephisto then fired the derringer, releasing his grip on the gun, which shot up into the air. All eyes were on Golconda falling to the floor. The derringer wound itself round the spar to which its cord was attached. In the confusion afterwards, doubtless, Mephisto meant to get rid of the evidence. What he did not reckon on was the presence of a Scotland Yard detective who would immediately take charge of the proceedings and confine him to his dressing room. But in the meantime there was absolutely nothing to show that he had just murdered his brother in cold blood. It was as though," the old man finished, shrugging, "the Great Golconda had indeed been shot with a phantom pistol."

"And being next in line," said Hopkins, "Mephisto would've stepped into the baronetcy and all them lovely golden sovs. Nice work, Mr. H. Nice work, indeed!"

# DOUG ALLYN

## STAR PUPIL

*Doug Allyn, author of several excellent short stories over the past five years, will have published his first novel by the time you read this. The third winner of the Robert L. Fish Memorial Award for promising new writers, Allyn has produced stories of both detection and suspense, with a wide variety of backgrounds. Perhaps none has been so powerful as this tale of a teacher of convicts in a prison school. It was second in the voting for this year's EQMM Readers Award.*

"**P**assion," I said quietly, "is the source of true literary power. Your own feelings, honestly described, can transform the simplest story into prose with tremendous emotional impact. It can give your writing—" I hesitated. Someone was sobbing at the back of the classroom. An oversized Chicano kid, twentyish, clad in faded dungarees like the rest of them, tears streaming down his stubbled cheeks. A new student this term. Martinez? Something like that.

"It can give your work value," I continued, "even before your writing skills develop. If you can express your emotions clearly, you can—" Some of the students in the front row were getting edgy, shifting around to see what the fuss was about. I decided to press on, to give the guy a chance to pull himself together rather than embarrass him by halting the class.

"Passion," I began again—It wasn't going to work. Martinez was blubbering openly now, and the other students were grinning and nudging each other, most of them eyeing me in open speculation as to how I'd handle the situation. Jailhouse games. The clock above the door showed twenty minutes left in the period, and since all penal-institution classes must begin and end exactly on time I couldn't even dismiss early. Terrific.

I glanced a wordless plea at Indio Zamora, top dog of the

Gusanos, the largest Chicano gang here at WaCoCo, the Wayne County Correctional Facility. Indio met my gaze for a moment, his dark eyes unreadable, then nodded a barely perceptible acknowledgement and glanced at Segundo, his second in command. A look, nothing more. Segundo, a slope-shouldered Neanderthal with his hair tied back in a ratty ponytail, slid out of his seat and shambled to the rear of the room. He bent down, murmured something in Martinez's ear. And the kid stopped crying, Instantly.

Segundo eased down beside him at the rear table and rested a blunt-fingered paw on Martinez's shoulder—for comfort or as a threat, I couldn't tell. But Martinez stayed stone-silent through the rest of my lecture.

In the six-odd months I'd been teaching creative writing at the prison, I'd seen this kind of thing before—a whisper here, a look there as effective as the crack of a whip. Detroit's street gangs are active in WaCoCo, and a boss con like Indio Zamora can have the power of life and death over other inmates. Still, as a writer, I've often wondered exactly what the men *say* at such times. Is the force in the message? Or the messenger?

The discussion period at the end of class was the usual stew of abysmal ignorance and surprisingly sharp insights. When I took this job, I frankly expected to be teaching illiterate semimorons, but though most of the cons are language-deficient and ill-educated, I'd guess the I.Q. levels in my prison class aren't much lower than the Detroit City College classes I teach the rest of the week. And a few of my student convicts, like Indio Zamora, or Ahmad Clark, enforcer for the Black Pharaohs, are intimidatingly bright, with a shrewd, feral intelligence probably superior to the best of my college students.

"Mr. Zamora," I said as the cons filed out to return to their respective cellblocks under the unblinking eyes of the corridor surveillance cameras, "can you spare a minute?"

"Sure," Indio said, "or ten years." Segundo hesitated as well, but, at Indio's nod, went out with the others. I wondered if the two men ever spoke at all, or if they simply communicated by some sort of wolf-pack ESP. Zamora sat on the edge of the front table, dark, hawk-faced, slender as a leather riding crop, his prison denims neatly pressed and tailored, a perfect fit.

"Thanks for helping out with Martinez," I said.

"No charge, Mr. Devlin," Indio shrugged. "He's one of my people and he shouldn't be cryin' in public. Bad for my image."

"Still, I appreciate it. Pity you can't help maintain order in my college classes."

"Maybe I will," he said, straightening, "sometime in the next century. That it?"

"No, that's not it," I said, annoyed. "Aren't you even curious about what my agent thought of your novel?"

"I figure if he said anything interesting, you'd let me know."

"He liked it as much as I do. In fact, he's already submitted it to a major publisher."

"And that's good?"

"Good? It's terrific. I wish he was half as enthusiastic about my work. He said to tell you your book has more commercial potential than anything he's handled in years."

"Sounds krush." Indio straightened. "So. How long will it take for anything to happen?"

"I can't be sure, but, as fired up as Rudolph was, possibly a month or so."

"Or longer?"

"Maybe longer," I admitted. "But the point is, Rudolph Herzel likes your work and he's not an easy man to impress. Damn it, Indio, you just don't realize what this means. For me to say you're talented is one thing, but for Rudolph to say so, and to give your book a special push, is quite another. It means that you can really write, that you can make a life for yourself after you get out of here."

"Or it might mean you two dudes have similar taste and the book does nothing. Look, Mr. Devlin, I know you mean well, but hope's a risky idea to buy into in the joint. You walk around with your head in the clouds, you can do a brodie down a sewer. So if your agent likes my book, that's cool, but maybe I'll wait till the check clears to start the fiesta, you know?"

"The book will sell," I said. "I may not be the world's greatest authority, but I know talent when I see it, and you have it. All you've got to worry about is what to write next."

"Wrong," Indio said evenly. "I've got a few other things to worry about, Teach, like stayin' alive and on top of the dungheap until tomorrow, and then the day after that. Be a shame if my book's a bestseller and I'm suckin' dirt in Forest Lawn, no?"

"I suppose so," I said. "Still, maybe late some night, after lights out and lockdown, you might want to think about what your life could be like as a writer. Because you're going to make it, whether you believe it or not."

"Okay, Mr. Devlin," Indio nodded, with a faint grin—the first one I'd ever seen. "Maybe I'll try thinkin' about it. Just a little, some night after lockdown. I'll see you next Thursday, And, ah, thanks. I won't forget this."

"No charge," I said. "You've earned it."

"Maybe," he said, "*pero*—" He swallowed, then turned and stalked out without a backward glance. But I was almost certain I'd caught a flicker of something in his dark eyes. Hope? I couldn't be sure. But if it was, it made all the headaches of teaching in this hellhole worth it.

I thought about Indio often during the next week, especially while reading the earnestly muddleheaded offerings of my junior college students. A few of them have potential, I suppose, the talent and the command of language necessary to become good writers, but they lack character. They simply haven't seen or done enough to develop original viewpoints. Their tales of puppy love and parental betrayal are as homogeneous as the pop/pap music they listen to. Not totally their fault. A generation ago a few literate role models still walked the earth. Who do these kids have?

And yet Indio Zamora, a young self-educated gangbanger from East Detroit, had, with minimal instruction from me, assembled a savagely honest first novel, a book so good I paid it the ultimate writer's compliment of wishing I'd written it myself.

I didn't really expect to hear more from my agent immediately—the process of selling a book can take months, or even years. Still, the following Thursday afternoon, I called Rudolph's office.

"Dev, good to hear from you," Herzel's honey-thick Georgian accent rumbled over the line. "Great minds must run in the same rut. I wrote to you today."

"Wrote to me?"

"About that student of yours, Zamora? Dee Grossman at Burke Edwards called me this morning, said she'd read the book at a single sitting, couldn't put it down. She's submitting it to the board on Wednesday, we should receive an offer by the end of the month."

"It's as good as sold and you didn't let me know?"

"I said I just dropped you a note—"

"Couldn't you have called?"

There was a silence on the line. "Yes," Rudolph said, "I suppose I could have, though it's not my usual practice—especially when there's nothing definite."

"It's just that—I think it's more important to Zamora than it would be to someone who's free."

"I see. Well, I'm sorry, Dev, but publishing is a business, and patience is one of its protocols. And if Mr. Zamora hasn't acquired that trait in his present circumstances, I doubt he ever will. How's *your* new book coming?"

"It, ah, it's coming. Slowly, and not as steadily as I'd like."

"You know I never press, Dev, but it's been a while. Are you sure you're not overextending yourself? With extra teaching, perhaps?"

"I'm all right," I snapped. "I'll work through it."

Despite the guff I'd given Rudolph, I didn't tell Indio the news before class that night. Instead, I glanced at him from time to time as I lectured, hoping to see some hint of anticipation or curiosity. Nothing. If anything, he was even less animated than usual, present in body only. I couldn't understand it. When my first novel was under consideration I hovered around my mailbox like an expectant father, and it irritated me that Indio seemed so disinterested. I was tempted not to tell him at all, to simply wait until he asked, but if we were having a war of nerves, I surrendered, and asked him to stay a moment after class.

"I talked to my agent today," I said. "He expects you're going to get an offer on it soon."

He stared at me blankly. "How soon?"

"I'm not sure—possibley by the end of the month. The point is—"

"It doesn't matter. I won't be here."

"Why not? Where are you going?"

"To hell, probably," he said evenly. "Unless writin' a book balances out the cutting I'm doin' time for."

"What are you talking about?"

"About hope, and how it can mess up your head in the joint. Remember what you said last week about doing some thinking after lights out? About how selling the book could maybe make a difference in my life? Well, I did think about it, and I decided you were right. And I took a shot at changing things." He hesitated, glancing uneasily at the open door, walked over, checked the corridor, then closed the door and leaned back against it. "Look at me," he said. "How much do you figure I weigh?"

"Weigh? I don't see what—"

"I weigh one seventy soakin' wet," he said. "You know what that means? It means I'm not big enough to survive in here on my own. If I'm not ganged up, I'm fresh meat for the first psycho with the hots for me."

"I still don't—"

"I'm alive because I'm a Gusano," he continued, raising his fist, showing me the worm tattoo that writhed up his right forearm from wrist to bicep. "And I'm not just some gangbanger—I'm a top dog, a boss. Not because I'm tough. Plenty of guys under me could break me in half. Segundo for one. But I'm smarter than they are, and they know it. So they follow me. And they trust me. And I hear things. Not just Gusano business, all kinds of things. I could write a book," he said dryly. "Anyway, I figured that maybe I could do just that to buy my way out. You remember a couple of months back two Feds from the Organized Crime Task Force hauled me outa class for a talk?"

I nodded. "I remember. A short conversation, as I recall."

"Had to be. Bein' around those guys is dangerous. People wonder if you're rollin' over for 'em. Thing is, they offered me a deal—give 'em enough information about the gangs and I could walk. They'd get my sentence reduced to time served if I cooperated."

"And you didn't take it?"

"No," he said. "I couldn't see givin' 'em anybody when we'd all be back on the same streets eventually. My life wouldn't be worth spit. Better to just stand up and do my time, you know? Only now I got a chance for somethin' better than bein' just another chump. So I dropped a dime to the Feds, see if the offer was still open."

"And is it?"

"Sure. The deal is, I talk, they'll fake some scam to take me outa the general population and park me in isolation while they follow up what I give 'em. If it checks out, I can be on the street in a couple of months."

"But there's a catch?"

"Sort of. There's this guard, Magruder. You know him?"

"I've seen him. Tall? Brushcut?"

"And crooked enough to screw into the ground. He wants a payoff. Five grand. Or he puts the word out about what's goin' down. And I'm a dead man."

"Can't you ask for protection?"

"No way. Even if the Feds believe me, they can't keep me alive. I'd get torched in my cell or maybe poisoned. The gangbangers'd get to me somehow. Which brings me to you."

"I thought it might," I said cautiously. "Only I didn't just get off the boat, Indio, I've been working here awhile and I've seen a few jailhouse games."

"You don't believe me?"

"It doesn't matter whether I do or not. Between my child support and car payments, I'm—"

"You didn't answer my question. Do you believe me or not?"

"I honestly don't know," I said, "but if I had any extra money do you think I'd be teaching in this place?"

Indio stared at me, frankly reading me, then shrugged. "Look at these," he said, tossing a pair of photographs on my desk.

I picked up the photos and felt a knot harden in the pit of my stomach. They were snapshots of my ex-wife and seven-year-old daughter, taken at the playground of my daughter's school. "You son of a bitch," I said softly.

"You don't understand. Look at them. When were they taken?"

I examined the photos more carefully. From the light and the clothes they were wearing—"Last fall, I suppose. September sometime. So?"

"September fourteenth," he said, "a few days after you started teaching this class. Do you know how big the Gusanos are, how many men? Maybe three hundred, maybe more. And I'm El Hombre, the main man in here. I have power. Real power. And I didn't get it by missing bets. I started looking for a handle on you the first day we met. I've had these pictures for months. I could've used 'em to pressure you anytime. But I didn't."

"Until now."

"I'm not using them now. I'm giving them to you. And putting my life in your hands. If Segundo or the others find out I'm dealing with the Feds, I won't live a week. Help me, Mr. Devlin."

"Even if I wanted to help, I don't have five—"

"Jesus, I'm not askin' you for money, Teach, I've got the damn cash! But I need to get it to Magruder, and he won't take his payoff from anybody but me. No corroborating witnesses that way. I can't use my own people to bring it in without making them wonder why I need it. You're my only chance."

"But even if I helped, you're searched before you go back to your cellblock, aren't you?"

"Yeah, but I go to work first, in the library. I can stash it there until I hook up with Magruder. Just bring it to me, is that too much to ask?"

"It wouldn't be if I believed you."

"You've read my book, Mr. Devlin, you've seen *mi corazón*— my heart. If you don't know me now, there's nothing more I can say. No hard feelin's. Maybe I'll see you around."

"Indio," I called after him. He paused in the doorway. "Look—" I swallowed hard. "What would I have to do?"

The Wayne County Legal Aid Cooperative Office was nowhere near as grand as its name. A one-story storefront with raw, graffiti-streaked plywood panels for windows on the wrong side of Montcalm Avenue, downhill Motown. The waiting room was jammed, its mismatched vinyl sofas filled with black and Hispanic street people, the air thick with the aroma of damp clothing, cigarette smoke, despair. I told the black matron at the front desk I had an appointment with Lia Alvarez and she thumbed me toward an office at the rear. I wandered down the narrow corridor, feeling pinpricks of resentment between my shoulderblades. Whitey gets waved on through. And what else is new?

Lia Alvarez glanced up at me over the rims of her half-framed reading glasses with eyes that were strikingly dark and intelligent. She was small, a pert raven in a conservative business suit. Olive skin, tightly curled, gleaming hair—not conventional cover-girl material, I suppose, and yet I found her oddly magnetic, almost familiar, though I was sure we'd never met.

"Can I help you?" she asked. Even her voice seemed familiar—husky, velvet, like Bacall's in *Key Largo*.

"I hope so," I said. "One of your clients asked me to see you. Indio Zamora?"

The room temperature chilled at least ten degrees. "Mr. Zamora is not my client," she said. "What is it you want?"

"I'm not sure," I said. "He asked me to see you—"

"You're Devlin, aren't you?" she frowned. "Thomas Devlin? The writer? *Poets and Promises?*"

"That's right," I said, surprised she recognized me.

"Indio told me he was taking a writing course from you at WaCoCo," she said. "And now you're running errands for him?"

"I'm not an errand boy, exactly," I said. "He's one of my students. I'm trying to help, that's all."

"I see." She eyed me thoughtfully. "Well, far be it from me to impede the educational process, Mr. Devlin. His *or* yours." She took a small envelope from the top desk drawer and pushed it toward me.

"What is this?"

"A key. To a locker at Metro Airport."

"The airport?"

"You seem surprised."

"Well, I guess I thought I'd just see you and—"

"Mr. Devlin, Indio Zamora is my stepbrother. He was my sole support through law school, and since I'm partly to blame for his incarceration I try to—"

And suddenly I realized why she seemed so familiar. There

was a slight family resemblance, of course, but it was far more than that. "You're Rena, aren't you?" I said.

"I beg your pardon?"

"In Indio's book, the hero has a sister who is—assaulted. He's sent to prison for avenging her. He describes you very accurately—perfectly, in fact."

"I see," she said, meeting my gaze. "Well, I suppose I should be flattered. Or something."

"It seems very odd to meet you like this. It's as though you stepped out of a story. Or a dream."

"If that's a compliment, I'll take it," she said brusquely, "but I assure you I'm quite real. And if you're wondering, the rest of it is true as well."

"I'm sorry," I said, "I didn't mean to—"

"It's all right," she said. "I've adjusted to what happened, more or less. What Indio did because of it, well, that's much harder. Because he shouldn't be in jail at all. It was a matter for the police, or maybe the Gusanos. Only Indio felt he had to handle it personally. And publicly. For the sake of my honor. Or his. I was never quite clear on that point. He's really written a book? He said he had, but with Indio—" She shrugged.

"He's not only written it, it'll probably be published within a year. Your brother has tremendous potential as a writer, Ms. Alvarez. He's the best student I've ever had."

"Indio has a great many talents—" she nodded coolly "—any one of which might have landed him where he is even if I hadn't been hurt. He also has admirable qualities, Mr. Devlin, but he's a complicated man. If I were you, I'd be a bit wary where Indio's concerned."

"And yet you're trying to help him, too," I said, picking up the envelope.

"He's my brother," she said, "he's not yours. And giving you that envelope is the extent of my involvement. Have a nice day, Mr. Devlin." She returned her attention to the papers on her desk, end of interview. I shrugged and turned away.

"Mr. Devlin?" she said as I opened the office door. "I enjoyed *Poets and Promises* very much. It's a wonderful book. When will we see your next?"

"It shouldn't be too much longer," I said. "I've been, ah, having a little trouble, but it should be finished soon."

"I hope so," she said. "I look forward to reading it."

"Thank you," I said. "So do I."

Airport security at Detroit Metropolitan is extremely tight, metal detectors, guards, the works which is probably why Indio chose it for a money drop. It's one of the few places in Motown you can carry cash without constantly looking over your shoulder.

The key Lia gave me opened a luggage locker just off the main concourse. It contained a leatherette briefcase with the K-Mart price stickers still on it. I glanced around, but no one was near, so I popped the latches on the case. A moneybelt was folded neatly inside, a cheap, pliable plastic, one-size-fits-all affair about four inches wide, with a velcro hookup and a narrow nylon zipper along half its length. I opened it and rifled through the cash to make sure it was all there, five thousand in old bills. For a moment I wondered where the money'd come from, whether Lia had dropped it off or someone else. A gang member? And it occurred to me that if I had the brains God gave a goose I'd leave the case where it was and walk away.

But somehow I couldn't. And it wasn't just my promise to a student, or that Lia Alvarez was a very interesting lady. It was pride, I suppose, pure and simple. My writing wasn't going well, and if I backed off now, would it be out of caution or because I was jealous of Indio's talent? I honestly wasn't sure. I closed the briefcase and took it with me.

Getting into the Wayne County Corrections Facility is almost as difficult as breaking out. There are three separate checkpoints at the employees' entrance to the prison, the first with a metal detector, then two more electronic gates monitored by television cameras. Cofer, the guard at the first checkpoint, seemed to sense immediately that something was wrong. He's a large man, fortyish, grey streaks in his Afro and moustache, and a pillow-sized paunch bulging at his blue uniform belt. We usually talk sports as he checks the contents of my briefcase, but he didn't respond when I asked how the Pistons were doing and he seemed to search my case with unusual thoroughness. He passed me through without comment, but by now I was sweating, and if the first electronic gate hadn't opened as I approached it I might've turned and sprinted for home. The second gate wasn't as easy. I stood facing the camera for roughly a year and a half before the damned relay clicked and the steel door slid open.

It was a lively class—good-natured banter from the students and a short story from a double-lifer that showed real promise. Still, by the end of the second hour the moneybelt around my waist weighed a hundred pounds. Or more.

After class, Indio closed the door behind Segundo, the last of the students to file out. "Mr. Devlin, you look awful." Indio grinned wryly, shaking his head. "You've got no aptitude for crime at all."

"Thanks, I think," I said, stripping the belt from under my shirt and passing it to him. "When you get your first publisher's advance, you owe me a steak dinner."

"I owe you a lot more than that," he said, unzipping the belt and setting the packets of bills out on my desk, "but this'll do for a down payment." He hitched up his blue-denim workshirt and slid the belt around his waist, leaving the money on the desk.

"What are you doing?" I said.

"Cash on delivery, Mr. Devlin, one belt, five grand. And one of my people deposited another five in your savings account today. Ten K for one night's work—not bad, no? You'll get another ten thousand next week, and ten more the week after that. Two more belts, that's all I ask, and then you're off the hook."

"What the hell are you talking about?"

"About power, Mr. Devlin, about how a guy my size stays alive in a place like this. With the cocaine that's sealed in the lining of this belt, I'll be richer than Hank the Deuce. It's worth more than diamonds inside. More than life."

I lunged at him, but he pivoted like a matador, seized my wrist in his left hand and whipped it up between my shoulder-blades. He flicked his left wrist and a seven-inch sliver of steel appeared in his palm like magic, an inch from my eyes. "Cool out, Teach—you make a scene and you're the one who'll take the fall, not me. They'll know you brought the junk in. And that you got paid. Cops hate it when straight people go bad, they'll love to bust you. Now you back off slow and sit down, you dig?"

"I don't understand," I said, backing to the edge of the desk. "You could get out of here, you have talent—"

"Be a writer, you mean? Somebody like you? Holdin' two jobs tryna make ends meet? Waitin' like a whipped dog for word from some friggin' editor?"

"Maybe it's not a great life," I conceded bitterly, "but at least I'm not in jail."

"Not yet, anyway—" Indio smiled "—and you better hope you never are. I don't think you got what it takes to make it in the joint. You should have read my book better. 'I am the Invictus Worm, buried by the world, yet I strengthen, feeding, thriving in the pit.' Or maybe you should reread Milton—better to rule in hell than to serve in heaven."

"The man who said that stayed in hell."

"But I won't," Indio said, stuffing his shirttails back in his trousers. "I'll cut a deal to get out, *after* I get some serious cash together, and this setup will do it for me. And you, too, if you think straight. Two more belts, thirty grand in the bank, that's not so bad. More than you got for your last book, right?"

"I won't do it," I said, straightening, trying to pull myself together.

"Yes, you will," he said, sliding the shiv back into his sleeve and opening the door. "I didn't use a plastic belt because it was cheap. I used it because it takes fingerprints real well, and yours are all over this one. If you figure you can explain that away, be my guest, but I hope you don't try. You're an intelligent guy, Mr. Devlin, too smart to risk ending up in here. With guys like me. You'll get the next key in the mail with another five grand on account. I'll see you next week. And don't do anything stupid, okay?"

He ducked out into the corridor and stalked away. And I was so furious at the betrayal that I almost shouted for a guard and to hell with the consequences.

But I didn't. Indio had read me well. Either I was too bright,

or more likely too cowardly to risk going to prison. So I didn't
call out, God help me. I couldn't.

He'd told me the truth. It was all there in his book. Later that
night I brewed a pot of coffee, sat down at the kitchen table of
my tiny apartment, and reread the original draft of his manu-
script from beginning to end, seeing it clear-eyed, minus the
glow of discovery. Indio hadn't concealed what he was. He
described his life in the gangs on the Cass Corridor without
glamorizing it or making excuses for himself. There was no
Sociology 101 "victim of a racist society" drivel that most cons
rattle off like a mantra. He was a street-smart ghetto delinquent
who'd become a successful criminal by dint of his own labor—
a dark mirror image of the American Dream. The stark honesty
of his account gave it strength and impact. My mistake had been
in assuming that his unflinching examination of his life implied
a rejection of it, that his intelligence and his talent had trans-
formed him. I'd been conned. By an expert. And by my own
need to validate my teaching by discovering a star pupil. And
the hell of it was that even after what had happened, I found it
difficult to believe I'd been so wrong about him.

I sat at the table for hours after I'd finished the book, sipping
black coffee and chain-smoking, though I'd quit years before,
trying to think the situation through. Nothing came. I was too
drained emotionally, running on empty. Still, I hadn't wasted
my time. Rereading his book had convinced me of two things—
one, that Indio was an even better writer than I'd first thought,
and two, that I was in deep, deep trouble. The man revealed in
that book was perfectly capable of destroying me without a
qualm.

I thrashed around in my empty bed like a beached trout for
what remained of the night, nightmaring, doing hard time in
WaCoCo. I gave it up around 5:00 A.M., slipped on my bathrobe,
put on the coffee, and paced restlessly around the apartment,
looking for an out. I could tell my sorry little tale to the
authorities, but even if they believed me I'd probably wind up
in jail. Working at WaCoCo had erased my illusions about the
criminal-justice system. It's an arcane game for professionals,
and Indio knew the moves and the players far better than I did.

He could cut a deal to testify against me and hit the street while I was still trying to explain my stupidity to a lawyer.

At some point in my wandering, I brushed the curtains aside and glanced out my living-room window at the empty street. Only it wasn't quite empty. A car was cruising slowly past, a teenager's car, black with yellow pinstriping, lowered, fender-skirted, it's glass pack mufflers rumbling hollowly in the early-morning stillness.

I stared after it as it disappeared around the corner, trying to remember if I'd seen it before. But somehow I wasn't surprised when ten minutes or so later it crawled past again. And suddenly I was galvanized, enraged. I'd tried to do a decent thing and I'd been betrayed. And maybe there was no way out for me, but, by God, the game wasn't over. Not yet.

First things first. Indio hadn't exactly threatened my family, but he obviously knew where they were. I wanted them out of harm's way while I worked things out. I mulled that over for a few minutes, then called my ex-wife, told her I'd won a non-refundable two-week Hawaiian vacation, and suggested she take our daughter and go, that I'd pick up the tab for everything. It was the first time since our divorce we settled anything without bickering. I thought about going with them, and continuing on to Tahiti or Australia or wherever, but dismissed it. Indio had a belt with cocaine residue in it and my prints on it. He could trade me for a reduced sentence even if I ran.

Still, the idea had its appeal. It was either run or take the payoff and deliver the belts. And who'd be hurt if I did? It wasn't as though he was selling the stuff to school kids, his only customers would be convicts. And he was right about the money. Thirty thousand *was* more than I'd received for my last book.

Books. I kept coming back to that. You've seen my heart, he said. And it was true. But had I seen anything else in his book? Any weakness? Just maybe. After all, Indio wasn't in prison because he was a gangster—he was there because he valued his honor. And because he loved his sister.

I cruised through my morning classes on autopilot, my mind like a gerbil in a jogging drum, ideas tumbling endlessly over each other. And always coming up the same way, with the same image. Lia Alvarez. If there was a way out for me, Indio's feelings for her were the key to it. By noon I'd assembled a crude plan. I didn't like it much, but at least it gave me something to do, and an excuse to see Indio's sister again. Or try to.

"Wayne County Legal Aid, Alvarez." Her voice on the phone was curt, all business, and for a moment my heart sank. Suppose she said no?

"Hi, this is Tom Devlin, the writer from Friday afternoon—remember me?"

"Of course, Mr. Devlin," she said coolly, "Indio's teacher and friend. Do you need a lawyer already?"

"Possibly," I admitted, "but that's not why I'm calling. I'm calling about food. Dinner, specifically, at someplace with candles and a view of the city. Does the Sky Room on top of the Renaissance Center sound at all interesting?"

"The Sky Room," she echoed. "My, my, my. Very posh. And very expensive. And what would we talk about? My brother, perhaps?"

"We can talk about anything you like, cats and kings, whatever. Or we can just enjoy the meal and the view. No strings attached."

"Sometimes I think I see Detroit all too clearly from my desk."

"Which proves my point. You need a change in perspective. About sixty stories' worth. What do you say?"

"Are you in trouble?" she asked suddenly.

"No," I lied, "why do you ask?"

"If you don't know already, then maybe I'd better enlighten you," she said brusquely, "and the Sky Room's as good a place as any. Is tonight at eight convenient for you?"

"Tonight?" I said, surprised. "Why, yes, tonight will be fine."

"Somehow I thought it might be," she sighed. "I'll meet you there, eightish. Have a nice day."

She rang off without waiting for a reply. I suppose I should have been offended, but instead my spirits lifted a bit. I was still in a jam, but at least I could look forward to a dinner high above the city with an interesting date. And if things didn't work out, I could always take a header off the roof after dessert.

I canceled my last class, drove over to the Cass Corridor, and prowled through a half dozen pawnshops before I found what I wanted—a duplicate of the plastic moneybelt I'd carried into WaCoCo. Then I stopped by the Renaissance Center, the five-tower, sixty-story complex of shops, restaurants, and offices that rises like a stack of poker chips beside the Detroit River, a half-billion-dollar gamble that the heart of Motown can be revived. A winning bet? It's too early in the game to be sure.

I took an express elevator from the mezzanine to the top floor, made reservations at the Sky Room for a table with a view of the river, and arranged for a special service the restaurant offers on request. A photographer.

By evening my upbeat mood had faded a bit, partly because if my little charade flopped I'd be out of options and partly because the more I thought about my idea the less I liked it. I wore my best suit and arrived well before eight to claim our table. I made sure the photographer understood her instructions, then took a seat at the bar while I waited for my date. Or my fate. Or both.

The Sky Room has a sensual, sophisticated ambience, embroidered linens, candleglow dancing on silver carafes, the lights of Detroit and the Canadian side of the river stretching away to the horizon as though the Milky Way had whispered down like snow. The waiters were white tuxed and black tied, but not snobbish. They joked with the diners and each other, typically Motown, where the only class line that counts is the balance in your bank statement.

And then Lia walked in, and the room seemed to brighten. She was wearing a twin of the dress I'd seen a few days before, a plain dun business frock adorned only with a scarlet wisp of a scarf, and yet I felt my breathing catch. She looked absolutely stunning, underdressed for the room perhaps, but, if anything, more attractive for it. She spoke to the maitre d', who escorted her to the table I'd reserved. I wandered over, carrying the small parcel I'd brought with me and wishing to God I was meeting her under other circumstances.

"Hi," I said, parking the package beside my chair as I sat, "I'm glad you could make it."

"So am I," she said. "You look very natty. I thought writers were supposed to be rumpled."

"Ordinarily I am, but this is a special occasion."

"Yes," she mused, scanning the room, "so it would seem. And yet—"

"And yet?"

"Look, Mr. Devlin—"

"Tom," I interjected.

"No, at this point it's still Mr. Devlin and Ms. Alvarez. And that may be as far as it gets. I'll be blunt, Mr. Devlin. The only times I've ever been here were on business. If this is a business dinner, fine, but can we deal with the agenda first? It might save you an expensive evening."

"I have no particular agenda other than getting to know you better."

"And that's all? There's nothing in particular you'd like to ask me? About my stepbrother, for instance?"

"I do have one question," I said. "Do you think working on the Corridor's made you just a teensy bit paranoid? Or were you always this way?"

"In this town, paranoia's just another name for reality."

"Maybe so," I admitted, "but everybody needs a break from reality now and again. So let's take one. Now, shall I ask for the wine list?"

"Just one last question," she said. "Why the Sky Room? For a first—date? If that's what this is."

"I think that's the term, yes."

"All right, then—why here?"

"Simple," I said. "I wanted to make sure you'd say yes."

"I see," she said slowly. "Well, true or not, that was the right thing to say. Tom. All right, let's ask for the wine list. Bearing in mind that I'm already impressed, so don't overdo it by choosing something terribly expensive, okay?"

"Ms. Alvarez," I said, "I think this could be the beginning of a beautiful friendship."

But it seemed more like renewing a friendship than a beginning. She really was familiar, in a way. I had Indio's description of her as background, but it was no more than a sketch, really. He saw her as a sort of streetwise madonna, and she was, but she was also bright and tenacious and compassionate, and funny. And as the evening flew past, I became almost certain that she wasn't involved in Indio's life, except as his sister and his friend. Which made me dislike my scheme even more. Still, I had no choice. And it was almost time.

"Oops, almost forgot," I said, picking up the parcel from the foot of my chair. I placed the moneybelt on the table, then lifted out the small gift-wrapped box and handed it to Lia.

She opened it. "A corsage?" she smiled. "You really take first dates seriously, don't you?"

"Only this one," I said. "Shall I help you put it on?"

"No, I think I'd like to save it, if you wouldn't mind. It's too pretty to wear. And a—moneybelt? Is this some sort of a bribe?"

"It's just something I picked up for a class," I said. "I forgot it was in the bag."

She knew I was lying. Whether it was her training as a lawyer or because we were simpatico, somehow she sensed it. But she would have let it pass, I think, except that the photographer chose that moment to take her shot. Lia glanced up, startled by the flash, then read my eyes and my soul like a cheap novel.

"Just part of the service," I said lamely. "A picture to—"

"Is it?" she said, cutting me off, her gaze still locked on mine. I looked away.

"What's going on here?" she asked.

"Nothing. Why do you ask?"

"Never mind," she said, rising. "Whatever it is, I wish you'd told me. It's been a lovely evening—Mr. Devlin. Thank you. This should cover my half of it." She fished two twenties out of her purse, tossed them on the table, then walked away, moving hastily through the crowd.

"Lia, wait a minute—"

"Here's your photograph, sir," the camera girl said, blocking my path. "It came out perfectly."

"Right, I'll be right back," I said, trying to brush past her as Lia disappeared into the corridor.

"Sir," the girl said, grasping my elbow gently, "didn't you say something about a tip? Fifty, wasn't it?"

It was too late, anyway. Lia was already gone. "Yes," I sighed, taking out my wallet. "Fifty, exactly." The girl handed me the Polaroid snap. She was right, it had turned out very well. And maybe I was off the hook. Instead of delivering the drugs, all I had to do was show Indio the picture of Lia with the moneybelt, tell him that her prints were on it, and that he couldn't burn me without destroying her as well. And he'd never do that. Stalemate. I was free of him.

I should have felt relieved, liberated. But I didn't. Maybe it was the damned snapshot, the glow in Lia's eyes as she held the orchid just as the flashbulb fired.

I called Lia's office the next morning, got put on hold by her receptionist, and, as I waited, realized I had no idea of what to say, anyway. The truth? More lies? I wasn't sure which would be worse, so I hung up before she came on the line. I thought of her often over the next few days and found myself taking out the photograph at odd moments and staring at it as though it held a message for me. And perhaps it did.

On Tuesday morning, after my ten o'clock class, there was an envelope waiting on the desk in my office. No postage, no return address, just my name on it. I asked the office girl if she'd seen who dropped it off, but she hadn't noticed anyone, and I wasn't surprised.

I closed the office door, sat down at my battered desk, and opened the envelope. Five thousand in cash and an airport locker key. I placed the envelope and Lia's photograph side by side. Did they balance out? Almost certainly. The photograph would neutralize Indio's hold on me. There was only one flaw in my little scheme. I couldn't do it. I just couldn't. I took a last, wistful look at the photograph, then tore it up and dropped the pieces in the wastebasket. Indio was right. I had no talent for this kind of thing. I was back to my original options—take my chances with the authorities, which almost certainly meant going to jail, or make another delivery. I was still staring at Indio's envelope when the warning bell sounded for the next class period. I slipped the envelope into my briefcase and walked out of my office. And into The Dream.

Every teacher has a personal version of The Dream—a vivid, recurring nightmare that shows up when you're under pressure. You're wandering through a strange school, knowing you're late for class, but can't find your room; or you're lecturing and suddenly realize you're only wearing underwear. Or less.

In my version of The Dream, I was addressing a class later that afternoon when I noticed the students seemed to be eyeing me strangely. And I realized I had no idea what I'd been talking about, or even which class this was. Western Civ? American Lit 202? My memory was a blank. Erased. And for a moment the spell of The Dream was so strong that I half expected to wake up in bed. But I didn't. Instead I stood there like an idiot for a century or so, trying to remember where I was, and then just said, "Class dismissed," picked up my case, and walked out.

I drifted down the empty corridor like my own ghost, ducked into the first empty classroom I came to, and collapsed into a desk at the rear. Sanctuary, a quiet place to think. *Think.*

I ran the situation over and over again in my mind, staring blindly up at the empty chalkboard, waiting for an answer to materialize. But nothing came. And after a while, Charlie Volk waddled in, a balding, three-hundred-pound Magoo in a stained white lab coat. He began assembling some sort of apparatus on his desk, humming contentedly to himself, then stopped as he noticed me at the back of the room.

"Hello, Devlin, what are you doing in here?"

"Nothing, Charlie. Just needed a place to hide. I'll get out of your way."

"No rush, my next class isn't for twenty minutes. I came in early to set up an experiment. How's the scribbling going? Still working on the great American novel?"

"When I find time," I said.

"Well, anytime you need a chemistry teacher for a hero, you know who to ask. It'd be nice to have somebody besides Disney write about us."

"Disney?"

"Walt Disney. Or whoever it was that made up that nonsense

for the movies. You know, *The Absent-Minded Professor, Son of Flubber,* all that drivel."

"Oh, that Disney. Sorry, I didn't make the connection."

"You know, you look a little like an absent-minded professor yourself, Dev. Something on your mind?"

"A small problem. Nothing I can't work out," I said, rising stiffly from the desk.

"With one of your stories, you mean?"

"A story?" I echoed. "Yes, I suppose it is in a way."

"Well? Solving problems is what we teach in here, maybe I can help. What is it?"

I stared at him blankly for a moment, then took a deep, ragged breath. I needed to talk to somebody badly. "It's just a plot I'm working out," I said. "About a teacher who gets himself in a jam."

The next night after class, I delivered the second belt to Indio. He seemed almost disappointed. I think he was looking forward to a confrontation, but I had nothing to say to him. He slipped the belt on under his shirt, eyeing me warily.

"You want to talk about this?" he asked.

"About what?"

"This situation we're into here. I know this can't be easy for you."

"I'm touched by your concern."

"Believe it or not, I do care about you, Devlin. You tried to help me and I haven't forgotten it. Plus I want to make sure you don't do anything stupid now and burn us both. Try thinkin' of this as an educational experience. You've taught me some things, now I'm returning the favor and you're gonna come out ahead of the game, wiser and richer both. Might even make you a better writer to know how the other half lives. So enjoy your walk on the wild side, Mr. Devlin. And be cool. You're doin' the smart thing."

"I hope so," I said.

"You are," he said. "Trust me."

"You've got to be kidding."

"Just a figure of speech," he grinned. 'I'll see you next week."

But he didn't. Indio was absent the following week. I asked Segundo where his boss was and he said he was in isolation block. There'd been a fire in the library. The guards knew it was arson, but couldn't nail anybody for it, so they punished all six of the cons who worked there—ten days in solitary each.

"Sorry to hear it," I said.

"You got any message you want to get to him?" Segundo asked.

"I thought you said he was in isolation."

"He is. But he's still El Hombre."

"Yes, I suppose he is," I said. "No. No message."

"You have a slight edge over writers on the outside," I said, facing the following Thursday-night class of thugs and felons. "You've seen and done things that most people haven't or you wouldn't be in here. It makes your viewpoint unique, and you can make that work for you." I continued on this tack for a bit, talking about former convicts who'd become respected authors—Eldridge Cleaver, James Ellroy, and others. Inspiration by example, I hoped. The class was edgy, unresponsive. I felt I was living The Dream again, lecturing to a Diego Rivera mural. Indio Zamora was back, sitting at a desk in the rear, silent as a stone idol, Segundo, as usual, at his right hand.

I managed to get through the session, made assignments for the following week, and dismissed them. Segundo ushered the others out into the corridor and took up a station on the hallway just outside the door. Indio unfolded from his seat and sauntered toward me. He looked like a man just out of solitary, hollow-cheeked, his dark eyes sunken, opaque.

"Maybe you think you're off the hook," he said quietly, stopping a foot or so away.

"Almost," I said. "I guessed you'd probably hide the belts in the same place, so they went up in smoke together. As for your money, it's in my bank in a savings account. In your name. You can pick it up when you get out. If you ever do."

"And if I told you I still have the first belt?"

"I wouldn't believe you. The guards knew the fire was arson and they turned the library upside down. If the belt was there, they'd have found it. They didn't. It burned. It must have."

"When you're right, you're right," Indio shrugged. "Both belts burned. An expensive fire. How did you do it? Some kind of chemical, right?"

"White phosphorous, and consulfuric acid. The acid ate through the lining, the phosphorous burns as soon as it's exposed to air."

"You're a chemist, too? I'm impressed."

"I'm not a chemist, just did a little basic research."

"And the coke that was in the belt?"

"I flushed it down the toilet where it belongs. By the way, Mr. Herzel called me while you were—away. Your book will be published—the advance will be ten thousand."

"Good, I can use the money. I'm about to change careers. I'm getting out of here, going into the witness-protection program."

"Is there an echo in here? I think I've heard this before."

"Maybe so—" he smiled narrowly "—only this time it's true. I took deposits to deliver merchandise, and then my stash gets torched. And now people figure I was runnin' a scam and burned the library to cover myself. They have no faith in humanity, you know? If I stay here, either some strung-out junkie'll waste me or there'll be a gang war and a lot of my people will get hurt. So I'm cutting a deal to get out, tryin' to trade the Feds enough to earn a walk without betraying any Gusanos. And then maybe I'll take my shot at the straight life."

"You'll do all right if you work at it. You're a bright guy, Indio, probably the best student I've ever had."

"No hard feelings, then?"

"Wrong," I said. "All kinds of hard feelings."

"Whatever," he shrugged. "But for what it's worth, I've worked a lot of hustles in my time, Devlin, but I never had a new blood beat me in a deal before. I guess that makes you my star pupil, no?"

"What it makes us is quits, Indio, dead-even. I don't want to see you again, in here or anywhere else."

"Like the song says, Teach, you can't always get what you want. If I'm really as good a writer as you say, maybe you'll see me around, like it or not."

"I doubt it. I think you're at home in prison, Indio. Afraid of the outside. I think you'll die in this place. Or one like it."

"Perhaps," he said softly, moving closer to me, his eyes only inches from mine, "but sometime, Devlin, maybe late some night, after lights out and lockdown, you'll think back on this and admit you learned as much from me as I did from you."

"I doubt that very much."

"No, I think you *will.* And you know what else you'll remember? What a rush it was to walk on the wild side. And you'll miss it. Maybe you'll even miss me."

"No," I said, "not a chance in hell."

"Maybe not," he shrugged, turning toward the door. "*Adiós,* Teach. Thanks for everything. It's been interesting."

"That it has," I said. "Good luck," I added, surprising myself.

He didn't reply. Segundo opened the door for him, then shambled after him down the corridor. I began erasing my notes from the chalkboard, but paused in mid-swipe, thinking about what Indio said about missing the wild side. And I knew he was wrong. If I'd learned anything from him, it was that some people need the adrenaline highs of that life but I wasn't one of them. Nor is there any chance I'll miss him. He's an amoral sociopath with no more conscience than that worm tattooed on his wrist. WaCoCo, or some other prison, is exactly where he belongs.

Still, wherever he ends up, I hope they give him a typewriter Because if not, I'll send him one myself. A teacher only gets one star pupil in a lifetime, and inside the walls or out Indio Zamora's going to be a fine writer. And in spite of everything, I can't wait to read his next book.

# BRENDAN DUBOIS

# FIRE BURNING BRIGHT

*Brendan DuBois's production of short mysteries has dropped off noticeably in the past two years, since the time when he was one of the most frequently published writers of short stories in the field. We hope there's a novel in progress, which will soon appear. In the meantime here's another of DuBois's powerful short stories. The crime of arson, so familiar to urban and rural life alike, is rarely dealt with in mystery fiction. Forty years ago Stewart Sterling wrote a whole series of novels involving arson investigation, but since that time there has only been a scattering of novels and short stories. The best of these remains Stanley Ellin's "The Nine-to-Five Man," but this tale of rural arson and murder is just as memorable in its own way.*

The first thing I did when the phone rang was to check the glowing red numerals of my bedroom clock radio, which told me it was four in the morning. Some people take a while to wake up when a loud noise—like a telephone—disturbs their sleep. Not me. Any loud noise at night is like a hand grenade rolled underneath my bed—it quickly gets my attention.

I swung around and switched on the side lamp, and by the time the third chime had rung, I had picked up the receiver and had a pen in the other hand.

It was Norma Quentin, night dispatcher for Franconia County. She didn't bother apologizing for waking me up. She knows me too well.

"Thought you'd be interested," she said, as she always does. "Purmort volunteer just responded up on Timberswamp Road—looks like a fire, suspicious origins and all the rest."

"Jesus," I murmured. "Tate Burnham?"

Her voice hesitated, just a bit. I'll always remember that.

41

"Don't know, Jerry. They've been gone about ten minutes—it'll take a while for you to get there, even if you hurry."

I heard the crackle of static and I imagined her, sitting in a darkened cubicle, in the basement of the county courthouse, linked by telephone and radio to the rest of the county, the console lights making her skin look bloodless. I was sure her two stainless steel crutches would be there, at her side, along with a .38 caliber revolver.

"Gotta go," Norma said. "Calls coming in."

Soon I was dressed and in my Ford pickup, driving north along Route 3, my reporter's notebook and camera bag on the cold and hard vinyl seat. The center of Purmort looked quiet enough—the few stores and two service stations darkened and empty—and in a few seconds I was back on Route 3, passing the small wooden building that held Justin's Plumbing Supplies, and the offices of the weekly Purmort *Sentinel* (Jerry Auberg, editor).

It was cold, very cold for October, and the lights from the truck caught the bright colors of the foliage of the trees along Route 3, which each fall enticed tourists to drive for hours. On both sides of the two-lane road, up beyond the trees and forests, were the ridgelines of the Purmort range. The mass of the mountains was impressive, like distant battleships sailing silently and without lights. I wondered what creatures lived up there at night and I shivered.

I missed the turnoff for Timberswamp Road and had to make a sloppy U-turn farther down. Timberswamp was a town-maintained road, unlike Route 3, which is maintained by the state. Purmort being Purmort, the road was cracked and bumpy and there were no streetlights at all. The few homes were set far into the woods, and all of them had bright and powerful yard lights on. I drove a mile and six-tenths by the truck's odometer before I saw the flashing lights of the fire trucks and police cruisers. I pulled up behind another pickup truck—one belonging to a volunteer firefighter, no doubt, since it had a slap-on red strobe light on its roof—and stepped out, swinging my camera bag over one shoulder. The cold hit me like a wet towel against my face, and I saw my breath in the frigid air.

There were lights everywhere, blue ones from the two

Purmort police cruisers and red ones from the two fire engines from the Purmort volunteer fire department. There was the loud crackling of radio static coming from the vehicles, and I walked along the road, nodding and looking at the huddled groups of volunteer firefighters, many in their nightclothes and wearing bunker jackets and heavy boots. It was then that an odd thing happened.

By that time, after all that had gone on over the summer, most of them had begun to at least accept me, if not quite trust me. But as I walked by none of them looked my way. They turned their backs and talked to one another, like tiny herds of animals in winter turning among themselves, protecting one another from an outside threat.

I walked up the road, a slight embankment of dirt and grass on the right, and that was when the smell of smoke and something else struck me, and I held onto the camera bag strap very tightly.

It began in spring, and innocently at first, with a few grass fires along some of the farms that dotted the outlying areas of Purmort. At first the firefighters and the chief of police, Randy Parnell, blamed the fires on kids smoking cigarettes or raising hell in preparation for summer vacation. Being the editor and sole reporter—and owner—of the *Sentinel,* I put the stories inside the paper. No cause for giving the kids publicity, I thought.

It was my fifth year in Purmort, and by the beginning of that fifth summer, I was beginning to feel that at long last Purmort was coming around to my presence. I don't blame them much for resenting me when I started there—I had come from that great hedonistic state to the south, and I was well-educated and a newspaperman, always a doubtful combination in a small town. But I came in with a large reserve of smiles and a willingness not to be pushed around, and in a while the *Sentinel* did all right. I didn't ignore the petty crimes and drunk driving arrests that every town offers, but neither did I go on investigatory rampages if the town road agent plowed out a few family driveways for free when times were tough in the winter.

The fires that spring meant nothing, and I was looking for-

ward to another round of Town Meeting stories, until a warm
May weekend when a summer cottage on Lake Arthur and a
barn on Swallow Reach burned down. Then the state came in,
with state police detectives and experts in arson, and in a while,
through a tersely worded press release, it was announced that
the grass fires and the fires at the cottage and barn were
connected. There was an arsonist at work in Purmort.

For the moment, at least, I found that hard to believe. I had
come to Purmort after thirty years of banging around in newspaper work in some of the larger cities in Connecticut and
Massachusetts, eventually reaching the top levels of editorial
staffs. And one warm spring day, as cliche-ridden as it may
sound, I decided I didn't want to be the top editor of one of
those large dailies anymore. I had gone to too many funerals of
my fellow editors and writers, and I decided I didn't want to be
remembered and then forgotten at a similar service. By then I
was by myself. My wife Angela had left me some years back,
after deciding she wanted to discover herself, and every now
and then she sends me an oddly written postcard from some
small community in New Mexico, where she makes pottery.
Our only son moved out to California, working in an esoteric
field of physics and computers I could never fathom, and twice
a year—as regular as elections—I get cards from him for
Father's Day and Christmas, each enclosing a hundred-dollar
check.

With that spring decision, I eventually made it to Purmort,
buying a failing weekly newspaper in the process. Now, five
years later, two parts of me reacted when I heard about the
arsonist: as a newspaper editor interested in a story, one more
exciting than anything else going on in the area, and as a
resident of Purmort, wondering if my home would be there
when I got home late from a selectman's meeting or county
fair.

I liked Purmort, and I liked my home. It was small and
sturdily built, with two woodstoves and a tiny barn, set on a
well-wooded lot on the Sher River. In the house and barn I had
thirty years of newspaper clippings, mementos and memories,
over a thousand books and years of colors slides from trips all
over Canada and the West, and Lord, how I didn't want to miss

that. For the very first time I thought of my past arrogance as an editor, spiking stories about house and apartment fires, or burying them far inside the paper. "Not news," I would say. "Happens all the time," and I never suspected then the gut-wrenching feeling of coming home with all of your thoughts and hopes and wishes of a quiet evening, and seeing only a blackened pile of rubble where your den used to be.

After hearing the news of the arsonist I had to travel to three towns before finding a store that hadn't sold out of smoke detectors, and I installed one in the basement, one on each floor of the house, and one in my barn. And, like so many of the townspeople in Purmort, I began going to bed at night with all the outdoor lights on and a loaded shotgun by my bed. I slept with a suitcase of clothes at my side and at night —no matter how cold—I kept a bedroom window open, to hear an approaching vehicle or footsteps along the grass.

Like so many others in Purmort, I never got a good night's sleep that summer.

For a week after the first spate of fires nothing happened, until one night, after a church meeting, the Olson family from Mast Road came home to see their two-hundred-year-old farmhouse burning bright, like a beacon upon a hill. It took Kerry Olson ten minutes to drive to his nearest neighbor to find a phone, and by the time the two engines from the Purmort volunteer fire department roared up, the house had collapsed and there was nothing left to do but wet down the embers.

And just when we started to appreciate the shock of that, a day later, half of Mrs. Corinne Everett's house burned before the Purmort department and some firefighters from Tannon arrived to save the other half. But she never went back home, Mrs. Everett, and she went to live in the county nursing home. I visited her once, for a follow-up story, and she sat alone in a wooden chair, staring out the window, and all she could talk about was her home, and her pet parakeet who had perished.

Oh, how the town started to change that summer. It was always another cliche that Purmort was a town where one could go to sleep at night with the house unlocked, but it was true, and the arsonist took that away. For a week or two the people in town, sitting around the Common Coffeeshop, or at

Tay's Tire, gossiped and complained and nodded and said that it had to be an outsider, some damn flatlander who was doing the burnings. But that talk faded away when it became apparent the arsonist knew the town, knew the people, and knew them both very well. When that became known, the people of Purmort stopped looking over their shoulders and started looking at each other.

One of the selectmen, Jeff Tamworth, talked to me one night, his leathery and wrinkled face puzzled and dismayed at the same time. "Jerry," he said as we sat in one of the booths and shared a meatloaf dinner at Ruby's Diner, "I've lived here all my goddamn life and I can't believe what I'm seeing. People are hushing up all the time now and staring at each other, and you know why? 'Cause you don't know who the son of a bitch is. He might be the guy sittin' next to you, having a smoke and a cup of coffee, and you sure as hell don't want to say you're going to visit your mom next weekend and the house is gonna be empty, or you don't want to talk about goin' on vacation. Christ, when you can't talk about stuff like that with your neighbors, it's almost as bad as it gets in the big cities."

Having spent years in the big cities, I was too polite to disagree with him, but two nights later Jeff Tamworth and I were in agreement.

That night I was out doing a story about Bob Reardon, who'd come back from a trip out to Alaska where he had done some big-game hunting. It would be a nice human interest piece, something to lighten up the *Sentinel*'s pages since the fires started. But while Bob might have been a demon behind a high-powered rifle, he was lousy at directions—probably couldn't tell you which direction the sun rises every morning.

So I found myself driving back and forth on Blueberry Hill Road, looking for a green house with white shutters and a dirt driveway. About the third time I made the round trip I pulled over next to a driveway to look at my notes again. But before I could switch on the inside light, the barrel of the biggest and blackest shotgun I ever saw came through my open window and stopped about six inches from my head. I froze, both hands in mid-air.

A voice from the darkness: "Now who the hell are you, and what are you doing out here?"

"Jerry Auberg, from the *Sentinel,*" I said, trying to keep my voice even. "I'm looking for Bob Reardon's place."

The shotgun barrel wavered, and then slowly pulled away. I turned and saw a heavyset man, with a thick and scraggly beard, looking in, chewing on a lower lip. He wore a red and black checkered hunter's jacket. "Got proof on that?" he said.

Luckily, I had a couple of copies of the newspaper with me, plus my driver's license. Within seconds the shotgun was by the man's side and he offered me his hand, which I shook, more to stop the trembling than anything else.

"Tyler Whitney," he said, motioning with his shoulder. "Live up there on the hill. I was standing watch tonight, my brother Ray, he takes the morning shift, and I saw your truck go back and forth a couple of times. Sorry if I scared you, but me and my brother are building a house up there. We don't want to lose it."

"It's all right," I said, though I sure as hell didn't feel all right. But I decided polite talk in the presence of a shotgun was the best approach.

"You're a newspaper man," he said. "They getting any closer to catching that fellow?"

I said, "No, not that I know of, and if they were, I'm sure the cops wouldn't tell me. Arson's such a tough crime to prove— you almost have to catch the guy lighting something off."

"Maybe so," Tyler Whitney said, picking up his shotgun. "But that fella better hope the cops catch him first. One of these nights he's gonna pick the wrong place to torch, and he's gonna get his damn head blown off, cops or no cops. And, buddy, you can print that in your newspaper."

When he left I drove a few feet, stopped and stepped out and got sick by the side of the road. If he had been any meaner, if he had been drinking . . . I remembered the closeness of that shotgun barrel, imagined smelling the gun oil and the gunpowder, tightly wadded up and ready to explode with a twitch of a finger, less than six inches from my head.

I'm afraid I never did the interview that night with Bob Reardon.

The fires stopped for eight days, and some residents started wondering aloud if the arsonist had gotten tired or scared.

And on the ninth night, he burned down the town garage.

The mood in Purmort grew worse. People were getting dark circles under their eyes from staying up so late, and arguments and even a few fistfights broke out over trivial things at the Common Coffeeshop or Ruby's Diner. Some children collected their favorite toys or dolls and mailed them to friends in other towns or states for safekeeping.

One of the worst nights was the night a benefit dinner was held at the Congregationalist Church, to raise money for the fire victims, four families who sat silenced and embarrassed in one corner of the church basement. The night was going along all right—the usual hams, casseroles, and baked beans—until a group of Purmort volunteer firefighters came in, dressed in their blue nylon windbreakers. And seeing that, Mrs. Olson— who had lost a hundred-year-old doll collection in her home— stood up and screamed, "I'll bet it's one of them, one of those volunteers. Why not? They know how to put fires out—I'll bet you they know how to set them!" Then some of the volunteers' wives shouted back at her, and it got worse.

And if the fires weren't bad enough, my friends and the townspeople of Purmort had to put up with another burden— the media.

For a short while the only stories about the burning of Purmort appeared in the *Sentinel,* or in stories filed to the statewide *Union Leader* by Amos Turin, a retired high school English teacher who lived in Tannon, the next town over. But after the town garage fire, and the fire at the Keefes' (where the eighty-seven-year-old grandmother survived by clambering out of her bedroom window and onto a garage), the wire services picked up the stories. And the avalanche started.

Boston newspapers and television stations. Camera crews from the four networks. *Time* and *Newsweek.* Reporters and writers and producers in fancy clothes, standing in the middle of the common, wanting to know where the "downtown" was and the taxi stands. When this onslaught started I had some serious thoughts to myself and spoke with Chief Parnell, finding him at his basement office in the Town Hall. He had lost a lot of weight, his usual sleek green police uniform a baggy and greasy-looking mockery. His eyes were red-rimmed and almost lifeless, like those belonging to a man fighting an invisible and spiteful foe.

I said, "Chief, when these media types get here, you be on your best behavior."

This stirred him some from his seat, huddled against a paper-filled desk. "What do you mean by that?"

"I mean these are pros, out-of-state, sent up here to do a story. They don't give a hoot about you or Purmort. They can buddy up to you and say, 'Don't worry, whatever you say will be off the record,' and it'll be on the six o'clock news that night. They're up here for one story and then they're gone, and you'll never see them again. They don't care what happens once they leave."

The chief seemed to take that to heart, but not Ryan Duffy, the volunteer fire chief who worked days in Tannon. He was quoted in almost every story, and his fat, bearded face was on a lot of newscasts. It backfired, of course, with some of his own men griping about him, and eventually the state police sat on him and told Ryan to shut up. Before that, unfortunately, there were two camera crews on hand the night Mrs. Olson started screaming at the firefighters in the Congregationalist Church basement. That made the evening news, with a lot of analyzing about "small town pressures" and "coping mechanisms" and a lot of false sympathy from the television people.

One afternoon I was halfheartedly typing up some deed transfers at the *Sentinel's* office when a familiar-looking man came in, dressed in casual clothes—designer jeans and sport shirt—that blinked a high price tag at you. He was about my age, beefy-looking and grinning, with dark, thinning hair. He had a gold watch about his thick wrist, and as he approached I stood up and stuck out my hand and said, "Well, I'll be jigged. Harmon Kirk. Harmon, I don't think I've spoken to you for five years."

His grip was strong. "Right with that, Jerry,"

I said, "Still with the *Courant?*"

"No, that was two papers ago. Got my own column, syndicated in a lot of dailies in the Northeast. Hope to go national next year."

Well, I knew what he was up here for, but for a while, at least, we were polite to each other, trading war stories and lies about past editors and stories. As we talked I admit I looked about my office, noticing the three mismatched desks and the piles of newsprint and the manual typewriters. A long distance from the many computerized newsrooms I had worked in.

Harmon finally said, "I guess you can figure why I'm here, Jerry. I'm doing a piece on your fires, and when I found out you were here, I knew I had to come by."

"Not my fires," I said, trying to smile. "And I'll be happy to tell you what I know, so long as I'm not quoted in any way."

Harmon's smile flickered a bit, like an old light bulb. "Not even for an old drinking companion?"

I tapped on my chair arm a few times. "Harmon, drinking companion or no, I've been interviewed and re-interviewed by a dozen of your colleagues and I'm—"

"They're your colleagues, too," he interrupted.

I said, "True, but I also live here. This is my home."

He said nothing for a moment, making me think he was going to leave, and he said, "Okay—off the record, I hear rumors that there are vigilantes up in the hills, trying to track down the arsonist. Any truth to that?"

I had heard the same rumors, but I didn't want hundreds of thousands of Harmon's readers thinking that we were all crazy hill people up here, armed with rifles and the like. I shook my head no.

It was a fairly dispirited interview. After a few minutes Harmon slapped shut his notebook and said, "Sorry to say, Jerry, you sure as hell have changed since we were in the same newsroom. I don't think the old Jerry would've stonewalled me like that."

"The old Jerry never had a home—just rental agreements," I said. "You can imagine I feel a sense of responsibility here."

"What about your responsibility to your readers?"

I tried to smile, tried to make him see what I had become. "My readers all live within ten miles of here—they're my neighbors. And all of them, even me, are scared of losing our homes. And they see you folks coming in, making fun of them and using their tragedies for your own gain. Harmon, I like this town, I like it a lot, and I'm proud of living here."

A few days later—after the Unitarian Church burned down—I ran across Harmon Kirk's column in one of the larger dailies, and he had quoted me, of course, but by covering up my identity and naming me only as a "local newsman." Being as I'm the only local newsman in Purmort, it didn't do much.

Another effect of the media barrage was to focus some of the townspeople's hostility on me. Even though I owned and wrote the local paper, and had done so for five years, the fires stripped away the thin layer of acceptability, which I had so diligently grown over the many months. Hardly anyone talked to me on the streets, and sitting down at the lunch or breakfast counters at Ruby's Diner or the Common Coffeeshop meant people on either side of me would silently pick up their plates and move elsewhere.

Subscriptions to the *Sentinel*—never big to begin with—started to dwindle, and I found myself caught in the middle of two opinions. Some people in Purmort thought my stories only encouraged the arsonist, and that I should report nothing (nothing!) at all about the fires. And another group of people felt I was hiding news and information, important items that the state police and the chief were hiding.

As for the first point, I could never have kept the *Sentinel* silent about what was going on in Purmort, and as for the second point, I had to plead a modified guilty—I never printed everything I knew.

For one thing, I accidentally learned—through a thoughtless comment by one of the state police boys in the chief's office—how the fires were set. A set of oil rags, jammed into a corner or in a woodpile, and then set ablaze with three wooden matches. Repeated, every time. Seconds after I found this out Chief Parnell was practically on his knees, begging me not to use it.

"Jerry, this is the only thing we've got on the son of a bitch," the chief said. "The only thing. You write it up in the *Sentinel* and he'll switch to something else, and we'll never be able to tie him in to all the fires when we get him."

I had to think long and hard on that one, but in the end, I gave in. I wanted to report the news, but most of all, like everyone else in Purmort, I wanted the arsonist caught. If this made me a bad newsman, well, it was something I could live with. I wanted to save my home.

On a Wednesday late in September, I gained back some of the acceptance and respectability of the people of Purmort.

I had spent the afternoon having lunch and doing some work at home, and I was a mile on the road into town when I realized I had forgotten some notebooks in my kitchen. I turned the pickup truck around in a school bus turnoff, and a few hundred feet from home, I saw a black cloud of smoke above the trees. I sped up, thinking maybe it was a car fire, or grass fire, or some kids camping out in my backyard.

I didn't bother to park the truck in the driveway—I drove across the lawn and into the backyard, watching the flames billow out and the smoke pour away from my barn.

It seemed like forever as I stood there by the truck, watching the flames grow larger, and watching the paint blister and blacken against the south wall of my house, and there was a quick, horrible debate going on inside my mind—call the fire department or grab the garden hose—what do do first?

Though the debate seemed to go on forever, it probably only lasted a few seconds. I ran to the garage, tossing aside rakes and shovels and grabbing the hard coil of a garden hose. My fingers and hands were trembling as I unrolled the hose in the backyard, and I broke two fingernails (and didn't notice it until the next day) screwing in one end to the outside faucet. As I worked I muttered a lot under my breath, hoping that someone, anyone, would see the smoke and call County Dispatch.

The smoke and flames rose higher and the heat was tremendous, blackening and curling the grass, blistering the south wall of the house. I turned on the hose and the water came rushing out, and when I turned it against the barn I realized what a pitiful stream of water it really was. I kept the hose on the barn for a few long minutes—remembering what was stored there— but I knew the barn was lost after there was a sharp *crack* as one of the windows on the south wall of the house burst from the heat. I shuddered and turned the hose onto the south wall, trying to wet it down.

The fire trucks came in a few minutes, and in that time the entire south wall was charred and two windows were broken, but the house was saved. That was at least some consolation, for the barn had collapsed upon itself by the time the trucks arrived.

The barn, with at least two hundred books, my only childhood photos of myself and my parents' wedding album, my winter clothes, slides from my trans-Canada trip, and two book manuscripts I had always wanted to finish, was gone.

I didn't bother picking through the rubble. It would have depressed me even more. Instead, I spent fifty bucks for Burke Farnsworth to come by with his backhoe and flatten everything and drive it into the cellar hole.

And seven days later—just a week!—Tate Burnham was arrested and charged with the arsons.

I must give Chief Parnell and the state police credit, for not once had Tate Burnham's name come up in any of my conversations with the chief or the state. But I learned he had been one of the handful of suspects from the start, and mainly because of the practically forgotten cottage fire that had started it all, on Lake Arthur. The cottage belonged to the Maynard family, and Tate Burnham—who worked in one of the mills in Tannon—had been dating seventeen-year-old Cindy Maynard. She had broken up with him and for revenge, perhaps, he had burned down the family's cottage. And to cover his tracks, the barn on Swallow Reach also went up in flames the same day.

Tate Burnham lived with his stepfather and mother in a trailer near the Purmont-Tannon line. And at one time, for about a year, he had been a volunteer firefighter in Purmont, until he dropped out last summer for no apparent reason.

The most-asked question, of course, was why? And in a private few minutes I had with Chief Parnell before Tate Burnham's court hearing, the chief had shrugged and said, "We think he started liking it, that's all. Simple as that. He started burning things down and enjoyed it."

Simple motive, and a simple capture. One Wednesday mem-

bers of the Greater Purmort Bird Club had been watching for a
Great Thrush Whacker or something up on Garrison Hill, and
they had seen Tate Burnham walk a ways across a field and go
into some woods. Some minutes later they saw smoke rising in
the distance and saw Tate run hell-bent-for-leather out of the
woods. One of the birdwatchers recognized Tate and the state
police and the chief were told, and they got search warrants
and found a collection of rags and a box of matches identical to
the ones used, a map marking some of the fires, and other
evidence.

Though I was happy he was captured, I wished he had been
caught sooner, but the fates didn't work that way. The smoke
rising the day the birdwatchers saw Tate Burnham came from
my barn.

A few days later I covered Tate Burnham's bail hearing, and
that's when the so-called Miracle of Purmort occurred.

In the basement of the Town Hall, next to the police station,
was the district court. On the day of Tate Burnham's hearing,
the benches were full and there was standing-room only against
the cement walls. I managed to get a seat up front. The rest of
the media horde had returned, including, I wasn't too happy to
see, Harmon Kirk. He gave me a half-wave and I responded with
a half-smile, and then Judge Temple came out, long black robe
flowing. After some legal jumbo Chief Parnell and a state
trooper came in, with Tate Burnham between them.

Tate was barely twenty, standing at least six feet and gangly.
He had an acne-scarred face and a scraggly beard, and he wore
army fatigue pants and a black T-shirt imprinted with a colorful
logo from one of those rock bands. There was a collective sigh
in the room when he walked in, and I wondered suddenly why
Chief Parnell or some county sheriffs hadn't frisked the crowd
as they came in. It would have been mighty easy to smuggle in
a pistol or a sawed-off shotgun, and Harmon Kirk caught my
eye and smiled again, and I knew the same thing was on his—
and others'—minds. No doubt the rest of the media were there
to cover the bail hearing, but I'm sure some were secretly
hoping for an outburst or a vigilante display.

After some more legal talk Judge Temple set bail at fifty

thousand dollars, cash or surety, meaning property or some such being put up for the bail amount. I heard a few low moans from the front right bench, and saw a heavy woman in black polyester stretch pants and a teary-eyed man, arm across her shoulders, and I imagined they were Tate Burnham's parents. That amount probably seemed as much as a million dollars to them, and I saw Tate turn and smirk at his parents, and at that moment I felt my jaw clench, knowing this smiling twerp had torn a part of my life out with his rags and matches.

Then a few people started coming forward, either with checks or pieces of paper in their hands, and the court clerk looked flustered and went up to the judge, and soon there was a line of people at the bench, all carrying something in their hands, and the courtroom started buzzing and I was scrambling to write in my reporter's notebook as Judge Temple rapped his gavel and said, "Tate Burnham, you should consider yourself one lucky soul. About twenty of your neighbors have come forward to pay your bail."

There was some shouting and crying from his parents, but after a few moments the handcuffs were off Tate Burnham and he was being hustled out of the courtroom, past the bright lights of the television cameras and the microphones of the reporters. The place became very crowded and I found myself wedged in among some reporters next to Wayne Ferguson, road agent for the town, who scratched at his bald head and explained why he had put up one thousand dollars for Tate Burnham's release.

Wayne Ferguson said, "Well, the boy's troubled, anyone can see that. I don't see what purpose or good it'd do, having him put in jail until the trial. No purpose at all. After all's said and done, he's from Purmort, he's a neighbor. And we take care of our own here."

With that he pushed some of us aside and I was next to Harmon Kirk, who carried one of those hand-held Japanese tape recorders.

Harmond said, "Hell of a good story, Jerry."

"That it is. But you must be disappointed—no vigilantes."

Harmon smiled at that. "Right. No vigilantes. My editors will be dismayed. Guess I'll have to pitch them a piece about a crazy town with a big heart."

"Guess so," and with that phrase, never had I been so proud to be a resident of Purmort.

That night, after my supper, I sat in front of my first-floor woodstove and watched the trapped flames flicker and dance, knowing my home was safe.

But I was up on Timberswamp Road, shivering in the late night cold, watching the hard gray in the east signal a slow-approaching dawn. I remembered how I talked to the county dispatcher, Norma Quentin, and how she hesitated when I asked her about this fire and Tate Burnham. The smell of the smoke was mixed with something else, a harsh, greasy smell, and I made my way farther up the hill, finding my way easily enough in the lights from the fire trucks and the police cruisers. Chief Parnell was there, with two of his officers, and I nudged past them, looking at the crest of the hill where the grass had burned away.

There was no wreckage there, no blackened timbers from a house or a barn. In the middle of the burnt-out grass patch was an oak tree, its trunk scorched by the flames. Next to the trunk was a gasoline can, turned on one side, its paint bubbled and smeared away. Wrapped around the base of the tree was a chain, and the chain ran down the hill a short way, where it ended up wrapped around the legs of a charred carcass, which at first looked like a cow or a goat or a . . .

Only by turning my head quickly and stepping away was I able to avoid getting sick. I breathed through my mouth, not wanting to smell that horrible, greasy odor again. Chief Parnell came over to me and grabbed my arm, and we walked a bit, down the darkened road, until my head cleared.

The chief said, "Got here quick enough."

"My sources. You know that." I looked back up the hill, and just as quickly at the chief. "Who is it?"

The chief shrugged. "Not an official I.D., but based on what we know and who was reported missing last night, I'll have to say Tate Burnham."

"Tate Burnham . . ." I turned and saw the chain again, imagining what it must've been like, to be chained there and engulfed in flames, not being able to escape or even move. I looked back at the chief and noticed the firefighters and the two other Purmort police officers, standing in a loose circle, all staring at me.

I said, "Who do you think did this to him?"

Again that casual shrug, and though the sun was beginning to rise, I was feeling colder. "Himself, I imagine," the chief said, his voice even.

"Himself?" I demanded, my voice rising. "Chief, you're saying he did it to himself?"

The chief's eyes narrowed and he said, "That's exactly what I'm saying, Jerry. The man knew we had him nailed to the wall, knew he wasn't going to escape a guilty verdict, knew he could never live in these parts again. Me, I think—and I'm gonna tell state police this—I think he came up here, depressed as hell, and he killed himself, just like those monks in Vietnam back in the sixties."

"Chief, the chain . . ."

The chief just raised an eyebrow. "He probably did it to himself, make sure he couldn't chicken out. Jerry, it makes sense, now, don't it?"

I tried to catch my breath and failed. My head seemed like it would burst, and I felt like grabbing the chief's shoulders for some reason. The firefighters and the police officers had stepped closer to me, still standing in that loose circle, and all of them were looking at me, and their expressions were all the same, a very cold expression, of a group or tribe looking at a dangerous outsider. For a moment I almost felt like laughing, remembering how suckered we had all been, at the so-called miracle as the townspeople lined up to pay for Tate Burnham's bail. Sure, out of the goodness of their hearts, to free Tate Burnham from the grasp of the state and to bring him back to the town where he belonged. I remembered what the road agent, Wayne Ferguson, had said: We take care of our own here.

They certainly do. The group of firefighters and police officers were closer, and again I felt like laughing at the horror of it all. I could live here for another ten or twenty or thirty years, and never would I belong, never would I be a part of what went on here in Purmort, below the surface and behind the headlines. I looked at all their faces, old and young, and they all looked like brothers.

I spoke up, loud enough so everyone could hear. "If you say so, but it's a pity, Chief. A real pity, that he died this way."

There were some smiles given to me by the group after that, and in a minute or so, I began walking quickly back to my truck, and once I glanced behind me, and I was happy to see I was alone. I went into my truck and locked both doors and before starting the engine, I placed my head on the steering wheel and wept.

I had lost my home.

# ANTONIA FRASER

# THE MOON WAS TO BLAME

*Lady Antonia Fraser, renowned historian and social ac-
tivist, somehow finds the time to produce mystery novels
and short stories, as well. Her novels and some of the
stories feature female sleuth Jemima Shore, while others
like "The Moon Was to Blame" are studies in suspense
and human weakness. Whatever her subject, Antonia
Fraser's name on a book or story marks it as one to be
read with anticipation and delight. This story appeared
in* EQMM *almost simultaneously with its publication in*
Winter's Crimes 21.

Isabel said afterward that we were really getting too old for
that sort of thing: which remains perhaps the best verdict on
the whole sad affair. Unless you take the line—as my wife did—
that the moon was to blame.

They've never found out who did it: just some ugly little
incident among a lot of drunken campers. Since clearly none of
us was involved, they let us all go and back we all came to
England. Not immediately—that would have looked odd since
we'd rented an expensive villa—but a little sooner than
planned. You could hardly blame us for cutting short our
holiday by a few days. A death on the beach below, police
crawling all over the place, *Greek* police what's more: not that
we put it like that to the charming young woman in the villa
rental office, given that she was a Greek. In any case, she was
most understanding. Especially as we showed no signs of asking
for a reduction in the rent.

Obviously none of us four were involved—how could we be
involved, up in that great big villa on the rock? How could a
smart villa party of well-off married people from London be

involved with some little scrubber camping down below? Different worlds. Utterly different worlds. Quite soon, the police took that line, too.

The world of the campers below was not only a different world, but a pretty horrible one to boot. Crowds—there must have been nearly fifty campers down there—and squalor, naturally, since there was no sanitation beyond the natural shade of the olive trees, those graceful trees whose leaves had flickered so exquisitely in the sunlight on the day we arrived, when the beach was still empty.

"Do you realize that apart from anything else—apart from the noise, ye Gods, the noise, we hardly slept a wink last night, did we, Isabel?—do you realize that it's *illegal?*" That was Nick. Isabel nodded vigorously, as she always agreed strongly with everything that Nick said in public. (In private, since the villa walls were not entirely soundproof, we were aware that matters were somewhat different.) But my wife, Dinah, did murmur to me afterward in that light voice of hers—the one she uses for her really snaky remarks—that it was wonderful to have Nick standing up for the law here on the tiny island of Bexi, it really must be the effect of the sun, since back on the great big island of Britain Nick sometimes took rather a different line about the law.

But I had better begin at the beginning. No, not at the very beginning, not from our very first business enterprise; suffice it to say that the four of us, Dinah and myself, Nick and Isabel, had become close enough over the years to take villas together in sunny foreign parts over a considerable span of time. The Algarve, Italy, Greece (Corfu followed by Paxos), all these have produced comfortable villas, more or less, and happy holidays, of which the same could probably be said. And frankly, a holiday which is more or less happy is way above most holidays you take: which is, I think, why we all persevered with the arrangement.

Did I mention that something else unites us—beyond the same line of work and living nowadays in the same part of London? We're all childless, or effectively childless. Nick did have a son by his first marriage, I believe, but either the mother kept him to herself or Isabel dumped him—the story varies. At all events, he never figures in our lives. As for ourselves, we've certainly never wanted children. We're enough for each other, always have been. I look after Dinah, she looks after me, as we're fond of saying, so that at the age when our contemporaries are spending all their time worrying over their ungrateful twenty-year-olds and a good deal of their money rescuing them from this, that, and the other, also without getting much thanks, we four have the luxury of our time to ourselves. And our money, too, come to think of it.

*Douceur de vivre:* that's our motto (and, yes, it does sound much better in French, but then we four are, I fancy, rather more enlightened in our enjoyment of luxury than the average couples who toast "the sweet life").

This year we decided to experiment with a lesser island and go to Bexi. An island paradise, said the brochure. And so I suppose it was—in a way. Much less spoilt than Corfu and much nearer to a decent airport than Paxos. Villa Aglaia was pretty near paradise, too. At first. Even my wife, who generally finds something to say about the washing arrangements or lack of them, approved the separate showers for each double bedroom, to say nothing of a water supply which actually did not run out. (Remembering that time outside Portofino!) And the view was so extraordinary, right there on the cliffs; we would look toward Albania at night and watch the moon rise. A thin crescent the night we arrived—amusing to be drinking retsina again, once the duty-free champagne ran out—but rapidly growing.

The moon: yes. Perhaps, after all, Dinah was right and the moon was to blame. Insofar as anyone else was to blame. Certainly the moon appears to have been to blame for what started to happen on the beach. When the first campers appeared—one large grey tent under the olives and one girl who slept under an old boat—we even thought them quite picturesque. The girl, anyway. "The local Samantha Fox," my wife dubbed her on one occasion, since she certainly had the most fantastic figure—the sort you could photograph for Page Three, as we couldn't help noticing since she seldom wore anything but a bikini bottom.

But Samantha Fox wasn't quite right since Brigitte—that was

actually her name—happened to be brown all over, having an amazing tan apart from having an amazing figure. As a matter of fact, I chatted to her quite a bit in early mornings when no one else was around, and she was really very polite and friendly— just a kid working her way around Europe as a waitress, taking a holiday on this beach in between. German probably—or was she Swedish? She had this special feeling about St. Peter's, Rome, I remember, the square at St. Peter's; she was absolutely deter- mined to see the square. We had quite long talks about it.

Not when the others were around, however. Then, I have to say, the conversation was on a very different level. Well, we were on holiday. There was one famous occasion when Brigitte, topless, wobbled so perilously near Nick, sunbathing on the stones, on her way to the sea that my wife and I both involun- tarily looked toward Isabel.

The fact is that Isabel, who does sometimes bathe topless (but always discreetly up at the villa), does have the most lovely slim figure, everyone agrees about that. But if Isabel has a fault, it's the fact that, good-looking woman as she is, she is totally flat-chested. Perhaps that explains why I've never really fancied her, and perhaps that explains again why we've all holidayed so happily together. Be that as it may, on this occa- sion Isabel merely smiled in her most tranquil manner and murmured something like, "I should be so lucky." Later in their bedroom, however, it was rather a less tranquil story. What a tigress! That serene, smiling woman. Still, the end of it sounded rather satisfactory—at least from Nick's point of view, and I assume Isabel's as well.

All the time, the moon was getting stronger at night—I should say bigger, but was it the increasing strength of the moonlight rather than the size of the moon itself which was so unsettling? Could you believe moonlight could be so white? Even when the moon was only half full. That strange, cold, ancient light illuminating the sea which washed the rocks beneath us, the sea stretching out to the Albanian coast in a vast series of black-and-silver eddies with that broad flare path in their center.

We took to sitting later and later on the terrace with our wine—a light Greek wine, for after dinner. "So light, it's like drinking water," Nick had said jovially on our second night. But of course it wasn't quite like drinking water, particularly not in the quantities in which we consumed it. Perhaps it was all that wine late at night which made us so unsettled. They were odd, quirky, even slightly sinister, those sessions we had on the terrace. Yet hadn't we drunk wine in the Algarve and Italy and Paxos only the year before, the result being mere pleasure, relaxation?

Most unsettling of all, after we finally left the terrace, my wife and I had to lie, silent, and sleepless, in our bedroom hot behind the shutters and listen to Isabel, the tigress of the night, who was growing more and more ferocious in the room alongside ours. Was *that* the wine? The wine coupled with the moonlight (I noticed they did not close their shutters)? Or was it the noises coming from the beach?

For the waxing moon brought campers, more and more campers. And given its provocative light, bathing the beach in its brightness like a too-well-lit stage where there had been nothing but discreet blackness before, we could hardly ignore their presence. There was—I can see it now, and my wife can see it, too—a feeling of working toward some kind of climax long before we heard the news about the party.

Besides, one or two fires began to flicker down below: those fires so dangerous to a wooded island depending on its olive groves, which was in fact the official reason for the banning of campers on Bexi. When we went down to swim in the early morning, we would find the black shells of night fires among the stones. There would also be cans of Coke, beer, and bottles abandoned. And other even more distasteful signs of what had taken place on the beach the night before. Signs of "safe sex" perhaps, but as my wife observed, wrinkling her nose (I hastily removed one of these signs from her favorite path into the water, burying it under a big cairn of pebbles), "Safe sex is all very well, but what about a beautiful beach?"

Oddly enough, Brigitte very much kept to herself, apart from it all. She was friendly enough with the campers—she was a friendly girl, as I've said—but she never joined in with them at their various unpleasant goings-on. I know that, because I used to watch her sometimes from the lookout up above, watch her gazing out to sea, smoking the odd cigarette. What was she thinking about? St. Peter's square in Rome, perhaps, something like that. But I kept all that to myself, just as I never mentioned our morning conversations before the campers came.

At least the Villa Aglaia remained airy and remote from the squalor. In the daytime, when the campers were asleep or away in the little town of Bexi, so long as you didn't go down to the beach or visit the lookout you could cut yourself off from the squalor altogether. My wife cut branches of myrtle from the bushes which lined the steep but short path from the villa to the beach and put them everywhere in vases in the big rooms. But as the noises grew in proportion to the number of campers, I asked her not to cut back any more of the myrtle, for the bushes did at least conceal the path to the villa. What if the campers, drunk—or drugged, I put nothing past them—all decided to surge up the path in the small hours?

"Then you, darling, will have to be a big he-man and protect me," Dinah said in her snaky voice. "I somehow don't think Nick and Isabel would notice."

It was Nick who brought back the news of the party which was going to be held on the beach on the night of the full moon. He had been into the little port in the Land Rover just before dinner, while Isabel was washing her hair, to cash some traveler's checks. He came back looking white, or as near white as anyone as perfectly cared for and turned out (which means tanned) as Nick can ever look.

"A bloody great notice!" he exploded. "In English, what's more. Full Moon Party. On Aglaia Beach—our beach. Everyone invited. Bonfires, dancing, naked bathing. Come by boat! Come by moped! On the night of the full moon. All this on a notice fixed to a tree just outside the town." He repeated: "And in English, too."

"If it hadn't been in English, Nick," my wife pointed out reasonably enough, "you wouldn't have understood it." But Isabel, short, carefully streaked hair in a shining halo, was busy giving Nick a rewarding pat.

"Well done, Nick. At least you've warned us."

"Warned us! I damn well have. Look, I'm going to have a whiskey. Have we got any left? It's a disgrace. Tomorrow I'm going to tell that little Greek girl in the office that I want it stopped, stopped without question."

"But tomorrow will be too late, Nick," Dinah continued in that same reasonable voice. "Tonight is the night of the full moon. Didn't you notice last night? It was very, very nearly full—only one tiny sliver missing."

I must say that I was surprised at the time that my wife had that kind of information at her fingertips, but then I read in one of the magazines you only read in airplanes that retaining the capacity to surprise your spouse is the secret of a happy marriage. I daresay it's Dinah's remarkable sense of order which made her interested in something equally regulated like the phases of the moon.

So we come to the party. I have to admit a certain reluctance in thinking about it all, even now, back in London W.11 in our beautiful house, the house which some people laughingly suggest is too big for us—"Too luxurious even for you two"—but is actually a wonderful monument to my wife's exquisite, cool, and above all fastidious taste. A showcase for a sense of order, somebody else said.

If that's true about our house, and it probably is, then you can just imagine how poor Dinah suffered during that nightmare buildup to the Full Moon Party on Aglaia Beach. The utter chaos, the noise, of course—the noise was indescribable—and let me not leave out the fear. The four of us, four sophisticated people, crouching there—I'm afraid after a while we were definitely crouching—as the car lights came toward the beach along the edge of the cliff, an army advancing on us, and the full moonlight lit up what went on below. In a way it reminded me of some medieval picture of Hell—all the couples writhing as though in torment, their white limbs gyrating. In fact, they were of course dancing and copulating. You would feel like using that word if you had seen what we saw.

"Supposing they do decide to come up here?" Nick said that, I know he did. "Just supposing?" Nick is a big man, very heavily built in spite of all the exercise he takes. We're both of us big men, come to that, two big men with two fragile wives—that was another thing we had in common. Dinah, like Isabel, is wonderfully slender—well preserved or whatever you call it. Naturally she takes marvelous care of herself. But even Nick sounded frightened. And I was frightened, too.

It was some time after that that it happened.

"Supposing you went down there? Just supposing." Who said that? Who spoke those words? It must have been my wife, for who else was present when those words were spoken? Nick and Isabel had gone off to bed at last, their shutters open to the noises of the hot inflaming night, and the light of the coldly lustful moon. We could hear that the tigress was already devouring her huge submissive prey when those words were spoken.

The excitement comes back to me now, the secret, thrilling fear of it all, and the whispered words which went on: "Take her—you want her. She's down there. Find her and take her. You want her, don't you? Take her, you want her. Take her, you want her."

Take her, you want her, wanton and naked, wanton and naked, the words became like a rhythm beating in my brain. Wanton and naked: but no, these last words were never spoken, even by my wife, but they, too, became like a rhythm in my brain.

Those were the words which continued to turn and tumble in my mind as I went down alone, down the myrtle path to the Aglaia Beach.

It wasn't difficult to find her—Brigitte, the brown goddess of the beach. She wasn't even dancing with the others round the fire; she was sitting by the upturned boat, alone in the dark shadow cast by the boat. She was smoking one of her cigarettes and looking out to sea. Perhaps she was thinking about Rome and St. Peter's. I rather hope so. I really rather hope she was thinking about something nice. Even by the boat, the noise of all the others was incredible, confusing, and they had transistors now, belting out their dance music across the moonlit sea, desecrating the moonlight, desecrating the whole beach.

I took her quite easily. I grabbed her, grabbed that round brown wobbly body. She was quite little in my arms, in spite of her fullness—much smaller than I thought she would be. So I took her and held her tight. She couldn't shout, either—not that it would have mattered much if she had, the noise was so loud, the other people so busy round the bonfire. All the same, I put my hand across her mouth.

"Now show me you're a man, after all—a real man. Take her!" But she didn't say "take" this time—she used something far rougher, cruder. That was my wife's voice again, she must have followed me down the myrtle path, but it was a voice so avid, so ferocious, that for a moment it even might have been the tigress, Isabel. And besides, I'd never heard my wife use a word like that in all our married life.

And I did take her. Didn't I? I would have taken her. If only she'd cooperated just a little, practiced a little of that love and friendship she talked about to me on the beach.

Instead, she struggled—struggled rather a lot. I mean, why flaunt yourself like that, half naked, sometimes wholly naked, if you're not prepared to cooperate just a little?

As to what happened after that, there's really no point in recounting it all. Sad and rather squalid, really, but a complete accident. Even a misunderstanding, you could say. If it hadn't happened with me, it would have happened sooner or later with any of the other men she led on and didn't satisfy.

Afterward I hardly remembered the details of it all, isn't that odd? Just coming back so carefully and silently up the myrtle path, my wife's eyes gleaming like a cat's as we felt our way. Afterward holding her in bed, and my wife, usually so fastidious, holding me, too. Nick and Isabel were silent by then. That night, very late, it was my wife who was the tigress at the Villa Aglaia. . . .

There's not much more to tell. As I said, the police didn't really bother us much, just a great many questions and all that, naturally, but mostly the obvious questions about the party and the noise and then the tragedy—had we heard anything, seen anything, that sort of thing. It went on for hours.

Heard anything! Nick really snorted at that one, I can tell you. For a moment I thought he was going to start up all over again about the noise and the camping being illegal and why didn't the police stop it? Which under the circumstances wouldn't have been quite appropriate. But as a matter of fact, Nick's pretty good with the police, officials generally, knows the value of politeness and all that. He also cut quite an impressive figure, all washed and shaved and tidy.

We all were—washed and shaved and tidy. And the Villa looked immaculate. As anyplace with my cool, collected wife at the helm invariably does.

As to Nick being so good with the police and officials generally, my wife did murmur afterward: "Well, he's had a certain amount of practice, hasn't he?" But then, as I already mentioned, my wife has always been a little tart—one can't say more than that—about Nick's sharp business practices. As usual, there's a good deal to be said for her point of view.

The conversation with Nick and Isabel after the police left really rather proved her point.

First of all, Isabel said, yawning slightly: "Listen, folks, we've been thinking it over. We're really getting a little old for this sort of thing—holidays *à quatre,* I mean. It's been great, of course, no need to say that, but it's a hotel for us next year. Villas on the sea can be noisy. You can hear everything. That's a fact. The most peculiar things. The later at night, the more peculiar. So it's a luxury hotel *à deux* for us, in future."

She didn't seem to expect an answer to what she had just announced and I suppose there wasn't much we could say. She didn't look at either of us as she spoke, I do remember that.

Then Nick chimed in. He'd been thinking overnight as well, it seemed. And what Nick had been thinking about was the next big deal—the one where there'd been a bit of an argument, seeing as I had done all the work from start to finish and couldn't see that he should have more than a very small cut. Well, on this particular deal, he simply stated that the split would be fifty-fifty. With no argument. He didn't seem to expect an answer to that one, either. . . .

As a matter of fact, I don't miss our joint holidays with Nick and Isabel. She was right, we really had grown out of all that. It's that fifty percent which still rankles. But whenever I say so to my Dinah—I groan and ask, "Why did I agree?"—she replies in her snaky voice (which, generally speaking, she uses a great deal less nowadays):

"You lost your head in Bexi, that's why." Then she adds more softly, "It was the moon that was to blame." There's even a voluptuous note in her voice when she asks in her turn: "Wasn't it all worth it?"

# Ruth Graviros

# TED BUNDY'S FATHER

*Fictional accounts of real-life murderers carry a special fascination, perhaps because the author is free to explore the mental processes of the killer and to speculate on what drove him to his crimes. Here the author carries the process one step further, with a riveting story of the father that serial killer Ted Bundy never knew. . . . . "Ruth Graviros" is a pseudonym of Eleanor Sullivan, the highly regarded editor of EQMM. Since she joined the magazine as Fred Dannay's managing editor twenty years ago, EQMM has occasionally published her short stories—always under a variety of pseudonyms because she wanted the stories judged for themselves without regard to their authorship. With "Ted Bundy's Father" she has produced her most successful effort, one which was nominated for this year's MWA Edgar Award.*

With his tendency to tune out the distasteful, Warner Chadason couldn't remember when he'd first heard or read about Ted Bundy. He'd had little personal experience with crime in his sixty-four years—the hit-and-run death of a classmate when he was in grammar school, a series of petty thefts on board ship when he was in the Navy, the burglary of the first house he and Jane had rented when they were married, the non-fatal shooting last summer of the manager of the store where they bought their liquor out on Route 138.

Except for several brief skirmishes in the North Atlantic in 1944, he had enjoyed an unthreatened life, growing up in an affectionate, comfortable home in the same serene town on the Rhode Island coast where he again now lived. His parents and his middle brother were gone, marriage had taken both sisters to distant parts of the country, and his oldest borther, a retired violinist with the Rhode Island Philharmonic, lived in Providence.

Warner's enthusiasms had always been simple. Beyond bring-
ing up a family and his work as a marine biologist, he enjoyed
reading, music, and fixing things. Wherever he'd lived since he
was a teenager, neighbors had called on him for help with
mechanical problems. Far from resenting it, he was sorry when
lack of time sometimes made it impossible to see a repair
through himself. He savored the hour or so with Jane over
drinks before dinner every evening, neglected his health a little,
and avoided television, aware that with his passive nature he
could easily watch to excess. One evening when he'd discovered himself idly watching *Wheel of Fortune* with Jane and
their visiting daughter Pat, whose husband was teaching an
evening class, he jumped to his feet, said, "Let me out of here,"
and headed for his study. "Too much for you, Daddy?" Pat said.
Jane laughed. "Can't take it, eh?"

So when *had* his awareness of Bundy begun? The question of
capital punishment had always been a bone of contention
between Jane and himself. Maybe it was during one of their
disputes about it. He was against the death penalty, no matter
how horrible the crime or the criminal. "It's not a civilized
solution, it doesn't address the problems these people are
acting out," was his unequivocal stand. He did recall one
evening early in the fall, the appetizing aroma of the lamb roast
in the oven urging them toward one last drink before moving
to the table, Jane spoke of Ted Bundy as if Warner naturally
knew who he was. "If we lived in another part of the country,"
she said, "one of the girls, or all three of them, could have been
his victim. I think you'd feel differently about it then."

Pat was thirty-five, Susan was thirty-three, and Elaine was
twenty-eight. "They would have been exactly the right age and
type of most of Bundy's victims when he was on his rampage in
the seventies," Jane said.

"The right type?"

"Intelligent, attractive, kind."

Warner frowned. "If I did go for the death penalty because
any of the girls were his victim, it would be because I couldn't
be impartial."

"You can't keep your distance from such an important issue because it hasn't happened to you!"

"I'm not saying the guy shouldn't be locked away for the rest of his life. I'm not even concerned about whether he lives or dies. But taking his life makes monsters of *us*. And it won't bring back his victims."

"He *has* been locked away, Warner, and he's escaped twice. In Colorado he jumped out of a second-floor window in the courthouse where he was about to go on trial, and later, when he was recaptured, through the ceiling in his jail cell. And he went on to Florida and killed and hurt some more young women. The ones who lived will never be the same. And even now on Death Row, they have to keep changing his cell because of his attempts to escape. It's all a game to him. Killing the girls was just the beginning. He's playing games with everyone: the police, the press, the psychiatrists, the courts, the taxpayers—"

Jane was the most persuasive woman Warner had ever known. When she walked into the lab at Woods Hole back in 1949 as a summer intern from Vassar, he'd known she'd be capable of dissuading him from some long-held convictions—which she had, for the most part painlessly. It was possible, he sometimes thought, that he'd married her as much for that quality in her as for the powerful physical attraction between them.

Her insistence on planned parenthood as a requisite to their marriage was a case in point. She wouldn't consider starting a family until they had sufficient means to give a child a healthy start in life. It was essential not only to their peace and happiness, she said, but to the peace and happiness of any children they would have—even to the peace and happiness of the community. "The unwanted child is the unwanted citizen," she'd concluded, never afraid of sounding the zealot. It was part of her passion. For all their reserved behavior in public and with the children, they were deeply passionate in private. He was, in his marriage, a very fortunate man, he knew, and Jane had made it clear every day of their years together that she considered herself as lucky as he did.

The children's slowness to marriage Jane attributed to the times—another judgment Warner could see to be true. His graduate students and the children of his friends and colleagues were definitely different in that respect from his generation. They seemed to fall in love just as haphazardly, but they were far more adept at protecting themselves from a chancy future. The cases of buck fever he'd witnessed back in the forties had no counterpart in the eighties.

Susan, their only child to marry young, was divorced and living in New Hampshire with her nine-year-old daughter Jess, not far from her former husband, whose lifestyle seemed able to accommodate little more than his carpentry jobs, skiing, drinking with his friends, and occasional "quality time" with his daughter. Pat had married at thirty-two. She and Bill, who taught drama at the university, were expecting their first child in March. Elaine, heedless of herself as the family beauty, so far seemed to thrive on her life as a journalist living alone in New York City. Over Thanksgiving weekend—which also happened to be the weekend of Warner's birthday this year—Tom, their fourth child, and associate professor in the humanities at the University of Chicago, had brought home a spirited young Dutch woman and announced their engagement at the holiday dinner. Meta was a psychologist with three years' more seniority on the faculty. Elaine declared herself to be delighted with Tom's catch but concerned that the weight of the family was falling so heavily toward the academic. "What's going on here?" she demanded.

"What can I tell ya?" Tom assumed *Saturday Night Live's* Dennis Miller's sweet smirk. "Knowledge is power."

"So think gossips and blackmailers, too." She shook her face close at him. "And spooks."

"And journalists," her brother said, sealing it with a kiss to her resolute jaw.

Warner spent a good part of the day after Thanksgiving helping Mark Roper, who had a glamorous house out near the beach, repair the damage after a plumbing leak that had all but ruined the Ropers' holiday. There was a half hour of daylight left when he drove in and saw Jane and most of the others settled in the old Adirondack chairs in the spacious fir-sheltered yard, bundled up in heavy jackets, drinking hot toddies. As he turned off the ignition and climbed out of the car, Jane poured from the thermos at her feet. "Welcome, pilgrim," she said, winding a cloth napkin around the glass and handing it to him.

"Hello, everybody." He took it from her to one of the empty chairs in the circle of conversation. Elaine was saying. "He murdered more women than we'll proabaly ever know. *He's* probably lost count."

"Don't you believe it," said Meta.

"When he was captured after killing that young girl in Florida, he told detectives he'd killed in six states, not four, and that they should add a digit to the FBI estimate that he was responsible for thirty-six murders."

"I wouldn't object to a change of subject," Jane said, taking the rubber ball Luther, the Labrador, had been holding in his mouth for her attention and tossing it toward the woods with a skilled arm.

"His is an amazing case of malignant narcissism." Meta's eyes behind her eyeglasses were bright. Did she know how pretty she was, Warner wondered, the blonde braid below her hand-knit cap so careless and healthy and young?

"Have they any idea even now what's genetic and what's not?" Jane asked her.

"Ha. We like to think we know. In Mr. Bundy's case, perhaps being born a white illegitimate child in the U.S. in nineteen forty-six when extramarital sex was still taboo, and being raised first in a household where he was led to believe his grandparents were his parents and his mother was his sister, then at the age of three being taken from the couple he thought were his parents by the sister a long distance away, where she soon presented him with a new 'father,' would prompt more than enough trauma to make any genetic factors irrelevant."

"Jack Nicholson grew up with that same mother-sister fiction," Elaine pointed out, "and he seems to have turned it into marvelous creativity."

Tom laughed. "He knows how to *play* malignant narcisism, for sure."

Elaine and Susan were pensive. "I wonder what makes the difference in how people react to desperate beginnings." Elaine said.

"The adults involved, I would think." A breeze blew up and Meta looked reflectively at the swaying trees. "Even if they can't be honest with a child regarding the facts, if they really love the child and show it in appropriate ways it should make a difference."

They celebrated Warner's birthday with dinner at their favorite restaurant in Newport on Saturday night. Through Sunday, the days and nights remained crisp and dry, with an ongoing fire in the living-room fireplace, impromptu conversations everywhere to be found in the house. Only one of those, to Warner's knowledge, disturbed the tranquility of the weekend.

Sunday morning, while the others slept late, only Susan, who was an insomniac, was awake to share breakfast in the sunroom with Warner and Jane. Susan, cursed with depression most of her life, had grown increasingly moody and fractious since her exuberant arrival in her battered Volvo on Wednesday night.

"I can't wait to get back and see Jess," she said gloomily.

"We can't wait to see her at Christmas," Jane assured her. "Have another popover."

" 'Have another popover.' My daughter finally comes up in the conversation and you say 'have another popover.' "

"I'm sorry, dear. I can't say we've missed her this weekend as much as you must have, but believe me we'd have loved for her to be here. You know we wish you'd move back to Rhode Island."

"She needs her father, too."

"Yes, of course she does. Susan, if we haven't spoken of her as often as we might it's not a case of out of sight out of mind, it—"

"I feel so out of it with all of you, you know?" Susan glared at each of her parents in turn and then focused her misty-eyed anger at the stack of firewood on the drive outside the window. "Last night at dinner I could have barfed at the new bonding going on across the table between Tom and his girl friend and the old bonding going on between Pat and Bill—like they couldn't wait to get back to their respective beds to hash about the rest of us."

"You'll marry again," Jane said—as Warner wished she hadn't even before Susan turned on her, furious.

"That's so typical, Mother! I'm not talking about me, I'm talking about them! You think you understand more than you understand—like Tom's smug little *clairvoyant* from the Netherlands. She has all the answers!" She returned her gaze to the driveway. "My dear brother's going to marry a girl just like the girl that married dear old Dad." Then, with the eye contact of a great actress, she told them both, "I'll leave you to *your* bonding, I've got to pack." She started out of her chair.

"Oh, shut up." Jane reached for her wrist and brought her back down. "Susan, I know that when you hurt, you want to hurt. And I know your father and I have made mistakes as parents and we're still making them—"

"What? Just by being models of contentment?" Susan said sarcastically. "Don't be silly. How could I object to that?"

"You could object to it, dear, if your courageous choice of a husband didn't live up to your expectations. Sam was a decent choice. He's a good man. But he's apparently not ready to be a husband and a father, and he may never be ready. You've dealt with that beautifully—"

"Spare me."

"I'm not being condescending."

"Oh, no? Spare me that, too."

Warner pushed back his chair, brought his half-empty plate and coffee cup to the kitchen, and leashed Luther for their morning walk.

When they returned a half hour later, Susan and Jane were still talking intensely but more quietly at the table. As Warner hung up his jacket in the mud room, thinking of how and where and whether to escape, he heard Susan complain that she bore the brunt of Sam's desertion in Jess's eyes, that all mothers bear the burden of a child's blame when a father is abusive or indifferent or absent and there wasn't a *word* for the unfairness of it.

Jane worked as a volunteer two days a week at a local thrift shop, the proceeds of which fed half a dozen charities. She was an insatiable reader and donated, borrowed, and returned books every day she went in. Several weeks before Christmas, she looked up after dinner from a copy of a dogeared paperback she was reading, thought awhile and said, "Bundy's game was easy for him to win because he didn't play fair. His victims weren't aware of the game—they hadn't been brought up to even dream they were being hunted when he came along in his well-mannered way with his casts and crutches and asked for their help."

"What's this obsession everyone has with this guy?" Warner objected. "Mass murder's a pretty morbid subject to begin with, and he's not the only one around."

"Well, for one thing he's due for execution soon. I should think that would be of interest to you, morbid as it is, you're so dead set against capital punishment."

Warner folded his newspaper closed. "What's the book?" He could see the author's name, Ann Rule, on the well-cracked binding from this distance, but not the title.

"It's called *The Stranger Beside Me.* The author's written other true-crime books and just happens to have known Ted Bundy since nineteen seventy-one when they were both night volunteers at a suicide-prevention clinic in Seattle. She was an unpaid volunteer, he was a paid work-study student."

"He was born in Seattle?"

"No, he was born in a home for unwed mothers in Burlington, Vermont, in late nineteen forty-six. His mother left him there alone for a few months, then returned to get him and bring him home to live with her parents in Philadelphia."

"And she pretended to be his sister," Warner remembered. "What about his real father?"

"His mother won't say, except that he was a sailor."

"There were a lot of us around then," Warner smiled.

"Abortion was illegal, of course, and anyway her family's religion forbade it. When she took him to Washington state, she started to use her middle name, Louise, instead of her first name, Eleanor."

"When did she tell him the truth about it?"

"She didn't. He knew something wasn't right—of course he would, a *sister* taking him away from his *parents?* When he was twenty-two he came back East and traced his birth to Vermont.

He went to Burlington, asked for his birth certificate under her name before she married John Bundy out in Washington, and there it was. It had to be some kind of shock."

"I can imagine," Warner said—then, as Jane returned to the book, he thought, No. No, I can't.

As Christmas drew closer and the university suspended classes, Warner helped Jane with the usual errands. Tom was flying to Apeldoorn with Meta to spend the holidays with her family, but Elaine was coming up by train from New York, possibly with a new suitor (but probably not, she said), and Susan was driving down from North Conway with Jess.

One rainy morning, Jane's Olds wouldn't start and Warner drove her to the thrift shop on the Post road. As she climbed out and reached back for the shopping bag of books she was donating and returning, he spotted the Ted Bundy book at the top. "Let me have a look at that before you return it," he said. That something inside him leapt at the prospect startled him.

That he was interested in reading it at all surprised Jane. "Do you want to pick me up at four-thirty?" she said, transferring the book from the bag to the passenger seat. "We have that heavy food-shopping to do."

He stopped at the lab for some papers and any mail, then drove home, made a cheese sandwich, poured a beer, and went to his study with the book.

Even reading comprehensively, Warner was a fast reader, and reading the book without skipping a detail he was halfway through it by midafternoon. He had stopped more than once to study the eight pages of photographs of Bundy, several of his victims, the scene of one of the crimes, a police sketch made of him in 1974, mug shots of him in 1975. At his most bedraggled, his hair curly and brown, his smile open, he was more attractive than average, even appealing. Warner could see he'd be very easy to relate to and trust on first meeting.

He was 5'10", which was surprising since his mother—of whom there was no photograph—was only a few inches over five feet. The more Warner read about his pretensions, his loving Mozart and good wines and gourmet food, the more impatient he became with the superficiality of the man. And as he read about the murders he had been convicted of and confessed to, the sicker he felt about Bundy. When the clock told him it was time to pick up Jane, he was relieved to take off his reading glasses and put the book aside.

As he went to the door, he stopped to take a brief, uncharacteristic glimpse of himself in the hall mirror—tall, his crisp salt-and-pepper hair still abundant.

If Bundy's mother was so short, he reflected as he unlocked the car a few minutes later, his height must have come from his father.

When they returned from shopping, Jane heated the pizza they'd picked up for dinner and served it with a green salad and wine. Warner didn't mention the cheese sandwich he'd had for lunch. He'd never had a cholesterol problem, but he was aware he was pushing it.

After coffee, Jane began her serious holiday cooking. She would start with the desserts tonight and tomorrow, and when the holidays rolled around a week from now she would have frozen or wrapped enough hors d'oeuvres, casseroles, bread, cookies, and desserts to see friends and themselves into the new year.

By the time the ingredients were organized and the oven was on temperature, Warner, in his study, was on page 397 of *The Stranger Beside Me:*

"Ted loved things more than he loved people. He could find life in an abandoned bicycle or an old car and feel a kind of compassion for these inanimate objects—more compassion than he could ever feel for another human being." For the firs time, Warner perceived Bundy involving himself in a genuine interest, not one he manufactured to impress. The skills must have served him well in his escape attempts.

Forty-five more pages and he'd finished. From the kitchen came the sound of foil tearing, of the oven, cabinet, and refrigerator doors opening and closing. Luther was in a deep sleep across the threshold, where he perversely liked to lie. Warner thought a while, then opened the book to study the

photographs once again and to reread parts of the second
chapter about Ted Bundy's start in life.

Eleanor Louise Cowell. The surname seemed familiar but far
from certain. Her illegitimate boy was born on November 24,
1946. Even allowing for the widest obstetrical vagaries in a full-
term birth, he was most likely conceived in February of that
year.

In February 1946, Warner had spent his last weekend fur-
lough prior to his discharge from the Navy in Philadelphia, off
the tanker on which he'd spent most of his almost two years of
college-interrupted service. Within the month, he was headed
home to Rhode Island, a degree, and, five years later, marriage.

His left hand and forearm were heavily bandaged because of
second- and third-degree burns he'd suffered in a fall against a
boiler during a heavy storm off Nova Scotia. But his sense of
freedom at his imminent release had more than compensated
for the pain. He and his best buddy, Alex Kessel, had signed off
and begun the weekend together, but Alex, who was engaged
to be married in May, went wild on the Friday night and spent
most of Saturday sleeping off a whopping hangover in their
hotel room.

After seeing to Alex's needs, Warner set out alone to see the
city of brotherly love. In the hotel coffee shop, he ordered
orange juice, scrapple (which he'd never had before), and eggs.
He went on to the zoo, then to the Museum of Art. It was there
that he'd noticed this tiny, dark-haired girl, first studying a
painting and then studying him. She spoke to him first, asking
him about his bandages. She told him how to care for burns and
the importance of keeping them clean and the bandages dry.
He thought she was a nurse at first, but she said no, she wasn't.

She hadn't, he recalled, answered any of his friendly personal
questions in detail. She told him her name was Ellie—if she
gave a last name it was lost to him. Remembering her and his
feelings now, Warner was newly impressed by her strange
secrecy and by the sadness of their predicament. She didn't
know what to do with her day and neither did he.

He suggested a movie and then, if she had no other plans,
dinner. She had no plans, she said—a movie and dinner would

suit her fine. They walked to where she knew the nearest theater to be. *To Each His Own*, which neither of them had seen, was playing, and though it held no attraction for him he could see she was drawn to it, so he reached for his wallet and paid for the best seats.

Afterward, he asked if she would be interested in a shore dinner and she said yes, she loved cole slaw, didn't he love cole slaw? Did he know it was sugar of all things that gave it that special taste?

The seafood restaurant they found was spacious and popular, with roomy booths and sawdust on the floor. They each had a cuba libre while they waited for their fried clams and although Warner couldn't actually remember what they'd talked about, he expected he'd done most of the talking and that it had been about his experiences on board ship, *his* interests, *his* aspirations. She wasn't shy so much as quiet and had given him the impression she preferred to listen and make the occasional— sometimes stupefying—comment.

She lingered so long over her ice cream and coffee, he guessed correctly that she was disinclined to go home and so he suggested that since the weather was on the mild side she, as a native Philadelphian, give him a walking tour.

First they observed the action on Market Street. Many servicemen during the war, Warner thought, had gone berserk on weekend leave because of the danger or boredom they were going back to—now they were going crazy for different reasons. The prospect of the real freedom soon to come, maybe, or the loss of their innocence or of their buddies—or, as in Alex's case, fear of a new commitment. He couldn't begin to say from his own experience what really drove the others.

From the busier streets, Ellie led him out past the length of Franklin Field to a college campus—which of Philadelphia's colleges another detail Warner couldn't recollect. It was while they were wandering there that she took him by complete surprise. They were alone on a path close to a dark two-story red-brick building when she faced him under a low-wattage streetlight, slid a hand under his pea jacket, under his winter middy, under his white T-shirt, and gave him an extended look that told him this was what the day had been leading to and that this was the place.

He followed her back around the side of the building and two steps up behind a row of white pillars to the deserted concrete terrace. Nothing about her previous, almost puritanical presentation of herself—her careful manners, the grey cloth coat over the black jumper and long-sleeved, high-necked white blouse—had prepared him for the ardor with which she met him, or the lust she evoked in him—a lust he'd never remotely, even in his loneliest fantasies, experienced until then.

The blank he draws now of almost everything that night after her climactic *"Oh!"* is terrifying. He does remember not seeing her home—at her insistence—and wondering if she could after all be married, or if it was his uniform she was ashamed of. He vaguely recalls wanting to phone her the next day before he and Alex returned to the ship, but she had left him with no information about herself and asked for none from him. Just as she had asked for no protection.

In 1969, while Ted Bundy was attending classes briefly at Temple University, a young woman was stabbed to death in the stacks of the library. Her murderer was never found.

In July 1971, in Burlington, Vermont, a young woman of twenty-four was beaten, raped, and strangled in her apartment. She had been working that summer at a motor inn directly next door to the home for unwed mothers where Ted Bundy was born twenty-five years earlier. The only indication that Bundy might have been in Burlington at the time, aside from his unaccountability elsewhere, was a notation in the dog catcher's records that someone named Bundy had been bitten by a dog that week.

Were Pennsylvania and Vermont the additional states Bundy meant when he laid claim to two in addition to Washington, Utah, Colorado, and Florida?

"You can't pronounce it centri*fugal* just because you want to," Elaine told Jess from her armchair. "It's cen*trif*ugal. You have to pronounce words properly or you don't get no respect." Jess, tall for nine, sat posture-perfect on the floor by the still aromatic

Christmas tree, considering her aunt doubtfully. "Besides, cen-*trif*ugal is more fun to say."

"I don't think so."

Elaine bounced her head against the back of the chair. "What can I tell ya, Tom?" she addressed her absent brother. "Knowledge is painful."

"Why *I* don't teach," Susan said from where she lay on the sofa, a chic-funky felt hat crunched low on her head.

"Why I don't teach too," agreed Elaine. She smiled at Jess. "I just preach, right?" It was Monday afternoon, the day after Christmas. She would be getting an early train back to New York in the morning. Susan and Jess were staying until Friday. She pulled herself out of the chair. "Well, it's my last chance to see the Canadian geese down by the salt marsh. Does anyone want to come with me?"

"*I* do." Jess was on her feet.

"I'm too comfortable," Susan told them, gazing into the fire and then at Elaine. "I'm sorry." Jess was already in the kitchen, asking if she could borrow her grandfather's binoculars.

"Listen, an outing for me is an everyday for you."

"And vice versa."

"So when are you coming to New York again? I've got two bedrooms now. Come and go as you please."

"With Jess?" Susan meant that was unlikely.

"With or without Jess. Either would be wonderful."

She meant it, Susan thought as Jess and Elaine slammed out the back doors. She didn't like remembering how relieved she'd been to find that Elaine was alone when she and Jess arrived on Friday, but she was in a self-forgiving mood and conceded that she had barely recovered from the Thanksgiving-weekend realization that the family was partnering out and she was being left behind. The first shall be last, etc.

Her father had been gone for hours, rescuing some students who had elected to stay over for the holidays and were having a problem at the lab. Her mother was concocting a fish chowder for dinner. The living room was a tangle from the day before. Maybe she could make herself useful and restore some order.

She rolled off the sofa onto her feet, taking off the hat, her gift from Elaine—from Putumayo, whose clothes Susan insisted were made with her specifically in mind. She looked around for a big box for the debris. The largest contained the portable fireplace her father had given her mother to make more comfortable the late-day and night outdoor sits she liked so much. They might want to keep it in the carton.

Searching further, she found the box with her fa⸱᷄er's gifts to her—a covered trashcan for the kitchen, because of a problem she was having with mice, inside it an ultrasonic-sound device that was supposed to drive pests away. It would do. She began gathering the discarded wrappings into it, setting aside any genuine ribbon of usable length in case her mother wanted it. If she didn't, Jess would.

"Here, let me help," Jane said, coming from the kitchen and kneeling beside Susan, who was reaching under the tree to realign a tumble of gifts.

"I see Father did his Christmas shopping at Payson's Hardware as usual," Susan observed.

"Jess told us on the phone you have 'horrible mice.' "

Susan shuddered. "They're making me paranoid. I'm all the time looking for sign of them. They're like tiny Houdinis." She stopped and looked at her mother. There had been an abstracted quality about her all weekend that Susan found disturbing. "Is there something wrong between you and Father?"

"Wrong!" Jane looked at her, alarmed. She slid some boxes around on the rug and stood up. "I've got to take out the bread," she said with a toss of the head that said "Come with me."

Lifting two hot loaves from the oven, a pair of quilted mitts on her hands, she said, "Something's bothering him. I don't know what it is."

"For how long?"

"A week." She started to glaze the bread with butter and gave Susan a wan smile. "Only a week."

"I hate to admit this," Susan said, inclining her head to her mother's flushed cheek, "but I like it better when you're both happy." She moved across the kitchen to the table and sat. "What did these students call him away for, anyway?"

"Oh, just the autoclave again. They're not used to it. They

were sterilizing the equipment for their tests and it malfunctioned. They were in a panic it was going to explode."

"Sounds familiar." How many times over the years Susan had heard her father on the phone saying, "Ground yourself well, unplug it, and I'll come by in an hour or so when it's cooled down."

"They keep building better mousetraps. When are they going to build a better autoclave?" Susan said. Then: "Don't they ever call on someone else to go fix it?"

"Why should they? He always says yes."

"Never be an expert." Susan took a pine branch from the arrangement in an old jar on the table and pinched the berries. "I have a streak of laziness two miles wide. Look at this family. I don't know where you got me."

"You don't?"

"I married Sam because I thought he was as lazy as me. In some ways he is, but he's up for every odd job anybody hands him. Wouldn't it be funny if I really married him because he's like Father?"

When Jess and Susan left at the end of the week, the house seemed not only emptier than usual, it seemed emptier longer. Warner's dark mood failed to lift and it seemed to Jane that the light had gone out of his eyes, that his skin was unhealthily darker. She wanted to suggest he see a doctor. It would have been ideal to be able to say it was time they both had a checkup, but she had had a thorough checkup as recently as September.

Late one evening toward the end of January, she came downstairs from an evening of estimating the taxes for the thrift shop and found him daydreaming in front of a dreary TV sitcom.

"What's on television?" she asked.

"Nothing too exciting," he said.

Ordinarily she would have clutched her heart and said, "Thank God," but he wasn't up for it and neither was she. Instead she went to the kitchen and brewed some tea for the *Eleven O'Clock News.*

In the middle of which Warner jumped from his chair with a stricken look, told her he thought he'd left an important matter unattended at the lab, he might be late getting back, put on his windbreaker, and was gone.

Dear God, she thought as the beams from the headlights flashed past the window, what now? What devil was driving him so far away from her?

With all the overhead fluorescents on and the night pitch-black beyond the windows, the laboratory was deathlike. Warner had shot the inside lock and gone directly to the autoclave—the highly pressured, overworked soul of the place. The heat it generated was tremendous and most of the faculty and students were afraid of the damage it was capable of. He had seen some very mean burns from it and was himself wary of such accidents after his at sea all those years ago.

Forty-two years ago.

Ted Bundy was to die in the morning at the age of forty-two. It had been announced on the news, as he had expected it would be. What he had not expected was a videotaped inter-view with him made earlier tonight at the maximum-security prison in Florida. Wearing what looked to be a shrimp-colored T-shirt over a white long-sleeved jersey, his handcuffed hands clasped together in front of his mouth as he listened to the interviewer's questions, he didn't look that age. Nor did he appear arrogant. When the man interviewing him—a minister, did they say?—asked what he thought should be done about mass-murderers like himself, he'd said, "Don't get me wrong, I don't want to die—but I think society should do whatever it has to do to protect itself." Was this a last-minute bid for mercy, Warner wondered, and was the claim he made about his obses-sion with hard-core pornography being the trigger for the killings as true as only he could know it to be, or was he playing yet another game with a world he did not love? Warner thought it was too simplistic an explanation for him killing as he did. He had to feel such an injustice had been done to him sometime in his life that he couldn't hurt enough to satisfy his rage.

People who favored the death penalty, it occurred to Warner, and those who put themselves on line for it seemed to share an inability to see beyond their terrible grievances. He was cer-tainly no more merciful than Jane. Luckier, perhaps, in a kind of sightedness that either could see beyond what she saw or not as far. Watching the interview with her, he had known they would have to discuss it when the news was over and he couldn't bear the thought of it. Nor could he bear to watch the rest of the interview itself, reading the terror in Ted's face in spite of the medication he must have been given—his mouth had been dry as he gave his carefully deliberated answers. How did a condemned prisoner live through his or her last hours? How did those who loved them? Why were they put through the long night?

The books and articles he had read about Bundy and other mass-murderers since he'd finished *The Stranger Beside Me*, in their attempts to shape some sense from their behavior, had only added to Warner's confusion. He was impatient when they focused on Louise Bundy as at the root of her son's pathology. Even though she had behaved peculiarly with Warner, even though she hadn't wanted any kind of protection, he couldn't excuse himself. True, she'd said no, but he could have insisted. That might have frightened her, but on the other hand she may have needed that kind of resassurance. He'd had an obligation to anticipate the possibility of a child and to protect against it. These past weeks he had looked up James Agee's comment in one of his letters to Father Flye, the Episcopal priest whose long friendship with the author dated back to when Agee was his student at St. Andrew's School in Tennessee. Jane had quoted it to him back when the *Letters* were first published in the sixties.

"I very much trust in the blindness of nature," he'd written, "but there is a great deal in that blindness which is repellent, too. Begetting a child is at least as serious an act as murder."

They had seen *To Each His Own* that same evening! Olivia de Havilland had won the Oscar for playing the mother of an illegitimate baby in the movie. He had thought it pure soap opera and had in fact fallen asleep through part of it. Ellie, this strange creature from some nether world like the Mariana Trench, as he had since come to think of her, had had tears in her eyes when the lights came back up in the theater. But in the movie Olivia de Havilland had put the baby out for adoption—why hadn't Ellie? And why had she left Ted alone for two months at the Vermont home before returning to claim him and bring him to her parents' home in Philadelphia? In one of the books Warner had read, it was estimated that half of all our knowledge is locked in our first year of life. With his fate uncertain those first three months, no one to bond to, and God only knew what happening the remaining nine months, Ted's destiny and that of his victims could well have been decided by his first birthday.

"It's a tragedy for this court to see such a total waste of humanity that I've experienced in this courtroom," the avuncular judge who was the first to sentence Ted to death in Florida had said. "You're a bright young man. You'd have made a good lawyer, and I'd have loved to have you practice in front of me. But you went another way, partner. Take care of yourself. I don't have any animosity toward you—I want you to know that."

That his hours with Ellie had been born of a kind of mild desperation, Warner had only recently acknowledged, and that everything he remembered and read about Louise Bundy told him that marriage with her would have been disastrous, couldn't absolve him of his absence in the boy's formative years. If he had given him a grounding and Ted had become a monster nevertheless, Warner could consider laying more of the blame elsewhere, or on the system. As it was, he recognized now, he was part of the system. The man he had thought he was—considerate, rational husband, father, mentor, neighbor—did not really exist.

Had anyone been observing Warner from outside since his arrival, they would have wondered at his almost catatonic stance before the silent autoclave. But now they would see him straighten and seem to address the problem it presented.

When the unit had last malfunctioned in December, Warner for reasons he hadn't fully admitted to himself until now, had repaired it only to meet its immediate functional and safety needs. Several pipes and the gauge needed replacement rather than first aid. He should have ordered the new parts and seen them installed by now, but he'd done neither. So that now all he had to do was remove the faulty parts, work at the already frayed cord so that it was dangerously exposed, pour water on the floor beneath the unit to simulate escaped steam, plug in the cord, grasp the exposed section, and precede his son to Hell.

The digital clock by the bed read 5:10. Jane had phoned the lab and Warner's office at the university with no luck. She knew he could have been at the lab and purposely not picked up. Instinct also told her not to go looking for him or to call the children.

Was it possible that Warner was lost to her forever? It could be happening, she knew that without having the slightest inkling why, and all she could do was wait for the news from some policeman or learn that this was simply another of the morbid apprehensions that had been hounding her since her sixtieth birthday. There was that, too, after all, to be considered in Warner's recent behavior.

She couldn't concentrate on anything but her thoughts. What Warner called "the great unread" in the bookcase by her side of the bed held no comfort for her tonight.

His ventures as a handyman, she thought. More often than not anymore they were an effort at keeping the peace in the families of friends and neighbors who had foolhardily entrusted their cars, TV sets, and lawn mowers, and sewing machines to each other. In trying to restore these things to the condition the lender perceived them to have been, he hoped to restore the amiability of the community.

Luther, who had kept a restless watch down by the back door most of the night, came upstairs and in from the hallway, leaning his face on the comforter—comforter himself, his dark gaze over his greying muzzle perplexed and concerned. "I've got two labs now," Warner had told him when he was a puppy, "but only one named Luther."

"I don't know, Luther," she said to him now. "I'd tell you if I knew, but I don't."

All she did know was that Warner had bounded from his chair in the middle of the interview with Ted Bundy. Pore over that as she had, she couldn't for the life of her see any significance in it at all.

She was down in the living room with a cup of coffee, Luther all but on her lap, when she heard a car turn into the driveway shortly after seven. As Luther ran barking to the door, Jane closed her eyes against the life that seemed to fall away from her in her fear of hearing the doorbell. Then there was the sound of the key in the lock and Warner let himself in. Bending wearily to hush Luther, he saw her. She ran to him from the chair and his arms closed around her. Hers encircled him in a grateful stranglehold.

In the pale cast of dawn, he had lost the name of action. But although he hadn't been able to end his life, he was left with serious doubt about the favor that would be to Jane. His recognition that all their life together had been a fool's paradise for him was not something he could shrug off. Had he had any conscience at all before he met her? Why had he aborted his plan for an accident? Did he not want to die? Had he not wanted to kill? Had he not wanted to be killed? There was that theory that those three elements are necessary for the commission of suicide, he remembered. Actually, he had no disposition for any of the three. More than that, though, the conscious thought that had stopped him was the certainty that Jane would know it had been no accident, however feasible it might seem to the police, the community, and perhaps the children.

He buried his face in her hair. They were both crying. And while she would probably never tell him why she was, he thought he knew. It would remain one of the few secrets they would ever have apart.

A few hours later on January 24, 1989, in a bar on the U.S. side of Niagara Falls, an observant stranger might have taken note of one of those ever-young, ever-attractive drifters, full head of curly hair, propped over a beer at the gummy counter, a loud, complacent woman at his side, both occupied with the news on the TV over the bar.

On the screen, crowds cheering a ghostlike white hearse moving through dawn light gave way to a replay of part of the Bundy interview of the night before.

"He sure was a good-looking guy," the woman said. "Just my type." she appraised her drinking partner. "He looks a lot like you, Gus. Look at him, Larry," she said to the bartender, "doesn't he look like Gus?" Larry checked the two faces out and agreed obligingly. "You could be father and son if you were older," she told Gus.

Gus smiled and stroked the stubble on his jaw, flattered at looking like the man on television and at being taken, as always, for younger than he was.

"Bastard never had a father," Larry commented, pouring himself the third cup of coffee that morning.

"My God, I can't get over it," the woman said, reaching for a cigarette. "You don't see a resemblance like this every day."

Just like her to go on and on about it, Gus thought, watching the dead man still talking on the television screen. And as he watched, the smile left his face and a penumbrous shadow fell across his calculating, worried eyes.

# CONNIE HOLT

# HAWKS

*This year's winner of the Robert L. Fish Memorial Award for the best story by a promising newcomer is a brief tale of mourners at a funeral in the Arkansas hill country. Though Connie Holt now lives in California, we can't help feeling that she knows her background very well indeed. This is the sort of memorable gem that tells us we'll be hearing more from its author.*

The mourners gathered in small groups on the hillside, some under the red-leafed oak and others before the monuments to their own dead in the overgrown Irish cemetery. Aunt Hattie was back home in the kitchen seeing to supper for the "hungry folks after a funeral." Aunt Sue, Uncle Joe's wife, stayed down to help her. So did Miss Tatum Harris, the telephone operator for Arkansas Bell in Republican. Miss Tatum had brought two of her lemon layer cakes to do for dessert. Her neighbor, Mrs. Loder Smith, the wife of the general store proprietor, went over to Miss Tatum's house to take the switchboard whenever trouble called the good lady away. Aunt Sue seemed low as she rolled and cut biscuits, but Aunt Hattie and the telephone operator kept up an effort to jolly her out of it.

The children—nieces and nephews of the dead man, Preacher's five young ones, and a few second cousins from Gilbert—were charged to be on their best behavior and to stay among the older graves at the top of the hill. Soon they were running through tall grass that tapped the spines of Irishmen one hundred years dead. Shrieks of happy laughter bounced off crumbling stone, and a game of marbles got under way on the bare, packed earth above Baby McDonough, 1865.

Sarah and Donald sat side by side in quiet dignity upon the granite slab of Lough MacDougal, the one stubborn old Scot to lie up in that Celtic hillock. They spoke in somber tones to

93

honor their uncle's funeral day, and to impress their maturity on the younger children.

"Preacher says Elmo ain't goin' to heaven 'cause he's a pagan," said Donald. At thirteen a deep furrow already showed between his brows.

"What's a pagan?" asked Sarah.

"Save they don't go to church and they're sinners, I'm not real sure," he replied.

"Daddy said Aunt Hattie says he ain't goin' too, 'cept' cause they cain't find him," Sarah said.

"Uncle Abe ain't goin' to heaven neither?" asked Donald.

"No, silly, not Daddy," she laughed, "Uncle Elmo. 'Cause they cain't find his body is how come he cain't get into heaven."

"What difference does that make?" Donald asked.

Sarah mused the point and decided. "I guess you got to have your body with you when your soul goes."

"'At don't sound right," said Donald with a knowing nod. "People don't use their bodies in heaven. Only your soul goes to Jesus. Nobody'd drag along to heaven somethin' that's been in a hole."

"All the same," she replied, "Aunt Hattie says there cain't be no Christian burial so he cain't go."

"Maybe so," Donald said, "but it don't matter none. If he was a pagan it ain't like he could of gone anyhow."

Just then Preacher's son, Lavon, yanked Sarah's long hair. She cried out in more surprise than pain, but Donald had to beat him smartly for it anyway.

The sun was high and hot when Sarah's mother came up to get them. Marble players had to dust off the knees of their good dark britches, and Lavon had to tuck in the tail of his white shirt.

"Quieten down now," said Mrs. Knox sternly, "and listen good." There was a deal of drawer tugging and grimacing . . . and here and there a shove. "This ain't no playparty. Y'all are goin' to go down there an' stan' with your mommas. Don't stan' with Abe ner Joe, you hear? You stan' with your mommas. All a' Joe's children, you stan' with me.

"There won't be no flibbity-jibs in the prayin', neither. I plan to pray with one open eye, an' I see anybody actin' flighty, I'll pray right then an' there they get their bottoms blistered. There ain't a grave but it's a funeral just the same." She surveyed the group with the cold blue eye she'd probably chosen to keep open. "Anybody here wunder anythin'?" All small heads wagged no. If anyone was nursing a question it wasn't likely to be about a point of etiquette. "Then you'll be walkin' down this hill behin' me."

The people stood in a loose circle with Preacher at the southern end to keep the sun out of his eyes. Abe and Joe Knox were on his right, a space carefully reserved between their dark presences and the rest of the bereaved. Across the circle Donald watched them. He watched his father's jaw muscles work. He watched something still and fierce lying back in his eyes. He saw Uncle Abe pick a spot in the weeds and stare at it stolidly, standing as still as a graven man. The children switched and twisted, and had their eyes all over, only accidentally including heavenward.

Preacher dropped his chin into his bow tie and clutched the Bible in both hands up to his wheezy chest. The circle grew silent waiting for him to call Jesus to the meeting. Only the brush rustle at the edge of the woods sounded until God came loud and sudden, like near thunder. All the children and a few grown men started visibly.

"Lord!" Preacher boomed out sharply. "Hear your children callin' your precious name in a wilderness of sorrow. Help this poor sinner to find the words that will open their hearts to you, so they can feel your healing power today. Show mercy to the soul of Elmo Knox. I pray, Lord Jesus, that when he was layin' out in that ditch somewhere, he had time to repent and ask you to come into his life. I pray that any wrong he ever did is forgiven. . . ."

Sarah listened at first, just like Sunday. The litany of Uncle Elmo's sins rolled out with the same cadence as mankind's from the pulpit, the sins written down in dark letters in Peter's book, the one he'll read from on the last day. Elmo Knox didn't go to church. He feared God so little that he didn't care who heard him blaspheme. He said God lived in trees and mountains and spoke in birdsong. He said river water was God's own blood. He said he was, himself, an animal no finer than a wood duck or worse than a bobcat. When he died off in the woods last summer, he lacked the foresight to make his remains available to box in fragrant Arkansas pine against the day of judgment. After a while Sarah ignored Preacher, just like Sunday, and dwelled in her mind on the dead man. She remembered the clear June day when she'd seen him last. . . .

They sat in the shade with their backs against an outcrop of stone halfway down Sugarloaf. Sarah appreciated the many colors of sunlighted green and blue before her, though she formed no thoughts about it. Elmo watched a redtailed hawk make wide circles above a bend in Latter's Run, and he thought about the hawk as he watched it.

"Hawks are patient birds," he said aloud. "They'll lay on the wind all day just waitin' for their best chance." Sarah began to watch the hawk, too. "They don't kill very often," he continued absently, " 'cause it's hard. Try to kill somethin' with sharp eyes an' quick feet." In a while the hawk drifted off his circle and headed east, away from the sun. Uncle Elmo spoke very point-edly then, and seemed to Sarah to be talking to the bird. "But sooner or later he'll kill. You can be sure of that. He has to."

He turned suddenly to the girl. "Good hunters are patient. You remember that. Your daddy an' Uncle Joe an' me are all good hunters. It's patience makes it so. You gotta watch hawks."

"I don't wanna kill animals," Sarah spoke solemnly. "I wanna catch 'um like you do. Just catch 'um to look at, see 'um up close, an' turn 'um loose."

"That's a good way," he agreed. "It gives all the fun of huntin' without hurtin' anybody. Seems like you hurt ever'thin' if you hurt one thin'. Now an' again I don't even like to walk on grass. Did you ever try to figger how many little grubs an' bugs are under your feet when you tramp aroun'? Or that the grass itself could maybe holler, only you cain't hear?" He shook his head and looked out to where the hawk had been, but Sarah was sure he was seeing inside his own head. "You gotta be real careful, though," he murmured. "Some animals ain't proper to catch."

"We oughta get on, Uncle Elmo," Sarah said half an hour later. "Momma'll have dinner on time we get there."

They walked together down Sugarloaf and out the dirt road toward home. Elmo showed her a nuthatch. "Any time you see a little bird headin' nose down a tree trunk like a fly, you know it's a nuthatch." He told her about the soft, pink pockets to be found in the pale belly fur of mother 'possums, and about their fearsome teeth and claws.

"You know, we could sure catch us a 'possum an' have a look," he said. "A box trap's all we'd need if we get real familiar with a partic'lar 'possum."

"We could fix up that ol' 'coon cage while we're waitin' to get to know a 'possum," Sarah suggested brightly, already able to see the small grey creature snug behind chicken wire.

"Knoxes start learnin' patience an' thinkin' ahead when they're little-biddy baby birds. . . ." said Uncle Elmo. His mouth smiled but his eyes didn't.

It was the next day that he walked alone into the woods. Even when her father and Uncle Joe had searched and come back without him, Sarah set about collecting a vegetable crate, heavy cord, and a stout stick to make a box trap for a mother 'possum.

Preacher was making his closing salvos on the flown spirit of Elmo Knox while the assembled mourners "amened" and praised God. The child, Sarah, was the only crier on the hillside.

After the funeral everyone drove back down the hill to Republican. Aunt Hattie had dinner waiting: fried chicken and frog legs, baked bass and biscuits, rice and gravy, greens . . . everything steaming in crockery bowls on the big kitchen table. There were sliced tomatoes, fruit salad, and cold milk in a tall pitcher.

The women and babies ate in the kitchen. The men ate outside, some sitting on their running boards and others hunkered down nearby. The children sat on the grey, planked porch crosslegged like Indians or dangling skinny ankles off the sides. Sarah and Donald had the north end of the porch to themselves.

"I been thinkin'," Sarah mused aloud between bites of chicken leg. "I figger Uncle Elmo ain't dead."

" 'Course he's dead," Donald returned flatly. "We were just to his funeral."

"Yeah, but we didn't bury nobody, now did we?" she said with her little pointed chin tilted smugly. "We didn't have no box 'cause we didn't have no body, an' we didn't have no body 'cause he ain't dead."

Donald considered this new thought carefully as his jaws worked over his plate.

"Looky here," continued Sarah reasonably. "Uncle Elmo never could of got lost in the woods on account of him knowing woods so good. And he'd have to of got bad lost for my daddy not to find him, on account of him bein' such a good tracker. Hey, even your daddy'd of found him 'cept he was bad lost, an' he cain't get lost! You see! It's just simple that he ain't dead."

"Well, where is he then?" asked Donald after a few moments to clear his mouth.

"New Orleans, I reckon," she said with an airy shrug. "He always said how he'd like to see that big causeway over Lake Ponchetrain."

The boy's eyebrows puckered and his lips pinched as he concentrated on Sarah's argument. At last he shook his head, slowly at first and then with violence.

" 'At's stupid. 'At's just real stupid!"

"No, it ain't!" she cried indignantly.

"He ain't a bird that just flies off," Donald sputtered, feeling angry without knowing why. "He ain't in New Orleans, neither! He's dead, you hear me?" He leaped sideways off the porch and ran around the side of the house.

Twilight was deep before Sarah went looking for her cousin. The air was cooling quickly with the sunset these autumn days, and the purple colors of evening added to the child's sense of summer's end. She found the boy behind the house, sitting on the "step box" beside the rain barrel.

"Hey, Donald," Sarah spoke gently into the shadows. "You wanna play checkers?" No answer came. "I got my checkers in the house. You wanna play?"

In that instant purple turned to black. It was that moment when day stops. If you see it happen, night seems very sudden.

"You mad at me?" she asked. But the boy was silent. "You're

actin' mad, but if we play checkers or somethin' you'll cheer up." Still no words came from the shadows by the rain barrel.

"Donald!" she snapped, finally in a huff. "You're about the sorriest thing I ever saw!"

"You're the sorriest thing in the whole world," said the boy at last. "Sayin' dead men ain't dead, they're only fishin' in Lake Ponchetrain. That's purely stupid. 'I'm at the funeral but I ain't sad,'" he mimicked her, "''cause Elmo ain't dead, he's in Paris, France.'" His voice was hard and angry. Sarah began to cry.

"You're so meanhearted," she whimpered, "I don't want even to mess with you."

"Aw, hush," he said, softening. "I ain't mad at you. 'At threw me how you said Elmo ran off. I think I wisht he had run off. I think I wisht he'd run off more'n anythin'. You understand?"

"Well, how come you're so dang sure he didn't?" she sniffed.

"Okay, listen an' use your head. . . ."

"Huh!" she pouted.

"What did Uncle Elmo take with him when he left?" he asked.

"A cane pole and a bag of cold biscuits," she replied. It was common knowledge. Everybody knew that.

"If he was goin' off travelin', would he of took that?"

"No," she nodded doubtfully. "I reckon he'd not of tooken off half cocked."

"'Course not," said Donald. "He always was careful what he took on a Sunday drive. If he had a pole an' a bite to eat he was goin' to the river an' no place else. Right?"

"I guess so," Sarah agreed sadly. "I just don't see how he could of got dead between here an' there, an' my daddy couldn't find him."

"I cain't either," he said through tight lips, "an' that's just what's botherin' me. Since our daddies are as good in the woods as Uncle Elmo, how come they cain't find their own brother on a gravel road? It don't make sense to me. Do you see what I'm drivin' at?"

"Not precisely, no," she answered.

"Ain't you seen Momma cryin'?" he asked.

"Gosh, yes," she said. "She's awful sad about Uncle Elmo. They was good friends, wasn't they?"

Donald was silent again. After a while Sarah knew he wasn't

going to play checkers at all. She went into the house where all the adult funeral-goers were gathered over Miss Tatum Harris's lemon cakes. They were in a deep discussion of the quarter horse auction in Fayetteville.

# PETER LOVESEY

# THE HAUNTED CRESCENT

*As regular readers of this series know, we usually avoid
stories involving ghosts or the supernatural. But there are
exceptions to every rule. . . . Peter Lovesey is perhaps
unique among modern mystery writers in that every one
of his thirteen detective novels to date has been set in the
past—often as far back as Victorian England. Although
"The Haunted Crescent" is set on Christmas Eve of 1988
in Bath, England, it deals with a 150-year-old crime there,
so once again Lovesey is using his unique talent to
conjure up images of what might have been.*

**A** ghost was seen last Christmas in a certain house in the Royal
Crescent. Believe me, this is true. I speak from personal experience, as a resident of the City of Bath and something of an
authority on psychic phenomena. I readily admit that ninety-
nine percent of so-called hauntings turn out to have been
hallucinations of one sort or another, but this is the exception,
a genuine haunted house. Out of consideration for the present
owners (who for obvious reasons wish to preserve their pri-
vacy), I shall not disclose the exact address, but if you doubt
me, read what happened to me on Christmas Eve, 1988.

The couple who own the house had gone to Norfolk for the
festive season, leaving on the Friday, December twenty-third.
Good planning. The ghost was reputed to walk on Christmas
Eve. Knowing of my interest, they had generously placed their
house at my disposal. I am an ex-policeman, by the way, and it
takes a lot to frighten me.

For those who like a ghost story with all the trimmings—
deep snow and howling winds outside—I am sorry. I must
disappoint you. Christmas, 1988, was not a white one in Bath.
It was unseasonably warm. There wasn't even any fog. All I can
offer in the way of atmospheric effects are a full moon that

night and an owl that hooted periodically in the trees at the far side of the sloping lawn that fronts the Crescent. It has to be admitted that this was not a spooky-looking barn owl, but a tawny owl, which on this night was making more of a high-pitched "kee-wik" call than a hoot, quite cheery, in fact. Do not despair, however. The things that happened in the house that night more than compensated for the absence of werewolves and banshees outside.

It is vital to the story that you are sufficiently informed about the building in which the events occurred. Whether you realize it or not, you have probably seen the Royal Crescent, if not as a resident, or a tourist, then in one of the numerous films in which it has appeared as a backdrop to the action. It is in a quiet location northwest of the city and comprises thirty houses in a semielliptical terrace completed in 1774 to the specifica- tion of John Wood the Younger. It stands comparison with any domestic building in Europe. I defy anyone not to respond to its uncomplicated grandeur, the majestic panorama of 114 Ionic columns topped by a portico and balustrade; and the roadway at the front where Jane Austen and Charles Dickens trod the cobbles. But you want me to come to the ghost.

My first intimation of something unaccountable came at about twenty past eleven that Christmas Eve. I was in the drawing room on the first floor. I had stationed myself there a couple of hours before. The door was ajar and the house was in darkness. No, that isn't quite accurate. I should have said simply that none of the lights were switched on; actually the moonlight gave a certain amount of illumination, silver-blue rectangles projected across the carpet and over the base of the Christmas tree, producing an effect infinitely prettier than fairy lights. The furniture was easily visible, too, armchairs, table, and grand piano. One's eyes adjust. It didn't strike me as eerie to be alone in that unlit house. Anyone knows that a spirit of the departed is unlikely to manifest itself in electric light.

No house is totally silent, certainly no centrally heated house. The sounds produced by expanding floorboards in so-called haunted houses up and down the land must have fooled ghost- hunters by the hundred. In this case as a precaution against a sudden freeze, the owners had left the system switched on. It was timed to turn off at eleven, so the knocks and creaks I was hearing now ought to have been the last of the night.

As events turned out, it wasn't a sound that alerted me first. It was a sudden draft against my face and a flutter of white across the room. I tensed. The house had gone silent. I crossed the room to investigate.

The disturbance had been caused by a Christmas card falling off the mantelpiece into the grate. Nothing more alarming than that. Cards are always falling down. That's why some people prefer to suspend them on strings. I stooped, picked up the card, and replaced it, smiling at my overactive imagination.

Yet I had definitely noticed a draft. The house was supposed to be free of drafts. All the doors and windows were closed and meticulously sealed against the elements. Strange. I listened, holding my breath. The drawing room where I was standing was well placed for picking up any unexplained sound in the house. It was at the center of the building. Below me were the ground floor and the cellar, above me the second floor and the attic.

Hearing nothing, I decided to venture out to the landing and listen there. I was mystified, yet unwilling at this stage to countenance a supernatural explanation. I was inclined to wonder whether the cut-off of the central heating had resulted in some trick of convection that gave the impression or the reality of a disturbance in the air. The falling card was not significant in itself. The draft required an explanation. My state of mind, you see, was calm and analytical.

Ten or fifteen seconds passed. I leaned over the banisters and looked down the stairwell to make sure that the front door was firmly shut, and so it proved to be. Then I heard a rustle from the room where I had been. I knew what it was—the card falling into the grate again—for another distinct movement of air had stirred the curtain on the landing window, causing a shift in the moonlight across the stairs. I was in no doubt anymore that this was worth investigating. My only uncertainty was whether to start with the floors above me, or below.

I chose the latter, reasoning that if, as I suspected, someone had opened a window, it was likely to be at the ground or basement levels. My assumption was wrong. I shall not draw out the suspense. I merely wish to record that I checked the cellar, kitchen, scullery, dining room, and study and found every window and external door secure and bolted from inside. No one could have entered after me.

So I began to work my way upstairs again, methodically visiting each room. And on the staircase to the second floor, I heard a sigh.

Occasionally in Victorian novels a character would "heave" a sigh. Somehow the phrase had always irritated me. In real life I never heard a sigh so weighty that it seemed to involve muscular effort—until this moment. This was a sound hauled up from the depths of somebody's inner being, or so I deduced. Whether it really originated with somebody or some *thing* was open to speculation.

The sound had definitely come from above me. Unable by now to suppress my excitement, I moved up to the second-floor landing, where I found three doors, all closed. I moved from one to the other, opening them rapidly and glancing briefly inside. Two bedrooms and a bathroom. I hesitated. A bathroom. Had the "sigh," I wondered, been caused by some aberration of the plumbing? Air locks are endemic in the complicated systems installed in these old Georgian buildings. The houses were not built with valves and cisterns. The efficiency of the pipework depended on the variable skill of generations of plumbers.

The sound must have been caused by trapped air.

Rationality reasserted itself. I would finish my inspection and prove to my total satisfaction that what I had heard was neither human nor spectral in origin. I closed the bathroom door behind me and crossed the landing to the last flight of stairs, more narrow than those I had used so far. In times past they had been the means of access to the servants' quarters in the attic. I glanced up at the white-painted door at the head of these stairs and observed that it was slightly ajar.

My foot was on the first stair and my hand on the rail when I stiffened. That door moved.

It was being drawn inward. The movement was slow and deliberate. As the gap increased, a faint glow of moonlight was cast from the interior onto the paneling to my right. I stared up and watched the figure of a woman appear in the doorway.

She was in a white gown or robe that reached to her feet. Her hair hung loose to the level of her chest—fine, gently shifting hair so pale in color that it appeared to merge with the dress. Her skin, too, appeared bloodless. The eyes were flint black, however. They widened as they took me in. Her right hand crept to her throat and I heard her give a gasp.

The sensations I experienced in that moment of confrontation are difficult to convey. I was convinced that nothing of flesh and blood had entered that house in the hours I had been there. All the entrances were bolted—I had checked. I could not account for the phenomenon, or whatever it was, that had manifested itself, yet I refused to be convinced. I was unwilling to accept what my eyes were seeing and my rational faculties could not explain. She could not be a ghost.

I said, "Who are you?"

The figure swayed back as if startled. For a moment I thought she was going to close the attic door, but she remained staring at me, her hand still pressed to her throat. It was the face and form of a young woman, not more than twenty.

I asked, "Can you speak?"

She appeared to nod.

I said, "What are you doing here?"

She caught her breath. In a strange, half-whispered utterance she said, as if echoing my words, "Who are you?"

I took a step upward toward her. It evidently frightened her, for she backed away and became almost invisible in the shadowy interior of the attic room. I tried to dredge up some reassuring words. "It's all right. Believe me, it's all right."

Then I twitched in surprise. Downstairs, the doorbell chimed. After eleven on Christmas Eve!

I said, "What on earth . . . ?"

The woman in white whimpered something I couldn't hear.

I tried to make light of it. "Santa, I expect."

She didn't react.

The bell rang a second time.

"He ought to be using the chimney," I said. I had already

decided to ignore the visitor, whoever it was. One unexpected caller was all I could cope with.

The young woman spoke up, and the words sprang clearly from her. "For God's sake, send him away!"

"You know who it is?"

"Please! I beg you."

"If you know who it is," I said reasonably, "wouldn't you like to answer it?"

"I can't."

The chimes rang out again.

I said, "Is it someone you know?"

"Please. Tell him to go away. If you answer the door he'll go away."

I was letting myself be persuaded. I needed her cooperation. I wanted to know about her. "All right," I relented. "But will you be here when I come back?"

"I won't leave."

Instinctively I trusted her. I turned and descended the two flights of stairs to the hall. The bell rang again. Even though the house was in darkness, the caller had no intention of giving up.

I drew back the bolts, opened the front door a fraction, and looked out. A man was on the doorstep, leaning on the iron railing. A young man in a leather jacket glittering with studs and chains. His head was shaven. He, at any rate, looked like flesh and blood. He said, "What kept you?"

I said, "What do you want?"

He glared. "For crying out loud—who the hell are you?" His eyes slid sideways, checking the number on the wall.

I said with frigid courtesy, "I think you must have made a mistake."

"No," he said. "This is the house all right. What's your game, mate? What are you doing here with the lights off?"

I told him that I was an observer of psychic phenomena.

"Come again?"

"Ghosts," I said. "This house has the reputation of being haunted. The owners have kindly allowed me to keep watch tonight."

"Oh, yes?" he said with heavy skepticism. "Spooks, is it? I'll have a gander at them meself." With that, he gave the door a shove. There was no security chain and I was unable to resist the pressure. He stepped across the threshold. "Ghost-buster, are you, mate? You wouldn't, by any chance, be lifting the family silver at the same time? Anyone else in here?"

I said, "I take exception to that. You've no right to force your way in here."

"No more right than you," he said, stepping past me. "Were you upstairs when I rang?"

I said, "I'm going to call the police."

He flapped his hand dismissively. "Be my guest. I'm going upstairs, right?"

Sheer panic inspired me to say, "If you do, you'll be on film."

"What?"

"The cameras are ready to roll," I lied. "The place is riddled with mikes and tripwires."

He said, "I don't believe you," but the tone of his voice said the opposite.

"This ghost is supposed to walk on Christmas Eve," I told him. "I want to capture it on film." I gave a special resonance to the word "capture."

He said, "You're round the twist." And with as much dignity as he could muster he sidled back toward the door, which still stood open. Apparently he was leaving, "You ought to be locked up. You're a nutcase."

As he stepped out of the door I said, "Shall I tell the owners you called? What name shall I give?"

He swore and turned away. I closed the door and slid the bolts back into place. I was shaking. It had been an ugly, potentially dangerous incident. I'm not so capable of tackling an intruder as I once was and I was thankful that my powers of invention had served me so well.

I started up the stairs again and as I reached the top of the first flight, the young woman in white was waiting for me. She must have come down two floors to overhear what was being said. This area of the house was better illuminated than the attic stairs, so I got a better look at her. She appeared less ethereal now. Her dress was silk or satin, I observed. It was an evening gown. Her makeup was as pale as a mime artist's, except for the black liner around her eyes.

She said, "How can I thank you enough?"

I answered flatly, "What I want from you, young lady, is an explanation."

She crossed her arms, rubbing at her sleeves. "I feel shivery here. Do you mind if we go in there?"

As we moved into the drawing room I noticed that she made no attempt to switch on the light. She pointed to some cigarettes on the table. "Do you mind?"

I found some matches by the fireplace and gave her a light. "Who was that at the door?"

She inhaled hard. "Some guy I met at a party. I was supposed to be with someone else, but we got separated. You know how it is. Next thing I knew, this bloke in the leather jacket was chatting me up. He was all right at first. I didn't know he was going to come on so strong. I mean I didn't encourage him. I was trying to cool it. He offered me these tablets, but I refused. He said they would make me relax. By then I was really scared. I moved off fast. The stupid thing was that I moved upstairs. There were plenty of people about, and it seemed the easiest way to go. The bloke followed. He kept on following. I went right to the top of the house and shut myself in a room. I pushed a cupboard against the door. He was beating his fist on the door, saying what he was going to do to me. I was scared out of my skull. All I could think of doing was get through the window, so I did. I climbed out and found myself up there behind the little stone wall."

"Of this building? The balustrade at the top?"

"Didn't I make that clear? The party was in a house a couple of doors away from you. I ran along this narrow passageway between the roof and the wall, trying all the windows. The one upstairs was the first one I could shift."

"The attic window. Now I understand." The sudden draft was explained, and the gasp as she had caught her breath after the effort.

She said, "I'm really grateful."

"Grateful?"

"Grateful to you for getting rid of him."

I said, "It would be sensible now to call a taxi. Where do you live?"

"Not far. I can walk."

"It wouldn't be advisable, would it, after what happened? He's persistent. He may be waiting."

"I didn't think." She stubbed the cigarette into an ashtray. After a moment's reflection she said, "All right. Where's the phone?"

There was one in the study. While she was occupied, I gave some thought to what she had said. I didn't believe a word of it, but I had something vastly more important on my mind.

She came back into the room. "Ten minutes, they reckon. Was it true what you said downstairs, about this house being haunted?"

"Mm?" I was still preoccupied.

"The spook. All that stuff about hidden cameras. Did you mean it?"

"There aren't any cameras. I'm useless with machinery of any sort. I reckoned he'd think twice about coming in if he knew he was going to be on film. It was just a bluff."

"And the bit about the ghost?"

"That was true."

"Would you mind telling me about it?"

"Aren't you afraid of the supernatural?"

"It's scary, yes. Not so scary as what happened already. I want to know the story. Christmas Eve is a great night for a ghost story."

I said, "It's more than just a story."

"Please."

"On one condition. Before you get into that taxi, you tell me the truth about yourself—why you really came into this house tonight."

She hesitated.

I said, "It needn't go any further."

"All right. Tell me about the ghost." She reached for another cigarette and perched on the arm of a chair.

I crossed to the window and looked away over the lawn toward the trees silhouetted against the city lights. "It can be traced back, as all ghost stories can, to a story of death and an unquiet spirit. About a hundred and fifty years ago this house was owned by an army officer, a retired colonel by the name of

Davenport. He had a daughter called Rosamund, and it was believed in the city that he doted on her. She was dressed fashionably and given a good education, which in those days was beyond the expectation of most young women. Rosamund was a lively, intelligent, and attractive girl. Her hair when she wore it long was very like yours, fine and extremely fair. Not surprisingly, she had admirers. The one she favored most was a young man from Bristol, Luke Robertson, who at that time was an architect. In the conventions of the time they formed an attachment which amounted to little more than a few chaperoned meetings, some letters, poems, and so on. They were lovers in a very old-fashioned sense that you may find difficult to credit. In physical terms it amounted to no more than a few stolen kisses, if that. Somewhere in this house there is supposed to be carved into woodwork the letters *L* and *R* linked. I can't show you. I haven't found it."

Outside, a taxi trundled over the cobbles. I watched it draw up at a house some doors down. Two couples came out of the building, laughing, and climbed into the cab. It was obvious that they were leaving a party. The heavy beat of music carried up to me.

I said, "I wonder if it's turned midnight. It might be Christmas Day already."

She said, "Please go on with the story."

"Colonel Davenport—the father of this girl—was a lonely man. His wife had died some years before. Lately he had become friendly with a neighbor, another resident of the Crescent, a widow approaching fifty years of age by the name of Mrs. Crandley, who lived in one of the houses at the far end of the building. She was a musician, a pianist, and she gave lessons. One of her pupils was Rosamund. So far as one can tell, Mrs. Crandley was a good teacher and the girl a promising pupil. Do you play?"

"What?"

I turned to face her. "I said, do you play the piano?"

"Oh. Just a bit," said the girl.

"You didn't tell me your name."

"I'd rather not, if you don't mind. What happened between the colonel and Mrs. Crandley?"

"Their friendship blossomed. He wanted her to marry him. Mrs. Crandley was not unwilling. In fact, she agreed, subject to one condition. She had a son of twenty-seven called Justinian."

"What was that?"

"Justinian. There was a vogue for calling your children after emperors. This Justinian was a dull fellow without much to recommend him. He was lazy and overweight. He rarely ventured out of the house. Mrs. Crandley despaired of him."

"She wanted him off her hands?"

"That is what it amounted to. She wanted him married and she saw the perfect partner for him in Rosamund. Surely such a charming, talented girl would bring out some positive qualities in her lumpish son. Mrs. Crandley applied herself diligently to the plan, insisting that Justinian answer the doorbell each time Rosamund came for her music lesson. Then he would be told to sit in the room and listen to her playing. Everything Mrs. Crandley could do to promote the match was done. For his part, Justinian was content to go along with the plan. He was promised that if he married the girl he would be given his mother's house, so the pattern of his life would alter little, except that a pretty wife would keep him company rather than a discontented, nagging mother. He began to eye Rosamund with increasing favor. So when the colonel proposed marriage to Mrs. Crandley, she assented on the understanding that Justinian would be married to Rosamund at the same time."

"How about Rosamund? Was she given any choice?"

"You have to be aware that marriages were commonly arranged by the parents in those days."

"But you said she already had a lover. He was perfectly respectable, wasn't he?"

I nodded. "Absolutely. But Luke Robertson didn't feature in Mrs. Crandley's plan. He was ignored. Rosamund bowed under the pressure and became engaged to Justinian in the autumn of 1838. The double marriage was to take place in the Abbey on Christmas Eve."

"Oh, dear—I think I can guess the rest of the story."

"It may not be quite as you expect. As the day of the wedding approached, Rosamund began to dread the prospect. She pleaded with her father to allow her to break off the engagement. He wouldn't hear of it. He loved Mrs. Crandley and his thoughts were all of her. In despair, Rosamund sent the maid-servant with a message to Luke, asking him to meet her secretly on the basement steps. She had a romantic notion that Luke would elope with her."

My listener was enthralled. "And did he come?"

"He came. Rosamund poured out her story. Luke listened with sympathy, but he was cautious. He didn't see elopement as the solution. Rather bravely, he volunteered to speak to the colonel and appeal to him to allow Rosamund to marry the man of her choice. If that failed, he would remind the colonel that Rosamund could not be forced to take the sacred vows. Her consent had to be freely given in church, and she was entitled to withhold it. So this uncomfortable interview took place a day or two later. The colonel, naturally, was outraged. Luke was banished from the house and forbidden to speak to Rosamund again. The unfortunate girl was summoned by her father and accused of wickedly consorting with her former lover when she was promised to another. The story of the secret note and the meeting on the stairs was dragged from her. She was told that she wished to destroy her father's marriage. She was said to be selfish and disloyal. Worse, she might be taken to court by Justinian for breach of promise."

"Poor little soul! Did it break her?"

"No. Amazingly, she stood her ground. Luke's support had given her courage. She would not marry Justinian. It was the colonel who backed down. He went to see Mrs. Crandley. When he returned, it was to tell Rosamund that his marriage would not, after all, take place. Mrs. Crandley had insisted on a double wedding, or nothing."

"I wouldn't have been in Rosamund's shoes for a million pounds."

"She was told by her father that she had behaved no better than a servant, secretly meeting her lover on the basement steps and trifling with another man's affections, so in future he would treat her as a servant. And he did. He dismissed the housemaid. He ordered Rosamund to move her things to the maid's room in the attic, and he gave her a list of duties that kept her busy from five-thirty each morning until late at night."

"Cruel."

"All his bitterness was heaped on her."

"Did she kill herself?"

"No," I said with only the slightest pause. "She was murdered."

*"Murdered?"*

"On Christmas Eve, the day that the weddings would have taken place, she was suffocated in her bed."

"Horrible!"

"A pillow was held against her face until she ceased to breathe. She was found dead in bed by the cook on Christmas morning after she failed to report for duty. The colonel was informed and the police were sent for."

"Who killed her?"

"The inspector on the case, a local man without much experience of violent crimes, was in no doubt that Colonel Davenport was the murderer. He had a powerful motive. The animus he felt toward his daughter had been demonstrated by the way he treated her. It seemed that his anger had only increased as the days passed. On the date he was due to have married, it became insupportable."

"Was it true? Did he confess to killing her?"

"He refused to make any statement. But the evidence against him was overwhelming. Three inches of snow fell on Christmas Eve. It stopped about eight-thirty that evening. The time of death was estimated at about eleven P.M. When the inspector and his men arrived next morning no footsteps were visible on the path leading to the front door except those of the cook, who had gone for the police. The only other person in the house was Colonel Davenport. So he was charged with murdering his own daughter. The trial was short, for he refused to plead. He remained silent to the end. He was found guilty and hanged at Bristol in February, 1839."

She put out the cigarette. "Grim."

"Yes."

"There's more to the story, isn't there? The ghost. You said something about an unquiet spirit."

I said, "There was a feeling of unease about the fact that the colonel wouldn't admit to the crime. After he was convicted

and condemned, they tried to persuade him to confess, to lay
his sins before his Maker. A murderer often would confess in
the last days remaining to him, even after protesting innocence
all through the trial. They all did their utmost to persuade
him—the prison governor, the warders, the priest, and the
hangman himself. Those people had harrowing duties to perform. It would have helped them to know that the man going
to the gallows was truly guilty of the crime. Not one word
would that proud old man speak."

"You sound almost sorry for him. There wasn't really any
doubt, was there?"

I said, "There's a continuous history of supernatural happen-
ings in this house for a century and a half. Think about it.
Suppose, for example, someone else committed the murder."

"But who else could have?"

"Justinian Crandley."

"That's impossible. He didn't live here. His footprints would
have shown up in the snow."

"Not if he entered the house as you did tonight—along the
roof and through the attic window. He could have murdered
Rosamund and returned to his own house by the same route."

"It's possible, I suppose, but why—what was his motive?"

"Revenge. He would have been master in his own house if
the marriage had not been called off. Instead, he faced an
indefinite future with his domineering and now embittered
mother. He blamed Rosamund. He decided that if he was not to
have her as his wife, no one else should."

"Is that what you believe?"

"It is now," said I.

"Why didn't the colonel tell them he was innocent?"

"He blamed himself. He felt a deep sense of guilt for the way
he had treated his own daughter. But for his selfishness the
murder would never have taken place."

"Do you think he knew the truth?"

"He must have worked it out. He loved Mrs. Crandley too
much to cause her further unhappiness."

There was an interval of silence, broken finally by the sound
of car tires on the cobbles below.

She stood up. "Tonight when you saw me at the attic door you thought I was Rosamund's ghost."

I said, "No. Rosamund doesn't haunt this place. Her spirit is at rest. I didn't take you for a real ghost any more than I believed your story of escaping from the fellow in the leather jacket."

She walked to the window. "It is my taxi."

I wasn't going to let her leave without admitting the truth. "You went to the party two doors along with the idea of breaking into this house. You climbed out onto the roof and forced your way in upstairs, meaning to let your friend in by the front door. You were going to burgle the place."

She gasped and swung around. "How did you know that?"

"When I opened the door he was expecting you. He said, 'What kept you?' He knew which house to call at, so it must have been planned. If your story had been true, he wouldn't have known where to come."

She stared down at the waiting cab.

I said, "Until I suggested the taxi, you were quite prepared to go out into the street where this man who had allegedly threatened you was waiting."

"I'm leaving."

"And I noticed that you didn't want the lights turned on."

Her tone altered. "You're not one of the fuzz, are you? You wouldn't turn me in? Give me a break, will you? It's the first time. I'll never try it again."

"How can I know that?"

"I'll give you my name and address, if you want. Then you can check."

It is sufficient to state here that she supplied the information. I shall keep it to myself. I'm no longer in the business of exposing petty criminals. I saw her to her taxi. She promised to stop seeing her boyfriend. Perhaps you think I let her off too lightly. Her misdemeanor was minor compared with the discovery I had made—and I owed that discovery to her.

It released me from my obligation, you see. I told you I was once a policeman. An inspector, actually. I made a fatal mistake. I have had a hundred and fifty years to search for the truth and now that I found it I can rest. The haunting of the Royal Crescent is at an end.

# MARCIA MULLER
# SILENT NIGHT

*A quite different Christmas story from the preceding one is this tale of Marcia Muller's private eye Sharon McCone, who prowls through the bleak underside of San Francisco on Christmas Eve in search of a runaway teenager who happens to be her nephew. McCone was the first of the modern female private eyes when she appeared in 1977, and she remains one of the best, due largely to her compassionate outlook and the well-researched backgrounds of her cases.*

"Larry, I hardly know what to say!"

What I *wanted* to say was, "What am I supposed to do with this?" The object I'd just liberated from its gay red-and-gold Christmas wrappings was a plastic bag, about eight by twelve inches, packed firm with what looked suspiciously like sawdust. I turned it over in my hands, as if admiring it, and searched for some clue to its identity.

When I looked up, I saw Larry Koslowski's brown eyes shining expectantly; even the ends of his little handlebar mustache seemed to bristle as he awaited my reaction. "It's perfect," I said lamely.

He let his bated breath out in a long sigh. "I thought it would be. You remember how you were talking about not having much energy lately? I told you to try whipping up my protein drink for breakfast, but you said you didn't have that kind of time in the morning."

The conversation came back to me—vaguely. I nodded.

"Well," he went on, "put two tablespoons of that mixture in a tall glass, add water, stir, and you're in business."

Of course—it was an instant version of his infamous protein drink. Larry was the health nut on the All Souls Legal Cooperative staff; his fervent exhortations for the rest of us to adopt

117

better nutritional standards often fell upon deaf ears—mine included.

"Thank you," I said. "I'll try it first thing tomorrow."

Larry ducked his head, his lips turning up in shy pleasure beneath his straggly little mustache.

It was late in the afternoon of Christmas Eve, and the staff of All Souls was engaged in the traditional gift exchange between members who had drawn each other's names earlier in the month. The yearly ritual extends back to the days of the co-op's founding, when most people were too poor to give more than one present; the only rule is Keep It Simple.

The big front parlor of the co-op's San Francisco Victorian was crowded. People perched on the furniture or, like Larry and me, sat cross-legged on the floor, oohing and aahing over their gifts. Next to the Christmas tree in the bay window, my boss, Hank Zahn, sported a new cap and muffler, knitted for him—after great deliberation and consultation as to colors—by my assistant, Rae Kelleher. Rae, in turn, wore the scarf and cap I'd purchased (because I can't knit to save my life) for her in the hope she would consign relics from her days at U.C. Berkeley to the trash can. Other people had homemade cookies and sinful fudge, special bottles of wine, next year's calendars, assorted games, plants, and paperback books.

And I had a bag of instant health drink that looked like sawdust.

The voices in the room created such a babble that I barely heard the phone ring in the hall behind me. Our secretary, Ted Smalley, who is a compulsive answerer, stepped over me and went out to where the instrument sat on his desk. A moment later he called, "McCone, it's for you."

My stomach did a little flip-flop, because I was expecting news of a personal nature that could either be very good or very bad. I thanked Larry again for my gift, scrambled to my feet, and went to take the receiver from Ted. He remained next to the desk; I'd confided my family's problem to him earlier that week, and now, I knew, he would wait to see if he could provide aid or comfort.

"Shari?" My younger sister Charlene's voice was composed, but her use of the diminutive of Sharon, which no one but my father calls me unless it's a time of crisis, made my stomach flip again.

"I'm here," I said.

"Shari, somebody's seen him. A friend of Ricky's saw Mike!"

"Where? When?"

"Today around noon. Up there—in San Francisco."

I let out my breath in a sigh of relief. My fourteen-year-old nephew, oldest of Charlene and Ricky's six kids, had run away from their home in Pacific Palisades five days ago. Now, it appeared, he was alive, if not exactly safe.

The investigator in me counseled caution, however. "Was this friend sure it was Mike he saw?"

"Yes. He spoke to him. Mike said he was visiting you. But afterward our friend got to thinking that he looked kind of grubby and tired, and that you probably wouldn't have let him wander around that part of town, so he called us to check it out."

A chill touched my shoulder blades. "What part of town?"

". . . Somewhere near City Hall, a sleazy area, our friend said."

A very sleazy area, I thought. Dangerous territory to which runaways are often drawn, where boys and girls alike fall prey to pimps and pushers. . . .

Charlene said, "Shari?"

"I'm still here, just thinking."

"You don't suppose he'll come to you?"

"I doubt it, if he hasn't already. But in case he does, there's somebody staying at my house—an old friend who's here for Christmas—and she knows to keep him there and call me immediately. Is there anybody else he knows here in the city? Somebody he might trust not to send him home?"

". . . I can't think of anybody."

"What about that friend you spent a couple of Christmases with—the one with the two little girls who lived on Sixteenth Street across from Mission Dolores?"

"Ginny Shriber? She moved away about four years ago." There was a noise as if Charlene was choking back a sob. "He's really just a little boy yet. So little, and so stubborn."

But stubborn little boys grow up fast on the rough city streets. I didn't want that kind of coming-of-age for my nephew.

"Look at the up side of this, Charlene," I said, more heartily than I felt. "Mike's come to the one city where you have your own private investigator. I'll start looking for him right away."

It had begun with, of all things, a moped that Mike wanted for Christmas. Or maybe it had really started a year earlier, when Ricky Savage finally hit it big.

During the first fourteen years of his marriage to my sister, Ricky had been merely another faceless country-and-western musician, playing and singing backup with itinerant bands, dreaming seemingly improbable dreams of stardom. He and Charlene had developed a reproductive pattern (and rate) that never failed to astound me, in spite of its regularity: he'd get her pregnant, go out on tour, return after the baby was born; then he'd go out again when the two o'clock feedings got to him, return when the kid was weaned, and start the whole cycle all over. Finally, after the sixth child, Charlene had wised up and gotten her tubes tied. But Ricky still stayed on the road more than at home, and still dreamed his dreams.

But then, with money borrowed from my father on the promise that if he didn't make it within one year he'd give up music and go into my brother John's housepainting business, Ricky had cut a demo of a song he'd written called "Cobwebs in the Attic of My Mind." It was about a lovelorn fellow who, besides said cobwebs, had a "sewer that's backed up in the cellar of his soul" and "a short in the wiring of his heart." When I first heard it, I was certain that Pa's money had washed down that same pipe before it clogged, but fate—perverse creature that it is—would have it otherwise. The song was a runaway hit, and more Ricky Savage hits were to follow.

In true *nouveau* style, Ricky and Charlene quickly moved uptown—or in this case up the coast, from West Los Angeles to affluent Pacific Palisades. There were new cars, new furniture and clothes, a house with a swimming pool, and toys and goodies for the children. *Lots* of goodies, anything they wanted—until this Christmas when, for reasons of safety, Charlene had balked at letting Mike have the moped. And Mike, headstrong little bastard that he was, had taken his life's savings of some fifty-five dollars and hitched away from home on the Pacific Coast Highway.

It was because of a goddamned moped that I was canceling my Christmas Eve plans and setting forth to comb the sleazy streets and alleys of the area known as Polk Gulch for a runaway. . . .

The city was strangely subdued on this Christmas Eve, the dark streets hushed, although not deserted. Most people had been drawn inside to the warmth of family and friends; others, I suspected, had retreated to nurse the loneliness that is endemic to the season. The pedestrians I passed moved silently, as if reluctant to call attention to their presence; occasionally I heard laughter from the bars as I went by, but even that was muted. The lost, drifting souls of the city seemed to collectively hold their breath as they waited for life to resume its everyday pattern.

I had started at Market Street and worked my way northwest, through the Tenderloin to Polk Gulch. Before I'd started out, I'd had a photographer friend who likes to make a big fee more than he likes to celebrate holidays run off a hundred copies of my most recent photo of Mike. Those I passed out, along with my card, to clerks in what liquor stores, corner groceries, cheap hotels, and greasy spoon restaurants I found open. The pictures drew no response other than indifference or sympathetic shakes of the head and promises to keep an eye out for him. By the time I reached Polk Street, where I had an appointment in a gay bar at ten, I was cold, footsore, and badly discouraged.

Polk Gulch, so called because it is in a valley that has an underground river running through it, long ago was the hub of gay life in San Franciso. In the seventies, however, most of the action shifted up Market Street to the Castro district, and the vitality seemed to drain out of the Gulch. Now parts of it, particularly those bordering the Tenderloin, are depressingly sleazy. As I walked along, examining the face of each young man I saw, I became aware of the hopelessness and resignation in the eyes of the street hustlers and junkies and winos and homeless people.

A few blocks from my destination was a vacant lot surrounded by a chain link fence. Inside gaped a huge excavation, the cellar of the building that had formerly stood there, now open to the elements. People had scaled the fence and taken up residence down in it; campfires blazed, in defiance of the NO TRESPASSING signs. The homeless could rest easy—at least for this one night. No one was going to roust them on Christmas Eve.

I went to the fence and grasped its cold mesh with my fingers, staring down into the shifting light and shadows, wondering if Mike was among the ragged and hungry ranks. Many of the people were middle-aged to elderly, but there were also families with children and a scattering of young people. There was no way to tell, though, without scaling the fence myself and climbing down there. Eventually I turned away, realizing I had only enough time to get to the gay bar by ten.

The transvestite's name was Norma and she—he? I never know which to call them—was coldly beautiful. The two of us sat at a corner table in the bar, sipping champagne because Norma had insisted on it. ("After all, it's Christmas Eve, darling!") The bar, in spite of winking colored lights on its tree and flickering bayberry candles on each table, was gloomy and semideserted; Norma's brave velvet finery and costume jewelry had about it more than a touch of the pathetic. She'd been sitting alone when I'd entered and had greeted me eagerly.

I'd been put in touch with Norma by Ted Smalley, who is gay and has a wide-ranging acquaintance among all segments of the city's homosexual community. Norma, he'd said, knew everything there was to know about what went on in Polk Gulch; if anyone could help me, it was she.

The photo of Mike didn't look familiar to Norma. "There are so many runaways on the street at this time of year," she told me. "Kids get their hopes built up at Christmastime. When they find out Santa isn't the great guy he's cracked up to be, they take off. Like your nephew."

"So what would happen to a kid like him? Where would he go?"

"Lots of places. There's a hotel—the Vinton. A lot of runaways end up there at first, until their money runs out. If he's into drugs, try any flophouse, doorway, or alley. If he's connected with a pimp, look for him hustling."

My fingers tightened involuntarily on the stem of my champagne glass. Norma noticed and shook her elaborately coiffed head in sympathy. "Not a pretty thought, is it? But what do you see around here that's pretty—except for me?" As she spoke the last words, her smile became self-mocking.

"He's been missing five days now," I said, "and he only had fifty-some dollars on him. That'll be gone by now, so he probably won't be at the hotel, or any other. He's never been into drugs. His father's a musician, and a lot of his cronies are druggies; the kid actually disapproves of them. The other I don't even want to think about—although I probably will have to, eventually."

"So what are you going to do?"

"Try the hotel. Go back and talk to the people at that vacant lot. Keep looking at each kid who walks by."

Norma stared at the photo of Mike that lay face up on the table between us. "It's a damned shame, a nice-looking kid like that. He ought to be home with his family, trimming the tree, roasting chestnuts on the fire, or whatever other things families do."

"The American Christmas dream, huh?"

"Yeah." She smiled bleakly, raised her glass. "Here's to the American Christmas dream—and to all the people it's eluded."

I touched my glass to hers. "Including you and me."

"Including you and me. Let's just hope it doesn't elude young Mike forever."

The Vinton Hotel was a few blocks away, around the corner on Eddy Street. Its lobby was a flight up, over a closed sandwich shop, and I had to wait and be buzzed in before I could climb carpetless stairs that stank strongly of disinfectant and faintly of urine. Lobby was a misnomer, actually: it was more a narrow hall with a desk to one side, behind which sat a young black man with a tall afro. The air up there was thick with the odor of marijuana; I guessed he'd been spending his Christmas Eve with a joint. His eyes flashed panic when I reached in my bag for my identification. Then he realized it wasn't a bust and relaxed somewhat.

I took out another photo of Mike and laid it on the counter. "You seen this kid?"

He barely glanced at it. "Nope, can't help you."

I shoved it closer. "Take another look."

He did, pushed it back toward me. "I said no."

There was something about his tone that told me he was lying—would lie out of sheer perversity. I could get tough with him, make noises about talking to the hotel's owners, mentioning how the place reeked of grass. The city's fleabags had come under a good bit of media scrutiny recently; the owners wouldn't want me to cause any trouble that would jeopardize this little goldmine that raked in outrageously high rents from transients, as well as government subsidized payments for welfare recipients. Still, there had to be a better way. . . .

"You work here every night?" I asked.

"Yeah."

"Rough, on Christmas Eve."

He shrugged.

"Christmas night, too?"

"Why do you care?"

"I understand what a rotten deal that is. You don't think I'm running around out here in the cold because I like it, do you?"

His eyes flickered to me, faintly interested. "You got no choice, either?"

"Hell, no. The client says find the kid, I go looking. Not that it matters. I don't have anything better to do."

"Know what you mean. Nothing for me at home, either."

"Where's home?"

"My real home, or where I live?"

"Both, I guess."

"Where I live's up there." He gestured at the ceiling. "Room goes with the job. Home's not there no more. Was in Motown, back before my ma died and things got so bad in the auto industry. I came out here thinking I'd find work." He smiled ironically. "Well, I found it, didn't I?"

"At least it's not as cold here as in Detroit."

"No, but it's not home, either." He paused, then reached for

Mike's picture. "Let me see that again." Another pause. "Okay. He stayed here. Him and this blond chick got to be friends. She's gone, too."

"Do you know the blond girl's name?"

"Yeah. Jane Smith. Original, huh?"

"Can you describe her?"

"Just a little blond, maybe five-two. Long hair. Nothing special about her."

"When did they leave?"

"They were gone when I came on last night. The owner don't put up with the ones that can't pay, and the day man, he likes tossing their asses out on the street."

"How did the kid seem to you? Was he okay?"

The man's eyes met mine, held them for a moment. "Thought this was just a job to you."

". . . He's my nephew."

"Yeah, I guessed it might be something like that. Well, if you mean was he doing drugs or hustling, I'd say no. Maybe a little booze, that's all. The girl was the same. Pretty straight kids. Nobody'd gotten to them yet."

"Let me ask you this: What would kids like that do after they'd been thrown out of here? Where would they hang out?"

He considered. "There's a greasy spoon on Polk, near O'Farrell. Owner's an old guy, Iranian. He feels sorry for the kids, feeds them when they're about to starve, tries to get them to go home. He might of seen those two."

"Would he be open tonight?"

"Sure. Like I said, he's Iranian. It's not his holiday. Come to think of it, it's not mine anymore, either."

"Why not?"

Again the ironic smile. "Can't celebrate peace-on-earth-good-will-to-men when you don't believe in it anymore, now can you?"

I reached into my bag and took out a twenty-dollar bill, slid it across the counter to him. "Peace on earth, and thanks."

He took it eagerly, then looked at it and shook his head. "You don't have to."

"I *want* to. That makes a difference."

The "greasy spoon" was called The Coffee Break. It was small—just five tables and a lunch counter, old green linoleum floors, Formica and molded plastic furniture. A slender man with thinning gray hair sat behind the counter smoking a cigarette. A couple of old women were hunched over coffee at a corner table. Next to the window was a dirty-haired blond girl; she was staring through the glass with blank eyes—another of the city's casualties.

I showed Mike's picture to the man behind the counter. He told me Mike looked familiar, thought a minute, then snapped his fingers and said, "Hey, Angie."

The girl by the window turned. Full-face, I could see she was red-eyed and tear-streaked. The blankness of her gaze was due to misery, not drugs.

"Take a look at the picture this lady has. Didn't I see you with this kid yesterday?"

She got up and came to the counter, self-consciously smoothing her wrinkled jacket and jeans. "Yeah," she said after glancing at it, "that's Michael."

"Where's he now? The lady's his aunt, wants to help him."

She shook her head. "I don't know. He was at the Vinton, but he got kicked out the same time I did. We stayed down at the cellar in the vacant lot last night, but it was cold and scary. These drunks kept bothering us. Mr. Ahmeni, how long do you think it's going to take my dad to get here?"

"Take it easy. It's a long drive from Oroville. I only called him an hour ago." To me, Mr. Ahmeni added, "Angie's going home for Christmas."

I studied her. Under all that grime, a pretty, conventional girl hid. I said, "Would you like a cup of coffee? Something to eat?"

"I wouldn't mind a Coke. I've been sponging off Mr. Ahmeni for hours." She smiled faintly. "I guess he'd appreciate it if I sponged off somebody else for a change."

I bought us both Cokes and sat down with her. "When did you meet Mike?"

"Three days ago, I guess. He was at the hotel when I got into town. He kind of looked out for me. I was glad; that place is pretty awful. A lot of addicts stay there. One OD'd in the stairwell the first night. But it's cheap and they don't ask questions. A guy I met on the bus coming down here told me about it."

"What did Mike do here in the city, do you know?"

"Wandered around, mostly. One afternoon we went out to Ocean Beach and walked on the dunes."

"What about drugs or—"

"Michael's not into drugs. We drank some wine, is all. He's . . . I don't know how to describe it, but he's not like a lot of the kids on the streets."

"How so?"

"Well, he's kind of . . . sensitive, deep."

"This sensitive soul ran away from home because his parents wouldn't buy him a moped for Christmas."

Angie sighed. "You really don't know anything about him, do you? You don't even know he wants to be called Michael, not Mike."

That silenced me for a moment. It was true: I really didn't know my nephew, not as a person. "Tell me about him."

"What do you want to know?"

"Well, this business with the moped—what was that all about?"

"It didn't really have anything to do with the moped. At least, not much. It had to do with the kids at school."

"In what way?"

"Well, the way Michael told it, his family used to be kind of poor. At least there were some months when they worried about being able to pay the rent."

"That's right."

"And then his father became a singing star and they moved to this awesome house in Pacific Palisades, and all of a sudden Michael was in school with all these rich kids. But he didn't fit in. The kids, he said, were really into having things and doing drugs and partying. He couldn't relate to it. He says it's really hard to get into that kind of stuff when you've spent your life worrying about real things."

"Like if your parents are going to be able to pay the rent."

Angie nodded, her fringe of limp blond hair falling over her eyes. She brushed it back and went on. "I know about that; my folks don't have much money, and my mom's sick a lot. The kids, they sense you're different and they don't want to have anything to do with you. Michael was lonely at the new school, so he tried to fit in—tried too hard, I guess, by always having the latest stuff, the most expensive clothes. You know."

"And the moped was part of that."

"Uh-huh. But when his mom said he couldn't have it, he realized what he'd been doing. And he also realized that the moped wouldn't have done the trick anyway. Michael's smart enough to know that people don't fall all over you just because you've got another new toy. So he decided he'd never fit in, and he split. He says he feels more comfortable on the streets, because life here is real." She paused, eyes filling, and looked away at the window. "God, is it *real.*"

I followed the direction of her gaze: beyond the plate glass a girl of perhaps thirteen stumbled by. Her body was emaciated, her face blank, her eyes dull—the look of a far-gone junkie.

I said to Angie, "When did you last see Mike . . . Michael?"

"Around four this afternoon. Like I said, we spent the night in that cellar in the vacant lot. After that I knew I couldn't hack it anymore, and I told him I'd decided to go home. He got pissed at me and took off."

"Why?"

"Why do you think? I was abandoning him. I could go home, and he couldn't."

"Why not?"

"Because Michael's . . . God, you don't know a thing about him! He's proud. He couldn't admit to his parents that he couldn't make it on his own. Any more than he could admit to them about not fitting in at school."

What she said surprised me and made me ashamed. Ashamed for Charlene, who had always referred to Mike as stubborn or bullheaded, but never as proud. And ashamed for myself, because I'd never really seen him, except as the leader of a pack jokingly referred to in family circles as "the little Savages."

"Angie," I said, "do you have any idea where he might have gone after he left you?"

She shook her head. "I wish I did. It would be nice if Michael could have a Christmas. He talked about how much he was going to miss it. He spent the whole time we were walking around on the dunes telling me about the Christmases they used to have, even though they didn't have much money: the tree trimming, the homemade presents, the candlelit masses on Christmas Eve, the cookie decorating and the turkey dinners. Michael absolutely loves Christmas."

I hadn't known that, either. For years I'd been too busy with my own life to do more than send each of the Savage kids a small check. Properly humbled, I thanked Angie for talking with me, wished her good luck with her parents, and went back out to continue combing the dark, silent streets.

On my way back down Polk Street toward the Tenderloin, I stopped again at the chain link fence surrounding the vacant lot. I was fairly sure Mike was not among the people down there—not after his and Angie's experience of the night before—but I was curious to see the place where they had spent that frightening time.

The campfires still burned deep in the shelter of the cellar. Here and there drunks and addicts lay passed out on the ground; others who had not yet reached that state passed bottles and shared joints and needles; one group raised inebriated voices in a chorus of "Rudolph, the Red-Nosed Reindeer." In a far corner I saw another group—two women, three children, and a man—gathered around a scrawny Christmas tree.

The tree had no ornaments, wasn't really a tree at all, but just a top that someone had probably cut off and tossed away after finding that the one he'd bought was too tall for the height of his ceiling. There was no star atop it, no presents under it, no candy canes or popcorn chains, and there was certain to be no turkey dinner tomorrow. The people had nonetheless gathered around it and stood silently, their heads bowed in prayer.

My throat tightened and I clutched at the fence, fighting back tears. Even though I spend a disproportionate amount of my professional life probing into events and behavior that would make the average person gag, every now and then the indestructible courage of the human spirit absolutely stuns me.

I watched the scene for a moment longer, then turned away, glancing at my watch. Its hands told me why the people were praying: Christmas Day was upon us. This was their midnight service.

And then I realized that those people, who had nothing in the world with which to celebrate Christmas except somebody's cast-off treetop, may have given me a priceless gift. I thought I knew now where I would find my nephew.

When I arrived at Mission Dolores, the neoclassical façade of the basilica was bathed in floodlights, the dome and towers gleaming against the post-midnight sky. The street was choked with double-parked vehicles, and from within I heard voices raised in a joyous chorus. Beside the newer early twentieth-century structure, the small adobe church built in the late 1700s seemed dwarfed and enveloped in deep silence. I hurried up the wide steps to the arching wooden doors of the basilica, then took a moment to compose myself before entering.

Like many of my generation, it had been years since I'd been even nominally a Catholic, but the old habit of reverence had never left me. I couldn't just blunder in there and creep about, peering into every worshipper's face, no matter how great my urgency. I waited until I felt relatively calm before pulling open the heavy door and stepping over the threshold.

The mass was candlelit; the robed figures of the priest and altar boys moved slowly in the flickering, shifting light. The stained glass window behind the altar and those on the side walls gleamed richly. In contrast, the massive pillars reached upward to vaulted arches that were deeply shadowed. As I moved slowly along one of the side aisles, the voices of the choir swelled to a majestic finale.

The congregants began to go forward to receive Communion. As they did, I was able to move less obtrusively, scanning the faces of the young people in the pews. Each time I spotted a teenaged boy, my heart quickened. Each time I felt a sharp stab of disappointment.

I passed behind the waiting communicants, then moved unhurriedly up the nave and crossed to the far side. The church was darker and sparsely populated toward the rear; momentarily a pillar blocked my view of the altar. I moved around it.

He was there in the pew next to the pillar, leaning wearily

against it. Even in the shadowy light, I could see that his face was dirty and tired, his jacket and jeans rumpled and stained. His eyes were half-closed, his mouth slack; his hands were shoved between his thighs, as if for warmth.

Mike—no, Michael—had come to the only safe place he knew in the city, the church where on two Christmas Eves he'd attended mass with his family and their friends, the Shribers, who had lived across the street.

I slipped into the pew and sat down next to him. He jerked his head toward me, stared in openmouthed surprise. What little color he had drained from his face; his eyes grew wide and alarmed.

"Ili, Michael." I put my hand on his arm.

He looked as if he wanted to shake it off. "How did you . . . ?"

"Doesn't matter. Not now. Let's just sit quietly till mass is over."

He continued to stare at me. After a few seconds he said, "I bet Mom and Dad are really mad at me."

"More worried than anything else."

"Did they hire you to find me?"

"No, I volunteered."

"Huh." He looked away at the line of communicants.

"You still go to church?" I asked.

"Not much. None of us do anymore. I kind of miss it."

"Do you want to take Communion?"

He was silent. Then, "No. I don't think that's something I can do right now. Maybe never."

"Well, that's okay. Everybody expresses his feelings for . . . God, or whatever, in different ways." I thought of the group of homeless worshippers in the vacant lot. "What's important is that you believe in something."

He nodded, and then we sat silently, watching people file up and down the aisle. After a while he said, "I guess I do believe in something. Otherwise I couldn't have gotten through this week. I learned a lot, you know."

"I'm sure you did."

"About me, I mean."

"I know."

"What're you going to do now? Send me home?"

"Do you want to go home?"

"Maybe. Yes. But I don't want to be sent there. I want to go on my own."

"Well, nobody should spend Christmas Day on a plane or a bus anyway. Besides, I'm having ten people to dinner at four this afternoon. I'm counting on you to help me stuff the turkey."

Michael hesitated, then smiled shyly. He took one hand from between his thighs and slipped it into mine. After a moment he leaned his tired head on my shoulder, and we celebrated the dawn of Christmas together.

# SHIZUKO NATSUKI
# THE LOVE MOTEL

*Writers are often asked where they get the ideas for their
stories. I have been in numerous hotel rooms containing
refrigerators prestocked with beverages for the guests, but
the idea for this story never occurred to me. Obviously it
did occur to Shizuko Natsuki, who has been one of Japan's
leading mystery writers for nearly twenty years. Her annual novels have been best sellers and award winners at
home, though only a few have appeared in America to
date.*

The part of Shibuya which is Dogenzaka 2 Chome has been
known as a shopping district. But if you go a short way farther
along this shopping street, the area around the main branch of
the Tokyu Department Store, you can turn off into a maze of
narrow, winding alleys, many no more than three meters wide.
Clustered on these narrow streets are the love hotels. Large and
small, there are more than a hundred of them altogether—
probably the largest congregation of love hotels in the city.

Since this is the very heart of Shibuya's busiest district, land
prices are extremely high, and yet the buildings here are not
particularly tall. Indeed, most of them are two- or three-story
structures jammed tightly together. The reason they are no
taller is that most of the buildings are flimsily constructed. On
the other hand, by having all the hotels clustered together this
way, they bring together throngs of customers, so that the
vacancy rate in the hotels is quite low and most of them are
busy and prosperous.

Among these hotels is one three-story building built like a
castle. The outer wall is faced with white tile and there are
three round turrets with bronze-colored roofs. On the whole,
it vaguely reproduces the effect of what may have been an
Arabian castle presented in a rather traditional and symbolic

133

manner. Because of the height of its turrets and the fact that it
has some twenty-three guest rooms, it rather stands out compared to the other hotels.

At 7:15 on a Tuesday evening in April, the house phone rang
at the front desk of the Castle Motel. The blinking red light
indicated that the call came from Room 305 on the third floor.
Since the people in that room had been there more than an
hour, the desk clerk supposed they were ready to check out.
Putting the phone to his ear, he was assaulted by a man's voice,
shrill to the point of hysteria and abnormally high-pitched.

"Come quickly! Something terrible has happened—something really terrible!"

The desk clerk, a man in his thirties, dropped the phone and
rushed from behind the counter. Since this sort of motel is
mostly used by people who would not care to be recognized
by colleagues, no one would call for help unless there was a
serious problem. In the past there had been two occasions
when elderly guests had died from their exertions. Another
time a young hoodlum had been there with a bar hostess he
had picked up. They had had a lovers' quarrel and it had ended
with her stabbing him and an ambulance had to be called.

The clerk took the elevator to the third floor. Above the door
to Room 305 glowed a small red light, indicating that the room
was occupied. The clerk knocked on the door, but there was
no immediate response. He continued to knock and rattle the
doorknob until someone on the inside unfastened the lock and
opened the door. The clerk pushed into the room past the man
who had opened the door. A nearly nude woman was sprawled
on the carpet where she had fallen. Her hair was fixed in a
permanent and tinged a light brown. The profile of her face that
was visible was white as parchment. She wore a bright-crimson
brassiere and the lower part of her body was wrapped in a bath
towel.

After his first shocked view of the woman, the clerk noticed
a small pool of vomit by her mouth and near her outstretched
hands was a bottle of orange juice which had spilled, leaving an
orange stain on the carpet. The man, clad only in boxer shorts,
cringed to one side, a stupefied look on his face. He had a thin,
bony chest and his hair and thick moustache were nearly silver.

His small, sunken eyes were wide with surprise. "Oh, this is terrible—just terrible," he said in a shaky voice.

"What happened?" the clerk asked him.

"Ru—I mean Sato—had just gotten out of the bath and got some juice from the refrigerator when she suddenly went into convulsions and collapsed."

"She got it from the refrigerator?"

The woman had collapsed in front of the refrigerator, which was stocked with an assortment of beer, juice, and isotonic drinks. The clerk suddenly realized that if that was true, it would make the situation very awkward for the hotel and he began to shake the woman roughly. "What's the matter with you?" he said to her. "Wake up." But the girl remained inert and unresponsive. She didn't appear to be breathing.

"I'd better call an ambulance," said the clerk, reaching for the house phone by the bed.

The ambulance arrived about five minutes later and the paramedics accompanying it immediately pronounced the girl dead. The emergency had also been called in to the Shibuya police and shortly a number of detectives and uniformed officers showed up, as well as a doctor dispatched from the emergency room of a nearby hospital.

After giving the girl a proper examination, the middle-aged doctor picked up the orange-juice bottle and sniffed it. "I would guess that the cause of death is poisoning, perhaps by some agricultural chemical," he said. "I can smell some sort of oil or tar in this."

"You mean poison was mixed in the orange juice," said Inspector Yazawa. He opened the refrigerator and examined its contents, then, slipping on a pair of gloves, took out two bottles of orange juice. These were the same brand the girl had been drinking. "It looks to me as though the cap has been removed and then replaced." The other detectives studied the bottle cap and expressed agreement with his observation.

"If it had been a carbonated beverage, it would have lost its fizz, but with orange juice you can't tell," said one.

The other bottle of juice appeared not to have been tampered with. Nor was there any evidence of tampering on any of the other beverages in the refrigerator. Inspector Yazawa spoke to the desk clerk and learned that as far as the beverages were concerned, the room-service maids replenished whatever had been consumed when they cleaned the rooms after a guest checked out.

"I'll find out when these were put here," the clerk told him.

At the moment, about sixty percent of the rooms—fourteen of the twenty-three—were occupied. Detectives were sent to every room to check the refrigerators while Inspector Yazawa listened to the desk clerk explain how the motel was run.

There was a garage that would accommodate no more than eight cars, but more than half of the guests came on foot. They entered the large, bronze-colored lobby through an arched gate. On the right side of the lobby was the front desk, which was screened off by a dark amber-tinted glass so that guests at the desk were spared the embarrassment of facing the desk clerk, even though the clerk had a clear view of the guests from his side. On a large plate-glass on the opposite wall were displayed color photographs of each of the twenty-three rooms available in the motel. If the picture was lighted up, it meant that that room was available. The guests would indicate the room of their choice by pressing the button beside it and the desk clerk would pass them the key to that room. Beside the desk was a sign indicating the room rates—6,800 yen to stay all night, 4,300 yen for those who chose to stay less than two hours.

Once the guests had received their key, they could take the elevator to the proper floor. The light over the door of the room would not be lit, but once the guests had entered the room and locked the door, the light would automatically go on to protect them from intrusion. There was an emergency exit at the end of the hall on each floor which was ordinarily kept latched on the inside. Inspector Yazawa checked to see that all the emergency exits were all still latched on the inside and then returned to Room 305.

There he found the man with silver hair sitting on the edge of the round bed that was hung with curtains made to resemble a Gobelin tapestry. The man was now dressed in a black suit.

He still appeared stunned by what had happened. Yazawa took him into the next room, which happened to be vacant. The room didn't have a round bed, but one of a more complicated design which could be illuminated by bright-blue lights. The bathroom was set apart by a smoked-glass panel so that someone on the outside could get a view, but only a hazy one, of a person in the bath. There was a TV set with a video player for showing porno movies—in front of it several chairs. The man sat in one of these while Inspector Yazawa and a young assistant sat facing him.

"What's your name?" Yazawa asked.

"Ogura Masaaki," the man replied in a faint voice. As he said his name, he traced the Chinese character for it on the palm of his hand. It occurred to Yazawa that there was something almost majestic about the man's name which seemed to go well with his grave, refined features. The man had an unusually large head for his slender build. This dignified man with his fine name seemed out of place in a love hotel.

"Your age?"

"I'm fifty-three."

"I believe you also know the name of the dead woman."

"Yes. She was Sato Rumiko."

"What sort of work did she do?"

"She worked in a bar in Shinjuku."

"How old was she?"

"I believe she was twenty-three."

"Have you known her for long?"

"Not really. I suppose I've known her for a year and a half."

There seemed to be a note of regret in his faint, nasal voice. He nodded his head and took a deep breath.

Today Sato had agreed to meet him at six o'clock at a coffee shop on Dogenzaka and they had walked to the motel from there. It had been about 6:15 when they checked in. They had selected Room 305 and gone directly about the business they had come to the motel for. Afterward, Ogura had gone into the bath first, then when Sato had taken a bath he had relaxed on the bed.

After a long soak in the tub, she had come out wearing a bra, with a bath towel around her waist. She had complained that her throat felt dry and went to the refrigerator. "Ru worked in a bar, but she almost never drank alcohol," Ogura said. "She took out a bottle of orange juice and took a big drink—she swallowed maybe two-thirds of the bottle in one gulp. Then she moaned and clutched at her throat. It all happened so fast there wasn't time for me to administer first-aid or anything."

He had been shocked for a moment, but once he recovered himself, he had called the front desk.

"Had either of you opened the refrigerator before she got the orange juice?"

"No. Neither one of us touched it."

"So you didn't drink anything yourself?"

"I took a drink of water while I was in the bathroom. That was all."

"Did anything seem odd or unusual when you first came into the room?"

"I didn't notice anything in particular."

"Had you come here before in the past?"

"No." Ogura shook his head. He was silent for a moment, then admitted, "Actually, we were here one other time—about six months ago—but we used a different room."

Yazawa began questioning the man about how often he used the hotel. Had he and Sato Rumiko met at love hotels once a month? Twice a month? Did they usually meet in this neighborhood? As the questioning went on, the man began to describe their relationship with a rather shameful expression on his face. Generally Ogura would meet Sato at Dogenzaka on his way home from work and they would spend an hour and a half or so at one of the love hotels before she hurried off to her job in Shinjuku.

"She was actually a very nice girl—not the sort you would expect to find among bar hostesses these days. She was a good girl. I always felt kind of sorry for her." Tears came to his eyes and he looked as though he were about to break down.

"You say it was customary to meet her on your way home from work. Where is it you work?"

"In Chiyoda Ward, near the Imperial Palace."

"Where exactly?"

A moment passed before the man could bring himself to

answer. But then he straightened his shoulders and sat more erectly. His expression was complex, but it seemed to Yazawa it was composed of equal parts defiance and embarrassment. He raised his hooded, deep-set eyes and said gravely, "I work for the Imperial Household Agency."

After all the refrigerators had been checked, it turned out that none of the drinks in any of the other rooms had been tampered with—only those in Room 305. After consulting with the desk clerks and the cleaning staff, the police learned that the previous guest had checked out of Room 305 around 5:30. Those guests had informed the front desk in advance that they would be checking out. They had, in fact, called the desk around 5:20. At that time the desk clerk asked if they had used any of the drinks from the refrigerator and had been told that they had taken one soft drink and one bottle of juice. Since the guests at the hotel who arrived by car tended not to drink alcohol, the consumption of soft drinks was high.

At 5:30, when the earlier guests had come down to the front desk, their bill had already been prepared and they paid and returned their room key. There had been no discussion.

Between the time they had checked out and the new guests checked in, a woman from the cleaning staff had been in the room. The first thing she had done was check the contents of the refrigerator and informed the front desk of what had been consumed. The desk clerk had then checked to make sure this tallied with what the guests had reported.

After that the cleaning staff had cleaned the room. Making sure the furniture was in the proper place, they dusted, vacuumed, cleaned out the ashtrays, and remade the bed with fresh sheets before cleaning the bathroom. The thing that guests to hotels such as these found most distasteful was evidence that the room had been previously occupied by someone else. After scrubbing the bathtub thoroughly, the staff dried it with clean towels. The entire process took about thirty minutes and when it was completed, the picture in the lobby was lighted indicating the room was ready for the next customer.

The maid who had cleaned Room 305 spoke very frankly about the drinks consumed by the previous guests. "They had a

soft drink and a bottle of juice. They left the two bottles and
two glasses on the table. I checked the refrigerator and reported
its contents to the front desk, then took the empty bottles to
the kitchen and replaced them with fresh ones. The new ones
had their lids sealed on properly—I don't know about the ones
that were still in the refrigerator. After that, I washed the glasses
and put them back on top of the refrigerator."

It appeared that the earlier guests had suffered no ill effects,
and that therefore the juice they had consumed had been
uncontaminated. And if the cleaning maid's testimony could be
believed, the new juice she had put in the refrigerator was also
uncontaminated. When Ogura and Sato had entered the room,
the refrigerator contained its usual stock of three bottles of
orange juice. Two of which contained poison. It was evident
that Sato had drunk one of these and had died as a result.

What remained of the juice she had drunk as well as the other
two bottles in the refrigerator were sent to the police lab for
analysis. The results showed that the two bottles which had
been tampered with contained quantities of the agricultural
poison, Malthion—a powerful insecticide that could be purchased at any department-store garden shop, and strong enough
so that, when mixed with juice, half a glass would be a fatal
dose.

Sato's body was taken to the university hospital for an autopsy. There it was determined that she had indeed died of
poisoning by Malthion. The estimated time of death was around
seven in the evening. She appeared to have died immediately
after ingesting the poisoned orange juice.

Who put the poison in the juice, and when?

There developed two theories regarding this case. One was
that it was the work of a random killer. This view was that some
person or persons entered Room 305 before Ogura and Sato
arrived and poisoned the bottles of juice. Sato had simply been
the unfortunate one to drink the poisoned beverage. As far as a
motive was concerned, it could either be a truly random killer
or someone who had a grudge against the Castle Motel and
wanted revenge.

The Shibuya police began checking on all the motel's employees and managers to verify their personal relationships. But if this *was* the work of a random killer, the motel could have been chosen at random—which would make the investigation very tough indeed. Seven years earlier, there had been a case where poison had been put in a soft drink, and that case was still unsolved. More recently, there had been a threatening letter in the newspapers, saying that the packaged cookies marketed by a certain company had been impregnated with cyanide. There were other cases—unfortunately not that rare—where people had left poisoned meat on the street so that dogs and cats would eat it and die. Thus it was entirely possible that someone who felt that love hotels and the people who used them were objectionable had sought retribution in this manner.

The second theory, of course, was that the killer specifically wanted to harm or kill Sato Rumiko.

At the beginning of the investigation, the police gave equal weight to both theories, but as the investigation proceeded and they learned more about Sato Rumiko's character and life style, it began to seem more plausible that she herself was the target of the attack.

Sato had claimed to be twenty-three years old, but it turned out that she was actually twenty-six. She had been born into a farm family in northern Japan and had dropped out of high school in her freshman year and made her way to Tokyo. There she had worked in a succession of jobs in massage parlors and bars. Back in her hometown, her father, who was now an invalid, lived alone, but Sato, who had been away for more than ten years, had never once returned home during that time.

Up until about a year ago, she had worked in a massage parlor in Shinjuku, but had quit in a dispute over money with one of her customers. Since then, she had been working in a small bar in the entertainment district. She lived in a small studio apartment in Kita Shinjuku. Having lived on her own in Tokyo since the age of fifteen, she seemed to have had the philosophy that it was all right to do anything as long as she was paid for doing it. Indeed, it seemed that the older she got the more committed she became to making money. Being young and attractive, she used her body as a weapon and made money from men in any way she could. In a locked box in the closet of her apartment,

the police found fixed-term deposit certificates and savings
bonds amounting to nearly $100,000.

This being the case, it seemed likely that among the men
whose money she had taken there were more than a few who
had been left feeling bitter or resentful. This made it necessary
for the detectives to check out the places she had worked to
try to sort out the web of liaisons and relationships she'd been
involved in. But despite all the legwork, they failed to turn up
anyone who might have a sufficiently strong motive to have
killed her.

Whenever she was propositioned by one of the patrons of a
bar where she worked, they would go to a hotel. For some time
her only steady, long-term patron had been Ogura Masaaki. So
in the end all the police had as the prime suspect in the case
was Ogura.

On the day of the murder and the next few days, Ogura was
brought to the police station in Shibuya for protracted questioning. He reiterated that he had known Rumiko for about a year
and a half. He had first met her while she was still working in
the massage parlor and had been captivated instantly by her
lovely, innocent face and amply endowed body. For a time he
had gone frequently to the massage parlor, but since he worked
at the Imperial Household Agency, he realized it would never
do to be seen there, so he had arranged their rendezvous at
love hotels, even after she left the massage parlor and began
working at the bar. "As far as that goes," he said, "I would have
been in trouble if I had been seen going into one of the hotels,
but the streets there are no narrow and usually deserted that it
seemed safer than meeting at a massage parlor."

"You told us you work in the library of the Imperial Household Agency. What exactly do you do there?"

"We mostly distribute publications, but for many years I have
been involved with the repair and restoration of old books that
have been damaged."

Although the police questioning went on for a long time,
Ogura seemed to have gotten used to it. He was beginning to
relax and talk more freely. He told them his father was a
bureaucrat in the Tokyo municipal administration and he him-

self, after graduating from a local high school, had taken a mid-level civil-service exam and won a so-called non-career position in the Imperial Household Agency. The non-career bureaucrats could expect to receive some promotions, but they would only rise to a limited level. For that reason, although he was already fifty-three years old, he had only recently been promoted to the position of section chief. At home he had a wife and two sons, one attending college and one in high school.

The interrogating officer looked at the suspect with his carefully trimmed silver moustache and noted that although the man displayed a certain formality there was something timid about him. "It seems to me that people who work at the Imperial Household Agency are accorded more respect than ordinary people and are expected to behave with dignity. But you went and got involved with a massage-parlor girl young enough to be your daughter. I think you wanted to drop her, but she wouldn't let you go. Men like you can never get away from women like Rumiko. I'll bet she was really taking you for a bundle. I think you finally reached the point where you couldn't stand it any longer. You got some poison, invited her to the motel, and while she was in the bath you—"

"That's not true! Rumiko wasn't that sort of girl. When it came to asking for money—well, that doesn't matter now. What you're saying simply isn't true. She had a good heart, even if she was a bar hostess. She was a sweet girl."

"Come on. You were being swindled."

"No! That's absolutely not true! I am still saddened by what happened to her. She was just a poor young girl who never wronged anyone. For her to be living in that shabby place was a shame. She only wanted me to find something better for her."

With these words, it seemed as if his real regret was being expressed for the first time. The police continued to try to get him to confess to the crime, but he refused.

"Look," he said, "there is one thing you're overlooking. It's clear that the poison must have been mixed with the juice before we went into the room. Even if you assume that I had some reason for wanting to kill Rumiko, why would I have chosen to do it at a motel like that? I've worked hard all my life to establish myself in the position I have achieved. Now that I have gotten involved in this affair, my career is ruined. After a lifetime of work and effort, my job and my prospects are gone. If I had actually done this, it would have made more sense for me to have run away rather than to have reported the matter. At a love hotel like that, they don't look at the guests' faces. I could have just walked away, but I did the right thing—I called the front desk and reported the death. What a naive fool I was."

Three days after the murder, Ogura continued to claim his innocence. It looked as though the investigation had come to a dead end. No other prime suspects emerged and this led some to revive the random-killer theory. A mood of frustration began to take hold of the homicide department.

But on the fourth day, on the Saturday, shortly before noon, a young man showed up at the Shibuya police station and said he wanted to talk to the officer in charge of the investigation. He appeared to be about thirty. He was of medium build and height, wore a blue suit, and in general gave the impression of being a serious sort of office employee.

Inspector Yazawa met with him in a small conference room.

"Forgive me for dropping in like this," said the man formally as he bowed. "Here is my card." According to the card, his name was Takei Makoto and his business address could only be termed a second-class location, but he did work for the trading department of a respectable securities-trading company. When asked his age, he said he was thirty.

"I really should have come to you sooner," he said, "but, well, the fact is that I am the guest who occupied Room 305 at the Castle Motel on Tuesday evening. I think I must have been there just before the girl died."

Inspector Yazawa stared at the young man in surprise. "If you were, you're the one who drank orange juice from the refrigerator and suffered no ill effects."

"No, that's not really the case."

According to the way Takei told it, shortly after 4:00 P.M. on Tuesday afternoon he had returned to Tokyo after being away on a business trip. He stopped at Harajuku to pick up a snack-bar hostess he knew and they drove around for a while in his car. At around 4:20, they checked into the Castle and quite by chance selected Room 305.

After they had made love, they went to the refrigerator and got out a soft drink for the woman and a bottle of orange juice, which Takei had poured into a glass for himself.

"When I opened the bottle, I thought the lid was rather loose, but I didn't think anything about it until I took a drink of the juice. It had a strange, oily smell and it tasted bad. I kept most of what I had drunk in my mouth and went to the bathroom and spit it into the sink. I poured the rest of the juice into the glass and tried to identify the oily smell, but all I could tell was that there was definitely something wrong with it. I ended up pouring it all down the sink."

"You washed it all away?"

"Yes. At the time it didn't occur to me that someone might have tampered with it and put poison in it—I figured some earlier guest had opened it some time ago and put it back in the refrigerator. I just thought it had spoiled."

Yazawa waited.

"There seemed to be nothing wrong with the soft drink, so I had a glass of that and it seemed to clean my mouth out. After that, I smoked a cigarette and then called the front desk to tell them we were ready to check out."

"Did they ask you if you had had anything to drink?"

"Yes. I was about to protest paying for the orange juice, but just at that moment I suddenly changed my mind—"

It was at this point that the thought occurred to him that something might have been put into the drink. He decided that if he said anything about the juice tasting funny, the motel might call in the police. If that happened, it might come to light that he had picked up a snack-bar hostess and gone to a love hotel on company time. So in the end all he had told the front desk was that they had consumed a soft drink and a bottle of orange juice.

They had then gone down to the front desk, where he turned in their key and received an itemized bill.

"The next day when I read in the newspaper that a guest who had come to that room after me had drunk poisoned orange juice and died, I was, of course, flabbergasted. In fact, I could only think how close I might have come to dying myself."

After that, he had known he should come to the police with his story, but he was very busy at work on Wednesday and by evening he was exhausted, so he had put it off until the next day. On Thursday morning he wasn't feeling well, but still he planned to stop by the police station on his way home from work. By noon, though, he was feeling nauseated and weak, and his arms and legs were leaden. He had gone to a nearby hospital with his symptoms and was told he was experiencing a slight muscle paralysis.

"Thinking about what had happened, I decided to ask the doctor about it. I said that two days previously I had drunk a mouthful of bad-tasting orange juice and asked him if that could have some bearing on my symptoms. The doctor said it was possible that that was the problem. He said that, depending on the quantity consumed, a deadly poison can show up as muscle paralysis after two or three days."

That day and Friday Takei had stayed home from work, and now he was feeling recovered.

"I realize now," he said, "that if I had only raised the question of the orange juice when I checked out, the next guest may not have been sacrificed. A terrible crime has been committed and I'm here now to help see justice done if I can."

He concluded by saying in a low voice that he hoped he could keep his name from being mentioned publicly in the matter.

The snack-bar hostess who had accompanied Takei to the motel was brought in for questioning. She confirmed the details of his story—he had taken a drink of orange juice in his mouth, made a funny face, and gone to the bathroom, where he had spit it out. Both at the motel and later in the car, he had complained of something wrong with the orange juice, but he had asked her not to say anything about it because he didn't want any trouble from the police.

The desk clerk at the motel remembered Takei's face and that of the girl.

Homicide next checked all the empty juice bottles that could be found at the Castle Motel. The cleaning maids rounded up all the empties that had been gathered from the various rooms and packed them in a box. From among these, the police lab found one that contained minute traces of Malthion. Because the bottle had not yet been washed, traces of the poison remained. The police were able to lift fingerprints from the bottle and when these were compared to Takei's prints, two of them matched. In this fashion, it was determined that the bottle had indeed come from Room 305.

At this point, the case took a new twist. Suspicion directed toward Ogura was suddenly greatly reduced. Takei had checked into the motel at about 4:20 and it now appeared that Malthion was already in all three bottles of juice in the refrigerator. Takei had drunk one, which was replaced by a fresh one brought in by the maid when she cleaned the room. Sato Rumiko had drunk the second bottle and had died. At that point there remained in the refrigerator two bottles of juice, one with poison in it and one without.

Suspicion that this was the work of a random killer begun to rise once again. The most likely prospect was that whoever had been in Room 305 before Takei had supposed that a later guest would drink juice from the refrigerator and so had mixed it with poison. It was clear that it would be a very difficult business to specify who that person was.

The next thing Homicide did was to investigate any connection linking Takei Makoto and Ogura Masaaki, or between Takei and Sato Rumiko.

Originally, Takei had come from Yamagata City in the far north. After graduation from the local high school, he had entered a university in Tokyo. He had worked at part-time jobs to pay for his school expenses and after graduation had immediately gone to work for the securities company where he was now employed. He had a wife and two children, a boy and a girl. They lived in a public-housing apartment in Akabane. Both his parents still lived in Yamagata. His father had worked for a local company and was now retired and living on his pension. Takei's record of performance in his company was undistinguished, but he had created no problems and caused no controversy.

For ten days, the homicide detectives pursued a thorough investigation to uncover any sign of a connection between Takei and either Ogura or Rumiko, but in the end they were unable to come up with anything. They had to acknowledge that Takei's testimony was believable, and as a consequence of that had to conclude that Ogura, too, was innocent. When they told Ogura they were beginning to believe his claim of innocence, he seemed only somewhat relieved. His shoulders still sagged and it appeared he still felt some remorse about what had happened. "That's fine," he wailed. "But what's going to happen to me at work? I'll either be fired or turned out to pasture. No matter what happens, it won't be good. This is terrible."

Seven months later the Poisoned Juice affair was closed by Homicide as unsolved. No new clues had turned up and it was supposed that some previous occupant of the room was a random killer.

Then, one Saturday evening at the end of November, Inspector Yazawa happened to be in Shinjuku for a school-class reunion. Afterward, he had gone out with a couple of old friends, and as they were walking down a crowded street in Shinjuku's entertainment district, he suddenly saw a sign on a bar that caught his attention. It took a second or two before he realized why he recognized the sign: it was the bar where Sato Rumiko had been working at the time of her death. "Let's try this place and see how it is," he said to his two friends, who were happy to accompany him because sometimes he talked about cases under his investigation and they enjoyed hearing the inside story.

The mama-san who ran the bar was about Yazawa's age. Her eyes lit up with pleasure when he entered the tiny bar. She had a thin face and wore a brightly colored kimono. She seemed to remember right away who Yazawa was.

"Well, it's been a long time," he said with a smile, noticing the pensive expression on her face. "I'm not here on business tonight."

"You're always welcome here," she said.

Somehow the three managed to cram their way into the crowded bar and were given stools at the counter next to the front door. Customers were being served by the mama-san and by a hostess in her twenties, evidently the girl who had been hired to replace Rumiko.

By the time each of the three men had consumed a couple of glasses of whiskey and water, the conversation had drifted from police investigations to certain rumors surrounding a friend they had in common. At that point, Yazawa slipped off his stool and headed for the restroom. When he came out, the mama-san was waiting for him with a fresh, hot towel for his face and hands. The customers who had earlier jammed the back of the bar had left, so they were alone here.

"Whatever happened to your investigation about Rumiko's death?" asked the mama-san in a low voice.

"Well, I'm afraid it wasn't cleared up," he admitted. He went on to explain that after the autopsy had been performed on Rumiko's body, it was supposed to be turned over to relatives, but because her father was bedridden her maternal aunt came to Tokyo from her hometown of Hakuseki in northern Japan to take care of the cremation and take the ashes home to Hakuseki.

Yes, the mama-san said, she herself had been particularly helpful to the aunt during that time: "The fact is, at the first of this month I was in Sendai on business, and afterward I went on to Hakuseki to pay my respects at Rumiko's grave. Traveling in that area is very convenient now that they've opened bullet-train lines in the northeast. It only takes about two hours to get to Sendai from Tokyo."

Yazawa nodded. "And a place like Hakuseki is really something. The station there looks like something that just sprang up from the rice fields. But a few shops and houses have begun to appear around the station and there is even a small apartment complex nearby. If Rumi had been born a little later, she might have found it worth staying."

"Yes," Mama-san said, "I don't think she realized what it is like there now. Land prices there have skyrocketed."

"Land prices? What are you talking about?"

"Well, I'd never been there before, so the first thing I did was go to her aunt's house—she'd told me to be sure to drop in and see her if I was ever in that area. So I did, and that was when I learned that Rumi's father had passed away in September."

Inspector Yazawa didn't interrupt this sudden revelation, so the woman continued. "He had had surgery in June of last year and they found that he had cancer. They didn't make any secret of it, but the old man hated being in the hospital, and since they couldn't treat the cancer anyway, they let him do as he liked and sent him home. During the summer he was in decent condition and living by himself. But once the weather turned, he took a turn for the worse."

"But what has that to do with skyrocketing land prices?"

"When he died, Inspector, he left several acres of land next to the new train station, and with land prices what they are today that parcel is worth something over a billion yen. All that would have gone to Rumi if she'd lived."

Yazawa remembered the facts about the victim. Rumiko was an only child. She had been born when her father was in his forties and her mother had died while Rumiko was in middle school. Her father had quickly found a second wife, but Rumiko had never gotten along with her stepmother and had gone off to Tokyo when she was in high school. Two years ago, the second wife had died and from that time on the old man had lived alone.

"In other words, you're telling me that Rumiko would have inherited all that land herself?"

"Yes. *If* she had lived. Rumiko was a hard worker and she saved her money, but she might as well not have bothered. Anyone could have seen that her father would die soon. But back when she left home, they hadn't even started building the bullet train. Back then it was just farmland, and that's why she never wanted to return home. I don't think the thought of owning that land ever occurred to her."

"I see. But in that case, does it mean there's no one else left to inherit the land?"

"No. There's one nephew. Her father's sister had gone off to Yamagata to be married and I heard that she had a son. He would be Rumi's cousin. If Rumi had lived, she would have inherited all the land. But with her dead, the whole estate went to the nephew instead."

"You mean he suddenly inherited a fortune he probably never even knew existed?" Even as he said it, Yazawa could feel his heart beginning to thunder in his chest.

"That's right," nodded the mama-san. "The cousin is about thirty years old and runs a coffee shop in Yamagata City, but even after Rumi's father fell ill he didn't bother to come visit the old man. Even his mother felt his behavior was disgraceful and was embarrassed to have him inherit the estate, but the law is the law and if it says he's entitled to the land he gets it."

"You say he's about thirty and lives in Yamagata," muttered Yazawa, calling to mind the features of Takei Makoto, who was thirty years old and from Yamagata.

Rumiko's cousin who had inherited her father's entire estate was named Sato Yoshio and he was just thirty years old. It was pure chance that he had the same surname as Rumiko. Sato is a common name in that part of Japan. His parents had been farmers on the outskirts of Yamagata City, but both of them had already passed away.

After graduating from high school, Yoshio had gone to work for a small company in the city because he hated farming. Three years ago, he was dismissed by the company and at the same time he sold a small piece of land he had inherited from his parents. With the money from that and some other money he was able to borrow, he opened a coffee shop in Yamagata City. He wasn't a very good manager, however, and apparently he decided that the only thing to do was get hold of his uncle's property any way he could.

In the end, he inherited his uncle's land, had the deeds transferred to his own name, and had already sold part of the land for about five hundred million yen.

Then it came to light that Sato Yoshio and Takei Makoto had been classmates at Yamagata High School. They, along with Ogura Masaaki, were brought in by the police and questioned separately.

The first to crack was Takei.

"The summer before last, I returned to Yamagata for a visit

and went to Sato's coffee shop to see him. That night the two
of us went drinking together and Sato told me that just a month
earlier his uncle had undergone surgery for a stomach ulcer—
or rather they had told his uncle it was an ulcer, but in fact it
was cancer. He was old, but they thought it might not spread
too fast. Sato told me the doctors said the old man had about a
year to live."

His uncle had a single daughter named Rumiko who had left
home and drifted with the wind. She was said to be working in
the entertainment business in Shinjuku. She hadn't been home
to see her father in more than ten years, but she would still
inherit all the property once the old man finally died. But if
Rumiko happened to die first, then everything would be inherited by Sato Yoshio, the old man's nephew.

"There were several acres of land which Sato estimated to be
worth over a billion yen. He figured that after he paid off the
inheritance taxes and all expenses, he would stand to gain
something like 400 million yen. He pointed out that all that
money was there, and it could all be his, but he wouldn't get to
touch a single yen of it as long as Rumiko was alive."

After returning to Tokyo, Takei went to a detective agency to
see if they could turn up anything of Rumiko's whereabouts. It
wasn't difficult for them to trace her to the entertainment world
of Shinjuku. After that, it took very little more investigation to
turn up the fact that once or twice a month Rumiko went to a
love hotel in Shibuya with a man named Ogura Masaaki who
was employed by the Imperial Household Agency.

"I'm the one who recruited Ogura," Takei told Yazawa. "The
method of carrying out the crime was also mine. I had never
met Ogura and had no connection with him, so when I reported
back to Sato I recommended him as a suitable third party for
the plan. We figured that as an employee of the Imperial
Household Agency, he would probably be above suspicion.
Besides, I thought, even if the police looked for some connection between Rumiko and me they would find nothing. After all,
she came from a completely different place than I do.

"Anyway, I proposed to Ogura that if he would poison
Rumiko for me, I would give him half the two hundred million
yen Sato would pay me.

"I was shocked at how readily he jumped at the offer. But I suppose, being on the non-career track, he could see what the future held for him. After six or seven more years of mending old books every day, he would reach the mandatory retirement age and receive his small retirement pension, which would amount to maybe two or three million yen—while what I proposed would bring him an easy hundred million yen. And while if it became known that Ogura had taken a bar hostess to a love hotel and thereby offended the dignity of the Imperial Household Agency, as a person on the non-career track, he would merely be reassigned to some regional office. So he agreed to it."

Once Takei had confessed, neither Sato nor Ogura had a leg to stand on. As expected, Ogura had lost his position as section chief and been transferred to a regional office.

"I really got burned for fooling around with Rumiko." Ogura's deep-set eyes glittered under his drawn eyebrows. "She appeared so sweet and naive at first, but after that she stuck me for as much money as she could. Every time I tried to leave her, she came up with something to prevent me—threatening to tell my boss and things like that. It was at that point that Takei contacted me. It was his idea to use an agricultural chemical.

"On the day of the murder, he went to the Castle Motel with a girl who knew nothing of what was going on and used Room 305. He put some of the poison in a bottle of juice and left the empty bottle there when he checked out. I calculated about how long it would take them to clean the room after he checked out and then showed up there with Rumiko.

"It was Rumiko's habit every time we had sex to have a long bath afterward and then drink some orange juice. While she was in the bath, I took the poison Takei had given me and put it into two bottles of juice. I believed that even if I were suspected of wanting to kill Rumiko, it was certain that a man in my position would never attempt such a thing in a love hotel. I thought it would be assumed that because of my position in the Agency, I would never do anything as cheap as this.

"Besides—" Ogura Masaaki smoothed his silver moustache, "—I was sick and tired of hearing all the time about how important the dignity of the Imperial Household Agency is."

—translated by Robert B. Rohmer

# ELIZABETH PETERS

# THE LOCKED TOMB MYSTERY

*Detective stories set in ancient Egypt are few in number. The most famous, of course, is Agatha Christie's* Death Comes As the End, *her 1944 novel set around 2000 B.C. Here Elizabeth Peters has ventured back to the 14th century B.C. for a story that John Dickson Carr might have envied. Whether writing as Elizabeth Peters or Barbara Michaels, the author never fails to entertain, and readers should especially note her series of Peters novels about Victorian archaeologist Amelia Peabody Emerson. Perhaps only an author like Peters, with a doctorate in Egyptology, could have written them, and the story that follows.*

**S**enebtisi's funeral was the talk of southern Thebes. Of course, it could not compare with the burials of Great Ones and Pharaohs, whose Houses of Eternity were furnished with gold and fine linen and precious gems, but ours was not a quarter where nobles lived; our people were craftsmen and small merchants, able to afford a chamber-tomb and a coffin and a few spells to ward off the perils of the Western Road—no more than that. We had never seen anything like the burial of the old woman who had been our neighbor for so many years.

The night after the funeral, the customers of Nehi's tavern could talk of nothing else. I remember that evening well. For one thing, I had just won my first appointment as a temple scribe. I was looking forward to boasting a little, and perhaps paying for a round of beer, if my friends displayed proper appreciation of my good fortune. Three of the others were already at the tavern when I arrived, my linen shawl wrapped tight around me. The weather was cold even for winter, with a cruel, dry wind driving sand into every crevice of the body.

"Close the door quickly," said Senu, the carpenter. "What weather! I wonder if the Western journey will be like this—cold enough to freeze a man's bones."

This prompted a ribald comment from Rennefer, the weaver, concerning the effects of freezing on certain of Senebtisi's vital organs. "Not that anyone would notice the difference," he added. "There was never any warmth in the old hag. What sort of mother would take all her possessions to the next world and leave her only son penniless?"

"Is it true, then?" I asked, signaling Nehi to fetch the beer jar. "I have heard stories—"

"All true," said the potter, Baenre. "It is a pity you could not attend the burial, Wadjsen; it was magnificent!"

"You went?" I inquired. "That was good of you, since she ordered none of her funerary equipment from you."

Baenre is a scanty little man with thin hair and sharp bones. It is said that he is a domestic tyrant, and that his wife cowers when he comes roaring home from the tavern, but when he is with us, his voice is almost a whisper. "My rough kitchenware would not be good enough to hold the wine and fine oil she took to the tomb. Wadjsen, you should have seen the boxes and jars and baskets—dozens of them. They say she had a gold mask, like the ones worn by great nobles, and that all her ornaments were of solid gold."

"It is true," said Rennefer. "I know a man who knows one of the servants of Bakenmut, the goldsmith who made the ornaments."

"How is her son taking it?" I asked. I knew Minmose slightly; a shy, serious man, he followed his father's trade of stone carving. His mother had lived with him all his life, greedily scooping up his profits, though she had money of her own, inherited from her parents.

"Why, as you would expect," said Senu, shrugging. "Have you ever heard him speak harshly to anyone, much less his mother? She was an old she-goat who treated him like a boy who has not cut off the side lock; but with him it was always 'Yes, honored mother,' and 'As you say, honored mother.' She would not even allow him to take a wife."

"How will he live?"

"Oh, he has the shop and the business, such as it is. He is a hard worker; he will survive."

In the following months I heard occasional news of Minmose. Gossip said he must be doing well, for he had taken to spending his leisure time at a local house of prostitution—a pleasure he never had dared enjoy while his mother lived. Nefertiry, the loveliest and most expensive of the girls, was the object of his desire, and Rennefer remarked that the maiden must have a kind heart, for she could command higher prices than Minmose was able to pay. However, as time passed, I forgot Minmose and Senebtisi, and her rich burial. It was not until almost a year later that the matter was recalled to my attention.

The rumors began in the marketplace, at the end of the time of inundation, when the floodwater lay on the fields and the farmers were idle. They enjoy this time, but the police of the city do not; for idleness leads to crime, and one of the most popular crimes is tomb robbing. This goes on all the time in a small way, but when the Pharaoh is strong and stern, and the laws are strictly enforced, it is a very risky trade. A man stands to lose more than a hand or an ear if he is caught. He also risks damnation after he has entered his own tomb; but some men simply do not have proper respect for the gods.

The king, Nebmaatre (may he live forever!), was then in his prime, so there had been no tomb robbing for some time—or at least none had been detected. But, the rumors said, three men of west Thebes had been caught trying to sell ornaments such as are buried with the dead. The rumors turned out to be correct, for once. The men were questioned on the soles of their feet and confessed to the robbing of several tombs.

Naturally all those who had kin buried on the west bank— which included most of us—were alarmed by this news, and half the nervous matrons in our neighborhood went rushing across the river to make sure the family tombs were safe. I was not surprised to hear that that dutiful son Minmose had also felt obliged to make sure his mother had not been disturbed.

However, I was surprised at the news that greeted me when I paid my next visit to Nehi's tavern. The moment I entered, the others began to talk at once, each eager to be the first to tell the shocking facts.

"Robbed?" I repeated when I had sorted out the babble of voices. "Do you speak truly?"

"I do not know why you should doubt it," said Rennefer. "The richness of her burial was the talk of the city, was it not? Just what the tomb robbers like! They made a clean sweep of all the gold, and ripped the poor old hag's mummy to shreds."

At that point we were joined by another of the habitués, Merusir. He is a pompous, fat man who considers himself superior to the rest of us because he is Fifth Prophet of Amon. We put up with his patronizing ways because sometimes he knows court gossip. On that particular evening it was apparent that he was bursting with excitement. He listened with a supercilious sneer while we told him the sensational news. "I know, I know," he drawled. "I heard it much earlier—and with it, the other news which is known only to those in the confidence of the Palace."

He paused, ostensibly to empty his cup. Of course, we reacted as he had hoped we would, begging him to share the secret. Finally he condescended to inform us.

"Why, the amazing thing is not the robbery itself, but how it was done. The tomb entrance was untouched, the seals of the necropolis were unbroken. The tomb itself is entirely rock-cut, and there was not the slightest break in the walls or floor or ceiling. Yet when Minmose entered the burial chamber, he found the coffin open, the mummy mutilated, and the gold ornaments gone."

We stared at him, openmouthed.

"It is a most remarkable story," I said.

"Call me a lair if you like," said Merusir, who knows the language of polite insult as well as I do. "There was a witness—two, if you count Minmose himself. The sem-priest Wennefer was with him."

This silenced the critics. Wennefer was known to us all. There was not a man in southern Thebes with a higher reputation. Even Senebtisi had been fond of him, and she was not fond of many people. He had officiated at her funeral.

Pleased at the effect of his announcement, Merusir went on in his most pompous manner. "The king himself has taken an interest in the matter. He has called on Amenhotep Sa Hapu to investigate."

"Amenhotep?" I exclaimed. "But I know him well."

"You do?" Merusir's plump cheeks sagged like bladders punctured by a sharp knife.

Now, at that time Amenhotep's name was not in the mouth of everyone, though he had taken the first steps on that astonishing career that was to make him the intimate friend of Pharaoh. When I first met him, he had been a poor, insignificant priest at a local shrine. I had been sent to fetch him to the house where my master lay dead of a stab wound, presumably murdered. Amenhotep's fame had begun with that matter, for he had discovered the truth and saved an innocent man from execution. Since then he had handled several other cases, with equal success.

My exclamation had taken the wind out of Merusir's sails. He had hoped to impress us by telling us something we did not know. Instead it was I who enlightened the others about Amenhotep's triumphs. But when I finished, Rennefer shook his head.

"If this wise man is all you say, Wadjsen, it will be like inviting a lion to rid the house of mice. He will find there is a simple explanation. No doubt the thieves entered the burial chamber from above or from one side, tunneling through the rock. Minmose and Wennefer were too shocked to observe the hole in the wall, that is all."

We argued the matter for some time, growing more and more heated as the level of the beer in the jar dropped. It was a foolish argument, for none of us knew the facts; and to argue without knowledge is like trying to weave without thread.

This truth did not occur to me until the cool night breeze had cleared my head, when I was halfway home. I decided to pay Amenhotep a visit. The next time I went to the tavern, I would be the one to tell the latest news, and Merusir would be nothing!

Most of the honest householders had retired, but there were lamps burning in the street of the prostitutes, and in a few taverns. There was a light, as well, in one window of the house where Amenhotep lodged. Like the owl he resembled, with his beaky nose and large, close-set eyes, he preferred to work at night.

The window was on the ground floor, so I knocked on the wooden shutter, which of course was closed to keep out night demons. After a few moments the shutter opened, and the familiar nose appeared. I spoke my name, and Amenhotep went to open the door.

"Wadjsen! It has been a long time," he exclaimed. "Should I ask what brings you here, or shall I display my talents as a seer and tell you?"

"I suppose it requires no great talent," I replied. "The matter of Senebtisi's tomb is already the talk of the district."

"So I had assumed." He gestured me to sit down and hospitably indicated the wine jar that stood in the corner. I shook my head.

"I have already taken too much beer, at the tavern. I am sorry to disturb you so late—"

"I am always happy to see you, Wadjsen." His big dark eyes reflected the light of the lamp, so that they seemed to hold stars in their depths. "I have missed my assistant, who helped me to the truth in my first inquiry."

"I was of little help to you then," I said with a smile. "And in this case I am even more ignorant. The thing is a great mystery, known only to the gods."

"No, no!" He clapped his hands together, as was his habit when annoyed with the stupidity of his hearer. "There is no mystery. I know who robbed the tomb of Senebtisi. The only difficulty is to prove how it was done."

At Amenhotep's suggestion I spent the night at his house so that I could accompany him when he set out next morning to find the proof he needed. I required little urging, for I was afire with curiosity. Though I pressed him, he would say no more, merely remarking piously, " 'A man may fall to ruin because of his tongue; if a passing remark is hasty and it is repeated, thou wilt make enemies.' "

I could hardly dispute the wisdom of this adage, but the gleam in Amenhotep's bulging black eyes made me suspect he took a malicious pleasure in my bewilderment.

After our morning bread and beer we went to the temple of Khonsu, where the sem-priest Wennefer worked in the records office. He was copying accounts from pottery ostraca onto a papyrus that was stretched across his lap. All scribes develop bowed shoulders from bending over their writing; Wennefer was folded almost double, his face scant inches from the surface of the papyrus. When Amenhotep cleared his throat, the old man started, smearing the ink. He waved our apologies aside and cleaned the papyrus with a wad of lint.

"No harm was meant, no harm is done," he said in his breathy, chirping voice. "I have heard of you, Amenhotep Sa Hapu; it is an honor to meet you."

"I, too, have looked forward to meeting you, Wennefer. Alas that the occasion should be such a sad one."

Wennefer's smile faded. "Ah, the matter of Senebtisi's tomb. What a tragedy! At least the poor woman can now have a proper reburial. If Minmose had not insisted on opening the tomb, her *ba* would have gone hungry and thirsty through eternity."

"Then the tomb entrance really was sealed and undisturbed?" I asked skeptically.

"I examined it myself," Wennefer said. "Minmose had asked me to meet him after the day's work, and we arrived at the tomb as the sun was setting; but the light was still good. I conducted the funeral service for Senebtisi, you know. I had seen the doorway blocked and mortared and with my own hands had helped to press the seals of the necropolis onto the wet plaster. All was as I had left it that day a year ago."

"Yet Minmose insisted on opening the tomb?" Amenhotep asked.

"Why, we agreed it should be done," the old man said mildly. "As you know, robbers sometimes tunnel in from above or from one side, leaving the entrance undisturbed. Minmose had brought tools. He did most of the work himself, for these old hands of mine are better with a pen than a chisel. When the doorway was clear, Minmose lit a lamp and we entered. We were crossing the hall beyond the entrance corridor when Minmose let out a shriek. 'My mother, my mother,' he cried— oh, it was pitiful to hear! Then I saw it too. The thing—the thing on the floor. . . ."

"You speak of the mummy, I presume," said Amenhotep. "The thieves had dragged it from the coffin out into the hall?"

"Where they despoiled it," Wennefer whispered. "The august body was ripped open from throat to groin, through the shroud and the wrappings and the flesh."

"Curious," Amenhotep muttered, as if to himself. "Tell me, Wennefer, what is the plan of the tomb?"

Wennefer rubbed his brush on the ink cake and began to draw on the back surface of one of the ostraca.

"It is a fine tomb, Amenhotep, entirely rock-cut. Beyond the entrance is a flight of stairs and a short corridor, thus leading to a hall broader than it is long, with two pillars. Beyond that, another short corridor; then the burial chamber. The august mummy lay here." And he inked in a neat circle at the beginning of the second corridor.

"Ha," said Amenhotep, studying the plan. "Yes, yes, I see. Go on, Wennefer. What did you do next?"

"I did nothing," the old man said simply. "Minmose's hand shook so violently that he dropped the lamp. Darkness closed in. I felt the presence of the demons who had defiled the dead. My tongue clove to the roof of my mouth and—"

"Dreadful," Amenhotep said. "But you were not far from the tomb entrance; you could find your way out?"

"Yes, yes, it was only a dozen paces; and by Amon, my friend, the sunset light has never appeared so sweet! I went at once to fetch the necropolis guards. When we returned to the tomb, Minmose had rekindled his lamp—"

"I thought you said the lamp was broken."

"Dropped, but fortunately not broken. Minmose had opened one of the jars of oil—Senebtisi had many such in the tomb, all of the finest quality—and had refilled the lamp. He had replaced the mummy in its coffin and was kneeling by it praying. Never was there so pious a son!"

"So then, I suppose, the guards searched the tomb."

"We all searched," Wennefer said. "The tomb chamber was in a dreadful state; boxes and baskets had been broken open and the contents strewn about. Every object of precious metal had been stolen, including the amulets on the body."

"What about the oil, the linen, and the other valuables?" Amenhotep asked.

"The oil and the wine were in large jars, impossible to move easily. About the other things I cannot say; everything was in such confusion—and I do not know what was there to begin with. Even Minmose was not certain; his mother had filled and sealed most of the boxes herself. But I know what was taken from the mummy, for I saw the golden amulets and ornaments placed on it when it was wrapped by the embalmers. I do not like to speak evil of anyone, but you know, Amenhotep, that the embalmers . . ."

"Yes," Amenhotep agreed with a sour face. "I myself watched the wrapping of my father; there is no other way to make certain the ornaments will go on the mummy instead of into the coffers of the embalmers. Minmose did not perform this service for his mother?"

"Of course he did. He asked me to share in the watch, and I was glad to agree. He is the most pious—"

"So I have heard," said Amenhotep. "Tell me again, Wennefer, of the condition of the mummy. You examined it?"

"It was my duty. Oh, Amenhotep, it was a sad sight! The shroud was still tied firmly around the body; the thieves had cut straight through it and through the bandages beneath, baring the body. The arm bones were broken, so roughly had the thieves dragged the heavy gold bracelets from them."

"And the mask?" I asked. "It was said that she had a mask of solid gold."

"It, too, was missing."

"Horrible," Amenhotep said. "Wennefer, we have kept you from your work long enough. Only one more question. How do you think the thieves entered the tomb?"

The old man's eyes fell. "Through me," he whispered.

I gave Amenhotep a startled look. He shook his head warningly.

"It was not your fault," he said, touching Wennefer's bowed shoulder.

"It was. I did my best, but I must have omitted some vital part of the ritual. How else could demons enter the tomb?"

"Oh, I see." Amenhotep stroked his chin. "Demons."

"It could have been nothing else. The seals on the door were intact, the mortar untouched. There was no break of the smallest size in the stone of the walls or ceiling or floor."

"But—" I began.

"And there is this. When the doorway was clear and the light entered, the dust lay undisturbed on the floor. The only marks on it were the strokes of the broom with which Minmose, according to custom, had swept the floor as he left the tomb after the funeral service."

"Amon preserve us," I exclaimed, feeling a chill run through me.

Amenhotep's eyes moved from Wennefer to me, then back to Wennefer. "That is conclusive," he murmured.

"Yes," Wennefer said with a groan. "And I am to blame—I, a priest who failed at his task."

"No," said Amenhotep. "You did not fail. Be of good cheer, my friend. There is another explanation."

Wennefer shook his head despondently. "Minmose said the same, but he was only being kind. Poor man! He was so overcome, he could scarcely walk. The guards had to take him by the arms to lead him from the tomb. I carried his tools. It was the least—"

"The tools," Amenhotep interrupted. "They were in a bag or a sack?"

"Why, no. He had only a chisel and a mallet. I carried them in my hand as he had done."

Amenhotep thanked him again, and we took our leave. As we crossed the courtyard I waited for him to speak, but he remained silent; and after a while I could contain myself no longer.

"Do you still believe you know who robbed the tomb?"

"Yes, yes, it is obvious."

"And it was not demons?"

Amenhotep blinked at me like an owl blinded by sunlight.

"Demons are a last resort."

He had the smug look of a man who thinks he has said something clever; but his remark smacked of heresy to me, and I looked at him doubtfully.

"Come, come," he snapped. "Senebtisi was a selfish, greedy

old woman, and if there is justice in the next world, as our faith decrees, her path through the Underworld will not be easy. But why would diabolical powers play tricks with her mummy when they could torment her spirit? Demons have no need of gold."

"Well, but—"

"Your wits used not to be so dull. What do you think happened?"

"If it was not demons—"

"It was not."

"Then someone must have broken in."

"Very clever," said Amenhotep, grinning.

"I mean that there must be an opening, in the walls or the floor, that Wennefer failed to see."

"Wennefer, perhaps. The necropolis guards, no. The chambers of the tomb were cut out of solid rock. It would be impossible to disguise a break in such a surface, even if tomb robbers took the trouble to fill it in—which they never have been known to do."

"Then the thieves entered through the doorway and closed it again. A dishonest craftsman could make a copy of the necropolis seal. . . ."

"Good." Amenhotep clapped me on the shoulder. "Now you are beginning to think. It is an ingenious idea, but it is wrong. Tomb robbers work in haste, for fear of the necropolis guards. They would not linger to replace stones and mortar and seals."

"Then I do not know how it was done."

"Ah, Wadjsen, you are dense! There is only one person who could have robbed the tomb."

"I thought of that," I said stiffly, hurt by his raillery. "Minmose was the last to leave the tomb and the first to reenter it. He had good reason to desire the gold his mother should have left to him. But, Amenhotep, he could not have robbed the mummy on either occasion; there was not time. You know the funeral ritual as well as I. When the priests and mourners leave the tomb, they leave together. If Minmose had lingered in the burial chamber, even for a few minutes, his delay would have been noted and remarked upon."

"That is quite true," said Amenhotep.

"Also," I went on, "the gold was heavy as well as bulky. Minmose could not have carried it away without someone noticing."

"Again you speak truly."

"Then unless Wennefer the priest is conspiring with Minmose—"

"That good, simple man? I am surprised at you, Wadjsen. Wennefer is as honest as the Lady of Truth herself."

"Demons—"

Amenhotep interrupted with the hoarse hooting sound that passed for a laugh with him. "Stop babbling of demons. There is one man besides myself who knows how Senebtisi's tomb was violated. Let us go and see him."

He quickened his pace, his sandals slapping in the dust. I followed, trying to think. His taunts were like weights that pulled my mind to its farthest limits. I began to get an inkling of truth, but I could not make sense of it. I said nothing, not even when we turned into the lane south of the temple that led to the house of Minmose.

There was no servant at the door. Minmose himself answered our summons. I greeted him and introduced Amenhotep.

Minmose lifted his hands in surprise. "You honor my house, Amenhotep. Enter and be seated."

Amenhotep shook his head. "I will not stay, Minmose. I came only to tell you who desecrated your mother's tomb."

"What?" Minmose gaped at him. "Already you know? But how? It is a great mystery, beyond—"

"You did it, Minmose."

Minmose turned a shade paler. But that was not out of the way; even the innocent might blanch at such an accusation.

"You are mad," he said. "Forgive me, you are my guest, but—"

"There is no other possible explanation," Amenhotep said. "You stole the gold when you entered the tomb two days ago."

"But, Amenhotep," I exclaimed. "Wennefer was with him, and Wennefer saw the mummy already robbed when—"

"Wennefer did not see the mummy," Amenhotep said. "The tomb was dark; the only light was that of a small lamp, which Minmose promptly dropped. Wennefer has poor sight. Did you not observe how he bent over his writing? He caught only a glimpse of a white shape, the size of a wrapped mummy, before the light went out. When next Wennefer saw the mummy, it was in the coffin, and his view of it then colored his confused memory of the first supposed sighting of it. Few people are good observers. They see what they expect to see."

"Then what did he see?" I demanded. Minmose might not have been there. Amenhotep avoided looking at him.

"A piece of linen in the rough shape of a human form, arranged on the floor by the last person who left the tomb. It would have taken him only a moment to do this before he snatched up the broom and swept himself out."

"So the tomb was sealed and closed," I exclaimed. "For almost a year he waited—"

"Until the next outbreak of tomb robbing. Minmose could assume this would happen sooner or later; it always does. He thought he was being clever by asking Wennefer to accompany him—a witness of irreproachable character who could testify that the tomb entrance was untouched. In fact, he was too careful to avoid being compromised; that would have made me doubt him, even if the logic of the facts had not pointed directly at him. Asking that same virtuous man to share his supervision of the mummy wrapping, lest he be suspected of connivance with the embalmers; feigning weakness so that the necropolis guards would have to support him, and thus be in a position to swear he could not have concealed the gold on his person. Only a guilty man would be so anxious to appear innocent. Yet there was reason for his precautions. Sometime in the near future, when that loving son Minmose discovers a store of gold hidden in the house, overlooked by his mother—the old do forget sometimes—then, since men have evil minds, it might be necessary for Minmose to prove beyond a shadow of a doubt that he could not have laid hands on his mother's burial equipment."

Minmose remained dumb, his eyes fixed on the ground. It was I who responded as he should have, question ; and objecting.

"But how did he remove the gold? The guards and Wennefer searched the tomb, so it was not hidden there, and there was not time for him to bury it outside."

"No, but there was ample time for him to do what had to be done in the burial chamber after Wennefer had tottered off to fetch the guards. He overturned boxes and baskets, opened the coffin, ripped through the mummy wrappings with his chisel, and took the gold. It would not take long, especially for one who knew exactly where each ornament had been placed."

Minmose's haggard face was as good as an admission of guilt. He did not look up or speak, even when Amenhotep put a hand on his shoulder.

"I pity you, Minmose," Amenhotep said gravely. "After years of devotion and self-denial, to see yourself deprived of your inheritance . . . And there was Nefertiry. You had been visiting her in secret, even before your mother died, had you not? Oh, Minmose, you should have remembered the words of the sage: 'Do not go in to a woman who is a stranger; it is a great crime, worthy of death.' She has brought you to your death, Minmose. You knew she would turn from you if your mother left you nothing."

Minmose's face was gray. "Will you denounce me, then? They will beat me to make me confess."

"Any man will confess when he is beaten," said Amenhotep, with a curl of his lip. "No, Minmose, I will not denounce you. The court of the vizier demands facts, not theories, and you have covered your tracks very neatly. But you will not escape justice. Nefertiry will consume your gold as the desert sands drink water, and then she will cast you off; and all the while Anubis, the Guide of the Dead, and Osiris, the Divine Judge, will be waiting for you. They will eat your heart, Minmose, and your spirit will hunger and thirst through all eternity. I think your punishment has already begun. Do you dream, Minmose? Did you see your mother's face last night, wrinkled and withered, her sunken eyes accusing you, as it looked when you tore the gold mask from it?"

A long shudder ran through Minmose's body. Even his hair seemed to shiver and rise. Amenhotep gestured to me. We went away, leaving Minmose staring after us with a face like death.

After we had gone a short distance, I said, "There is one more thing to tell, Amenhotep."

"There is much to tell." Amenhotep sighed deeply. "Of a

good man turned evil; of two women who, in their different ways, drove him to crime; of the narrow line that separates the virtuous man from the sinner. . . ."

"I do not speak of that. I do not wish to think of that. It makes me feel strange. . . . The gold, Amenhotep—how did Minmose bear away the gold from his mother's burial?"

"He put it in the oil jar," said Amenhotep. "The one he opened to get fresh fuel for his lamp. Who would wonder if, in his agitation, he spilled a quantity of oil on the floor? He has certainly removed it by now. He has had ample opportunity, running back and forth with objects to be repaired or replaced."

"And the piece of linen he had put down to look like the mummy?"

"As you well know," Amenhotep replied, "the amount of linen used to wrap a mummy is prodigious. He could have crumpled that piece and thrown it in among the torn wrappings. But I think he did something else. It was a cool evening, in winter, and Minmose would have worn a linen mantle. He took the cloth out in the same way he had brought it in. Who would notice an extra fold of linen over a man's shoulders?"

"I knew immediately that Minmose must be the guilty party, because he was the only one who had the opportunity, but I did not see how he had managed it until Wennefer showed me where the supposed mummy lay. There was no reason for a thief to drag it so far from the coffin and the burial chamber— but Minmose could not afford to have Wennefer catch even a glimpse of that room, which was then undisturbed. I realized then that what the old man had seen was not the mummy at all, but a substitute."

"Then Minmose will go unpunished."

"I said he would be punished. I spoke truly." Again Amenhotep sighed.

"You will not denounce him to Pharaoh?"

"I will tell my lord the truth. But he will not choose to act. There will be no need."

He said no more. But six weeks later Minmose's body was found floating in the river. He had taken to drinking heavily, and people said he drowned by accident. But I knew it was

otherwise. Anubis and Osiris had eaten his heart, just as Amenhotep had said.

---

*Author's note:* Amenhotep Sa Hapu was a real person who lived during the
fourteenth century B.C. Later generations worshiped him as a sage and scholar;
he seems like a logical candidate for the role of ancient Egyptian detective.

# JAMES POWELL

# A DIRGE FOR CLOWNTOWN

*The Canadian writer James Powell, a resident of Pennsyl-*
*vania for many years, has written only short stories thus*
*far in his mystery career of twenty-three years. Almost all*
*of his stories—about eighty to date—have appeared in*
EQMM, *though he has also been published in* Playboy.
*Powell once wrote that he sees himself as a writer of*
*humorous fiction who is attracted to the mystery story. A*
*perfect example of his work is the following story, winner*
*of the* EQMM *Readers Award as their favorite of the year.*

"**R**ingling-ringling!" shouted the bedside telephone. When he
fumbled the receiver out of its cradle, a familiar voice at the
other end of the line said, "We've got a live one, Inspector.
Three seventy-one Pagliacci Terrace, Apartment 2C."

Forcing a grunt as close to "I'm on my way" as he could
muster, the man in the bed got his feet on the floor and
staggered toward the bathroom, hitting a chair and the door-
jamb on the way. Grabbing two tight fistfuls of sink porcelain,
he stared down at the drain for a long moment. Then he raised
his head and saw himself in the mirror. By Jumbo, he looked as
bad as he felt! The dead-white skin, the great bloody slash of
smile, the huge round maraschino nose, the perfect black
triangles of his eyebrows, the dead white skullcap with the two
side-tufts of bright-orange hair. There he was, Clowntown's
finest, Inspector Bozo of the Homicide Squad. Talk about a
three-ring hangover! Bozo ran the tips of his trembling fingers
across his cheek. A trip to Makeup was long overdue. Well, it
would have to wait. When Homicide said they had a live one,
they meant they had a dead one.

Splashing water on his face, Bozo hurried back to the bed-

171

room. The clock-radio on the bedside table said 11:15 in the morning. Shaking his head at himself, he got into his baggy pants, pulled the suspenders up over his shoulders, and sat down on the edge of the bed to put on his long yellow shoes. (Shoe length indicated rank on the Clowntown force. When two deputy chiefs met toe to toe, they had to raise their voices to communicate.)

Next came the high celluloid collar with the big bow tie of fluorescent orange and purple lightning bolts. Then he slipped into the paddy-green-plaid trenchcoat with all the belts and flaps, tabs and buttons, and the three-pound brass police badge pinned to a lapel. Slapping the pockets to make sure he had his revolver and his bicycle horn, he headed for the front door. He took the expensive pearl-grey fedora from the hatrack, set it carefully and properly on his head, and stepped out into the hall. Years ago, when he'd designed his outfit, he could have chosen one of those little umbrellas with the water spout in the ferrule or a squirting flower as the finishing touch. Instead he'd picked this perfect hat, feeling it set off the rest of his exaggerated costume. Yes, all in all he'd put together a damn good act. Why was it starting to fall apart?

As he passed through the lobby, Bozo exchanged horn-honk greetings with the building superintendent. Outside, a crew of Sanitation Department clowns armed with pushbrooms were sweeping spotlights out of the gutters. The Saturday-morning street was cold and blustery beneath an elephant-grey sky. Clowntown's wind was legendary, with newspapers scuttling around every corner and flags snapping like tent canvas overhead. The rawness came with early December.

Bozo decided to walk. Pagliacci Terrace wasn't that far and he needed to clear his head. He stumbled going up a curb and felt his nose budge. Damn, not that again. Almost twenty years on the force and the best nose he could afford was a wobbly mail-order number from Mr. Snoot. Last month, coming down the crowded city-hall steps with some buddies from Vice, the thing had dropped right off and gone bouncing high, wide, and handsome down the steps with Bozo cursing and chasing after it.

Oh, no one laughed. His embarrassed friends pretended not

to notice. His Honor and the police chief and the rest of the brass looked the other way. They were all great admirers of his father, Big Bozo, who'd made the family name synonymous with clown. But Bozo knew they'd soon be clucking among themselves about how Big Bozo's boy was hitting the bottle, how he was going to seed, how he'd been in a tailspin since his divorce.

No, Bozo couldn't let that happen again. He made a mental note to have the nose looked after at the next sporting-goods store. The same people who custom-drilled the holes in bowling balls did nose refitting. And they always tried to sell him one of those flashy new Japanese noses all the trendy young clowns were wearing. But ever since the india-rubber-cartel people got their act together, the price of noses had gone through the roof.

Bozo reached the Pagliacci Terrace address and took the steps two at a time. The uniformed clown policeman guarding the apartment door saluted, using the hand holding his nightstick, rapping himself on the head and knocking his tall blue helmet askew. It was a stunt he did well and Bozo could see he was proud of it.

The dead clown lay on his back on the floor, toes pointed at the ceiling, the wreckage of a whole custard pie on his face. He was dressed in a convict's uniform of broad black and white horizontal stripes and brimless cap and had a black-plastic ball and chain shackled to one leg. Retrieving the victim's wallet, Bozo found the man's union card. He recognized the ferret face staring out at him from the photograph. Yes, he knew Clown Bunco very well. Like a few other clowns on the shady side of the law, Bunco, a small-time confidence man and hustler, had taken to wearing a convict outfit as if to openly challenge society and its values. Bozo glanced at the card again. Today was Bunco's birthday. Sending a friend a custard pie in the face on his birthday was an old Clowntown custom.

Over in the corner, the police medical examiner was cramming an immense cleaver, a butcher knife as big as a scimitar, and a vast hypodermic needle back into his black bag. "Well, Doctor?" asked Bozo coldly as he knelt down to clear away some of the custard and make sure it really was Bunco under the mess. He'd never cared for the medical examiner. The man had fled Clowntown soon after graduating from the Emmett Kelly School of Medicine to take a fling at burlesque, slouching across the stage and leering at females in low comic routines. When burlesque died, he'd crept back, happy to eke out a living as a police medical examiner. His lewd eyebrows, glasses, red nose, and moustache looked made from one piece and he walked like his tie was caught in the zipper of his fly. For Bozo the man would always have the smell of the rim-shot about him.

"Strychnine," said the doctor. "A massive dose in the birthday boy's custard pie." Reading Bozo's look of disbelief, he gave a take-it-or-leave-it shrug and loped for the door, adding over his shoulder, "The delivery man's waiting for you in there."

Bozo followed the direction of the medical examiner's cocked thumb into the bedroom, where a clown wearing a bright-yellow bellboy's uniform sat waiting with a very depressed look. His chest was decorated with large brass buttons and the words MIDWAY BAKING COMPANY were printed in chartreuse on his pillbox hat. "What the hell happened?" demanded Bozo.

"Search me," said the delivery man in a reedy, nervous voice. "This was almost my last stop of the day. I parked my van on the street. Up I came and honked at his keyhole. When he opened the door, I was standing there holding the pie behind my back. 'Clown Bunco?' I asked. 'Yeah, so what?' sez he. 'So Happy Birthday,' sez I and I let him have it right in the kisser. You know, the secret of my marksmanship is never taking my eyes off the target.

"But it's funny the reaction you get in that split second while the pie's in the air. Clown A's pleasantly surprised. Clown B's smug—he's already had so many pies in the face he hasn't gotten the custard out of his ears from the last one and I know there are three more pie-delivery men stacked up out on the staircase. But Bunco there gave me the kind of look you don't see very often, a kind of tearing up in the eyes like he was remembering how long a time it had been since anybody'd remembered his birthday. Then the pie hit." The delivery man looked at Bozo helplessly. "Then he fell over dead."

"The doctor says the pie was poisoned," said Bozo. "Which would mean he got custard in his mouth or up his nose. Well, I can't buy that." One of the first things a clown learned was the right way to take a custard pie in the face. Just before impact you closed your mouth tightly and breathed out through your nose.

"Believe me, it was the finger schtick that did him in," insisted the delivery man.

The great clown, Josef Schtick, the originator of many little routines clowns still use, came up with the business in question as a follow-up to being hit with a custard pie. He would stand there, a forlorn laughingstock, with the mess sliding down his face. Then he would take a scoop of the custard on his forefinger, look at it curiously, taste it, smile, smack his lips, and start eating. Bozo cursed his own obtuseness. The finger schtick. Of course.

Bozo sent the delivery man home, confident he couldn't have known the pie was poisoned. Clowns were totally incapable of causing direct physical harm to another person. That didn't mean a clown couldn't commit murder, only that he couldn't do it directly.

Bozo spent a good hour searching the apartment for something that might give him a clue to the murderer's identity. He found nothing until almost the last place he looked. In an envelope taped to the underside of the drawer in the telephone table, he discovered a manila envelope. Inside were a sheaf of sales receipts for furniture and other household furnishings made out to Bunco. He skimmed through them quickly. It was all expensive stuff and it wasn't anything here in the apartment. Strange.

But stranger still, why would a man hide sales receipts? Bozo made the envelope into a tube and stuffed it into his pocket. He left the apartment not sure what his next move should be. But back out on the sidewalk, he saw a Dinero's hamburger place across the street. All he'd found in Bunco's refrigerator was a wizened lemon and a moldy quart of buttermilk. Well, the guy had to eat somewhere. And that reminded Bozo he could use a shot of the feedbag himself.

The girl behind the lunch counter wore a blonde fright wig, a fashionable nose, an immense greasepaint smile, and, under her uniform, a big set of inflatable breasts. The portside one seemed to have a slow leak. When Bozo came in, she put down her copy of *Big Top Tid Bits* and ducked behind the coffee urn. He was sure he heard several strokes of a tire pump before she reappeared in full repair. "What'll it be?" she asked.

Bozo ordered his burger and sat watching the waitress prepare it. He knew her type well. The young girl fresh from Pratt Falls comes to Clowntown with stars in her eyes, so sure she'll land a job with the circus she can already smell the cotton candy. It ached to think about it. It made him remember his ex-wife, Calliope. She'd been new in town, too, the first time he met her, and hell-bent to make her name in the circus. What a knockout she'd been, with her carrotred hair done up in braids and her great big freckles and the tasteful way she'd only blacked out a single tooth.

Those first years of their marriage had been times of big change for Clowntown. Until then, the city'd been a solidly blue-collar community. A lot of clowns worked for Ringmeister, the center-city brewery, or in the textile mills of Clowntown Tinsel and Spangle. But one of the biggies bought out Ringmeister and closed it down and the Japanese computerized the hell out of the spangle industry. Center city declined, and the clowns began their flight out to the suburbs, to Carneyville and Highwire.

Bozo and Calliope hadn't made the move. He was glad they hadn't. He had watched the suburban clowns trade in their floppy shoes for expensive sneakers and their baggy pants for designer jeans. And he saw their red-nosed faces at the commuter-train windows on the elevated tracks, looking sad—not clown sad, but stark, lonely, three-piece-suit sad. And he knew how their stories would end. Each year they'd buy a smaller-size nose until they got down to one no bigger than an angry boil. One morning they'd arrive at work with a band-aid on their nose and tell their secretary they'd had the boil lanced. When the band-aid came off, it would be goodbye, Clowntown.

But looking back on it, Bozo knew that he and his wife should have started a family. They put it off too long. Then all of a sudden Calliope wanted her own career. Bozo had argued strongly against it, but Calliope stood firm. "I can hear my slapstick clock ticking," she insisted. "It's now or never."

"Then it's never!" Bozo had shouted.

After the divorce, Calliope went to circus winter quarters in Florida. Bozo missed her. He tried not to think of her down there, just one more big red smile among a thousand big red smiles waiting for the big break. He got a card from her now and then. Sometimes he sent her money. But he knew he'd never see her again.

Bozo's food arrived. He ate it warily, unsure of his stomach, and set about organizing his thoughts on the case. So what did he have? The business of breathing out through the nose when you take a custard pie in the face was a clown trade-secret. So the murderer had to be a clown, a clown who knew Bunco well enough to know he still did the finger schtick.

And what about the hidden envelope? Bozo pulled it out and examined the contents again. A receipt from Crystal Palace Furniture for a bedroom and a living-room set. Another from S-T Molding and Shelving for a fireplace mantel. A third from a company called PlexiGrandi for a piano. All were marked with the special instruction that the customer would pick them up at the warehouse. Why was stuff like this important enough for Bunco to hide? And was it connected with his murder?

Bozo pondered for a moment and then called the waitress over and showed her Bunco's union card. "Ever see this guy in here?"

She looked at the picture. "Him and his ball and chain? Sure—he was a regular," she said. "My first day here he gave me the honk and said if I played my cards right he'd introduce me to his bigwig pals in the circus. What a laugh. I sure told him where to get off."

"Somebody just told him where to get off permanently," said Bozo. "Bunco's been murdered." He waited for that to register before asking her, "Did he ever come in with anybody else?"

She snapped her gum thoughtfully before answering. "There was Waco. He was a rodeo clown—purple suspenders, hairy chaps, red-flannel long johns, a cowboy hat with the brim turned up in front—the whole ten yards. Distracting Brahman bulls from thrown riders was his life until rodeos went the way of the buffalo. He was a nice guy, Waco. Too nice to have anything to do with Bunco, I always thought. They used to sit over in that corner booth and talk. I haven't seen Waco for— how long's it been? Two months? Six weeks?"

She thought for a minute. "I let him take me out once. Oh, it was no big deal. He'd just come into some money and wanted to celebrate. He took me to one of those new wine bars where the mimes go. How harmless can it get, right, standing around for an hour or so pretending to drink?"

Bozo wasn't sure. In a recent try at cutting down on his own intake, he'd visited a wine bar some mimes had opened where Trapezio's, the great old Italian clown restaurant, used to be. It'd been a pleasant evening. A couple of those mime women would've been real knockouts if only they'd had big red noses. And the drinks had gone down smooth. But there'd been nothing pretend about the hangover he woke up with next day.

Over the past few years, mimes had started moving into center city Clowntown, renting apartments, restoring brownstones. Now they were a familiar sight every weekday morning, going off to their jobs wearing the tight jumpsuits of their class, striped jerseys, a white oval on the front of their faces, their hats decorated with a flower or a butterfly on a wire. And all of them, all, relentlessly walking against some wind that only they could feel. A lot of clowns resented the mimes, claiming they were standoffish and wouldn't give you the time of day. Bozo knew that wasn't true. Mimes were kind, gentle folk, quick, at the slightest encouragement, with the big smile and the gift of an imaginary flower.

"Boy, Waco really got a charge out of watching those mimes go through their paces—like sitting on bar stools that weren't there or leaning on empty air like it was the most natural thing in the world," said the waitress. " 'I've seen the future and it works,' he said as we walked out the door. Afterward we went around the corner to his place. He didn't try anything funny. We just had coffee and he showed me pictures of his kids."

"Where was this?" demanded Bozo.

"Corner of Pantaloon and Rigoletto," she said. "But don't waste your time. That was a couple of months ago. He said he was moving. He said the owner of his apartment building wanted to renovate and rent the place out for big bucks to the mimes. Hey, maybe he left his landlord a forwarding address."

She thought for a moment and said, "The only other guy I ever saw with Bunco was this big-jawed, big-chested clown in a red bowler and a tight orange suit."

Bozo drummed four fingers against his white cheek. "A tough-looking customer with a skull-and-crossbones on his left hand?" he asked. When she nodded, he had his clown. The only trouble was Mugo had been in jail for the last ten days on the charge of mimebashing. But he had friends. Mugo could have arranged to have Bunco killed from there.

Mime-bashing was the crime of the moment among trendy clown criminals, a shameful business made all the more so by the victims' peaceful natures. Where clowns were incapable of harming another directly, mimes couldn't knowingly do harm to anyone, period. Except, of course, to themselves.

Unfortunately, a bad clown element had gotten wise to this. They would prowl the streets at night with their noses in their pockets so they couldn't later be identified in a police lineup. If they ran across a mime, they'd take a swing at him, being careful to miss by a good six inches. But mimes being what they were, they had to snap their heads around as though struck or hurl themselves backward into the nearest wall or down a flight of steps. Last month Mugo and a bunch of his friends had set upon four mimes, throwing punches at them until the mimes knocked themselves unconscious. Then the clowns had stripped them and left them naked and bloody in the street. Fortunately, two of the victims had been able to identify Mugo by his tattoo. Could Mugo be the murderer? Why would he want to kill Bunco?

"Hey," said the waitress, looking down at Bozo's empty plate. "It's fresh—how about a slice of custard pie?"

Bozo headed off for Pantaloon and Rigoletto. But in the next block he saw a sporting-goods store and decided to get his nose tended to.

The dark, old-fashioned shop smelled of leather and the rosin bag. Bozo's honk was answered by one from the back room and a moment later a dusty old clown with a burly grey moustache appeared, cleaning his wire-framed glasses on his striped apron. He spotted Bozo's problem at once and without a word ushered the Inspector into a small curtained alcove.

There Bozo handed over the nose and sat with a hand modestly covering his naked undernose. The old man put a jeweler's loupe in his eye and examined the inside of the rubber nose. He sighed and was about to start his sales pitch when he saw Bozo's name inscribed on the rim of the hole. "Inspector," he asked in a voice filled with awe, "was your father by any chance Big Bozo?"

Bozo nodded. His father had been a three-star general in the Clown Marines. Strutting out there at the head of his crack clown drill-team in his uniform of electric-blue with all the gold frogging and gold stripes on the sleeve and his shako with its immense pompom, he'd been the hit of every parade. The drill-team's trips and stumbles were all coordinated to perfection. When one marching clown slipped on a banana peel, a hundred did.

"Let me shake your hand," said the little old clown, doing just that. "The way I see it, Big Bozo and his drill-team set war back a hundred years. And isn't that what the military's supposed to be all about?" Then he returned to the matter at hand. "Inspector, this nose of yours has gone to the well once too often. I can fix it for now, but what you really need—"

"Is a new nose? Forget it," said Bozo. "Not on a police inspector's salary."

"I was thinking of maybe something nice in the second-hand line," said the nose-auger man.

Bozo frowned. Since the india-rubber cartel, there'd been a sharp rise in the theft of noses for resale. There were even stories of ghoulish clowns haunting midnight cemeteries to desecrate the graves of the recent dead.

The old man had produced a small box lined with white velvet. Inside was a smart red nose. "This has you written all over it," he said. "A match made in heaven. That undernose of yours is a real honker. This little honey belonged to one of your small-nosed rodeo clowns. It'll auger out real nice."

Bozo blinked and snatched the nose. The name *Waco* was inscribed around the rim. "How'd you come by this?"

"Last week this rodeo clown in chaps and cowboy hat walked in off the street," explained the old man. "He said he had this spare that was just collecting dust. He said he could use the cash. So we struck a deal. Trust me. Like I said, it'll auger out real nice."

The old man was clearly disappointed when Bozo told him he'd have to get back to him on that. He shrugged and set about repairing the old nose as best he could.

Bozo sat there patiently, considering this new development. Here was this rodeo clown, a friend of Bunco's who comes into some money and then drops out of sight. A couple of months later, Waco pops up again out of nowhere to sell a spare nose. A week later more or less and Bunco gets killed. What the hell did it all mean? Bozo didn't know. But as he paid for the repair job, he decided to flash Bunco's picture. "Seen this guy around?"

The old man looked at him like he was joking. "The outfit's all wrong, of course," he said, "but I swear that there's the Waco character I was just telling you about."

Bozo strode down the street puzzling out this new development. Then he heard an approaching siren and stopped to watch as a Clowntown Fire Department ladder truck, a caricature of a vehicle, rushed down the street with clown firefighters falling off and chasing after it on all sides. Bozo smiled, knowing the bumble and ineptitude was part of the clown's art. That ladder truck would arrive at the fire as quickly if not quicker than any non-clown ladder truck. And, yes, the buckets of confetti they threw on the fire would extinguish it as effectively as any modern chemical mix. Clowns were proud of that.

As he resumed his walk, Bozo mused on why some clowns hated the mimes so much. He thought he knew the answer. It'd come to him a while back when he'd been eating his lunch on a park bench. Along came this mime, walking against the wind, and sat down across the path from him as though there was a bench there, which there wasn't. From an imaginary brown bag, he drew this imaginary napkin and tucked it under his chin. Next came an imaginary sandwich, which he unwrapped and smiled down at before eating with visible relish, scattering the crumbs for the real pigeons.

Then he peeled and ate an invisible banana while he watched the birds crowd around his feet. When he was through, he put the sandwich wrapper and banana peel into the paper bag, which he crushed into an imaginary ball and tossed at a wire trash-container twenty feet away. The mime's anxious face told Bozo about the flight of the ball. He knew it rimmed the target once, twice, three times before body English knocked it into the container. Delighted, the mime got up and strode happily back in the direction he'd come, still walking against the wind.

Sitting chewing on his baloney sandwich, which now tasted like ashes, Bozo decided clowns resented mimes not because the pigeons preferred their imaginary bread crumbs to a clown's substantial ones or because a mime's invisible tears seemed larger, his silent laughter louder than clown sorrow or joy. No, in the end he decided that the mimes made the clowns feel clumsy, coarse, material, and utterly earthbound.

Not that that justified mime-bashing.

The brick facade of Waco's old apartment building had been sandblasted. A spanking new canopy flapped over the front door with *Pierrot Plaza* written across it in cursive script. While Bozo stood there at the curb, a mime couple arrived, pushing their child in an imaginary stroller. As more mimes entered and left the building, Bozo noticed the fat clown in top hat, cutaway, and baggy striped trousers standing nearby watching the come and go with a big red smile and rubbing his gloved hands together vigorously. The man was the epitome of the old plutocrat clown so popular in the twenties and thirties. Here was clown avarice—greed carried to the point of laughter. Here was the Pierrot Plaza's landlord.

Honking his horn and wagging his badge with a thumb behind his lapel, Bozo stepped forward. "Bozo's the name, Homicide's the game," he said. "I'm trying to track down an old tenant of yours, a rodeo clown called Waco."

The landlord clown turned pale. Glancing quickly left and right, he led Bozo by the elbow down the sidewalk to the next apartment building. "If we're going to talk murder," he murmured, "let's do it here in front of my competitor's building. Violence makes mimes very nervous. But Waco didn't leave any forwarding address, if that's what you're after. I guess he's living somewhere in the high-rent district. Did you know he hit it big with the ponies a couple of months ago? He bet his bankroll. 'Play Animal Act in the fifth,' he told me. I wish I had. It paid a bundle."

Bozo frowned. Without a forwarding address, where did he go from here? "I don't suppose you caught the name of the people who moved his furniture?" he asked.

"That junk?" said the landlord. "He gave it all to the Poor Souls Rescue Mission. They fix up stuff like that for resale and use the money to help tramp and hobo clowns." He shook his head. "Boy, what a bunch of dodos they sent round to pick it up! Those clowns broke half the stuff on the way down, not counting what they did to the paint on the stairwell."

The landlord winced at the memory. Then he chuckled. "You want to hear something real funny? A month later when I'd fixed the place up for my new tenants, I was down in the lobby when this mime Pip, who I rented Waco's old apartment to, drives up in a truck with four mime buddies and they go through the rigmarole of unloading invisible furniture and carrying it up the stairs. Laugh, I thought I'd die. But here's what really got to me. Those mimes were a hell of a lot more careful moving furniture that only existed in their heads than those rescue-mission clowns were with the real McCoy.

"No, sir, I've got no complaints with the mimes," he continued, counting the reasons on his gloved fingers. "They're polite as hell. They're neat as pins. Maybe they're a bit emotional, but they don't talk your arm off. They don't trash the building. They pay their rent on time."

Warming to his subject, he added, "Look, I'm as big a clown booster as the next guy. But the circus doesn't stop here anymore. We've got to move with the times. Sure, Waco was a nice guy and he got lucky—good for him. But he never did a lick of work, nothing but mope around in his apartment all day or hang out at the track. Now take the mimes. Five mornings a week there they go, all heading for the financial district, all walking against the wind. And after work, here they all come back, still walking against the wind."

Bozo knew the mimes were highly favored by the financial community. The banks and brokerage houses liked them because of their honesty. As the saying goes, there are no pockets in mime jumpsuits.

The landlord barked a short laugh. "No, what I just said isn't quite right, come to think of it. They go and come back together, all except this Pip I was telling you about. He works down in the financial district like the rest of them, but with him you never know what way he's going to go when he leaves for work or which way he'll come back. Strange, right?"

"Well, maybe not," said Bozo thoughtfully. "Wasn't it the great clown philosopher Plato who said that the only thing you could say for sure about the wind was that it didn't always blow from the same direction?"

He left the puzzled landlord scratching his head, went into the apartment building, and took the elevator to the fifth floor where the directory said this Pip character lived. Suppose the guy wasn't a mime? Suppose he couldn't fake the walking-against-the-wind bit? Suppose he actually had to be walking against the wind? That would mean sometimes he'd have to head off in a different direction from the others. But if the guy wasn't a mime, who was he? Bozo thought he knew.

The door to Pip's apartment was wide open. The place was quite empty of furniture. A pug-nosed man in the usual mime getup sat in midair in the middle of the room, seemingly engrossed in the play of his wrists and fingers along the keys of a baby grand that wasn't there. Bozo's polite horn-honk made the mime jump and look up quizzically.

"I'm Inspector Bozo of the Clowntown Police, Mr. Pip," said Bozo. "I'm selling tickets for our annual Policeman's Ball."

Pip smiled broadly and nodded his head. Crossing the room, he seemed to sit down at an imaginary desk, pull out an imaginary drawer, take out an imaginary checkbok, and, with a visible flourish, make out an invisible check, which he handed over.

"You're very generous, Mr. Pip," said the police inspector. When the mime cocked his head modestly, Bozo continued,

"You'll get your tickets in the mail, sir." Politeness made him add, "It's a nice place you've got here."

The mime beamed and, getting up, reached out his elbow and leaned with perfect ease on the precarious perch of a mantel Bozo could not see.

Back in the elevator, Bozo had to admit that Pip was one of the best mimes he'd ever seen. Boy, that mantel routine, that was really some— Bozo frowned and tugged thoughtfully at the ends of his bright bow tie. Reaching in his pocket, he pulled out the manila envelope of sales receipts and went through them until he came to the word he was looking for. When the elevator doors opened, he crossed to the lobby phonebooth and skimmed through the classified ads, stopping to read in several places. Then he phoned for a police backup.

Rejoining the landlord out on the street, Bozo asked, "Did one of the mimes who helped Pip move in have a skull-and-crossbones tattoo on his hand?"

"Now that you mention it, one did. Strange. Mimes aren't much for tattoos. What's going on?"

"That's easy," said Bozo. "Those weren't mimes moving mock furniture. They were clowns in stolen mime outfits lugging real furniture up the stairs."

The landlord looked bewildered.

"Okay," said Bozo. "Do you know what the S-T in S-T Furniture Company stands for? See-Through, that's what. They make transparent home furnishings like fireplaces and mantels. And Crystal Palace Furniture only deals in glass tables and chairs and things like that. And surprise, surprise, PlexiGrandi Company makes Plexiglas pianos."

"So what're you telling me?"

"That your old tenant, Waco the clown, moved right back in again as Pip the mime. For him, clowning was a dead-end street. He dreamed of sending his kids to mime school to learn the basics—the tough stuff, like sitting on chairs and leaning on mantels that aren't really there. That meant passing himself off as a mime. Transparent furniture seemed the easiest way."

"So he wants his kids to have a better future than he did," said the landlord. "Since when was that a crime? Just between us, and in case you hadn't noticed, being a clown isn't what it used to be. So big deal. Listen, you don't tell anybody about Waco, I won't either."

"I wish it was that simple," said Bozo. "You see, Waco paid a shady clown named Bunco to set up his operation, like getting the fake mime union card, the furnishings, and the bogus mime movers. It looks like Waco gave this Bunco his clown nose as payment for all his help. And his costume, too. After all, he wasn't going to need the stuff anymore. But Bunco had a little shakedown in mind. He calculated that Waco would end up in some mime job with a lot of money or insider-information lying around. Well, he was right. Where he made his mistake was thinking Waco would sit still for a lifetime of being blackmailed. Waco decided to have him killed with a custard pie."

As he spoke, a little fluorescent-yellow car with a big star on the door pulled up to the curb. Bozo's police backup had arrived. Fourteen uniformed officers got out and lined up in order of height, from a seven-foot beanpole to a dwarf no more than three feet tall. Back in the days before the cuts in the police budget, they could have gotten nineteen men out of the same car.

They were a smart-looking bunch of clowns, full of ginger and bicycle horns, eager to get the job done. Bozo divided them into two groups, one to take the stairs and his own assault group that would go up by elevator. At Bozo's signal, the policemen started tripping over themselves, bumping into each other, and trying to get through the apartment-building door-way at the same time. They were a crack unit. Even with a good dose of gaston-and-alphonsing on top of the obligatory clowning around, they were in position in record time.

The door to the false mime's apartment was closed. Signaling his men to keep clear, Bozo honked his bicycle horn at the keyhole and shouted, "Open up, Waco, it's the police! We're onto your game!"

From inside, a voice shouted, "There's nobody here named Waco! I'm Pip! I'm a—" Then, realizing he'd given himself away, Waco snarled a defiant, "Come and get me, coppers!"

Bozo heard the sound of a window opening. He signaled his

men to break down the door, and followed in after them. Later he would remember the sorry dash of the Clowntown Police across a room filled with transparent furniture with a smile, but at the time the sight filled him with dismay. His men looked like a charge of stumblebums, barking their shins on the crystal coffee table and crashing into the Plexiglas piano and falling over the sofa and chairs.

Bozo rallied his men and, hot on Waco's trail, he led them out the window and up onto the roof. They got there just in time to see the fugitive clown cross over to the neighboring roof on a narrow plank. Sprinting as fast as his big shoes would allow, Bozo reached the edge just as Waco toppled the plank down between the two buildings. Bozo knew there'd be no catching him now.

Waco knew it, too. He lingered for a moment as Bozo's men came running up. "Doing things on too big a scale was my only mistake!" he called. "Next time I'll make do with a glass cardtable and folding chair, max! I'll sleep on the floor! I'll send the kids to mime boarding school! I won't tell them the truth about their daddy until they're old enough to understand! Then it'll be our little secret!"

"You'll never pull it off!" shouted Bozo earnestly. "Every time you sat down, it'd be a lie! And what kind of life would it be for your kids, always afraid to invite their friends home, always having to hide the dark secret that their dad was a clown?"

"I'm not a clown! I never was a clown! I'm a mime!" Waco cried in a fury. Then, as if he realized his anger belied his words, he forced himself to be calm. "All my life I've felt like an outsider," he said. "I told myself it was because I was a rodeo clown in a world where the rodeos are few and far between. But deep down in my bones, I always knew I was a mime. I think maybe the Gypsies stole me from a mime cradle and sold me to a nice childless couple of rodeo clowns. Okay, I can't recapture my mime heritage for myself, but I can damn well do it for my kids."

"You lost any chance of that when you killed Bunco," said Bozo.

"Bunco deserved what he got!" shouted Waco, turning away from the edge of the roof and starting toward the top of the metal ladder that would take him down to a fire escape and safety. "He would have sucked me dry! Then he'd have started on my kids! I don't regret what I did!"

It was cold on the roof. The sun poked through the dull winter sky like a nose of brass. A mere summer ago the same sun had set, a perfect fit, soft, warm, and red, down the slot of any Clowntown street. Bozo sighed to himself. He knew what he had to do. "I've got to take you in, Waco!" he called.

The murderer continued walking toward the ladder.

Bozo's men were lined up along the edge of the roof. They turned to him for instructions, honking their horns nervously. Bozo had hoped it wouldn't come to this, but police regulations were clear—he knew what he had to do. He drew his weapon. "Stop or I'll shoot, Waco!" he ordered.

The fugitive clown had reached the roof parapet now, his hands on the metal uprights of the ladder. He gave Bozo and the other policemen standing with their drawn weapons a pitying look and shook his head.

Bozo had no other choice. As humiliating as it would be, he pulled the trigger and the flag popped out of the end of the barrel. BANG! said the flag. In the next moment, all the clown policemen fired and all the flags at the ends of their pistol barrels said BANG! One policeman had a submachine gun. Its longer flag read RATATAT! What other kinds of weapons would be issued to clowns who by nature were unable to hurt anyone directly?

Waco knew that and he should have made his escape, but when the barrel flags appeared his body gave a sudden jump and spun as though hit with a fusillade of bullets. The horrified clowns watched Waco's grip on the ladder give way finger by finger until he fell back into that long emptiness that led to the street below.

Bozo watched in sad amazement. Could Waco's parents really have been mimes? Or was his desire to be a mime so strong that when the flag fire came he'd done what any real mime would have done even if it cost him his life?

Bozo sat on the edge of his unmade bed massaging his big bare left foot, which rested on his knobby right knee. He'd been thinking about the day's events. But now he turned his thoughts to Calliope hanging around circus winter quarters with clown stars in her eyes. It seemed to him that she'd been right to go and try. And he'd been right to stay, to see in his own small way that clowns got a fair shake and gave a fair shake. After all, wasn't justice as rare as stardom?

And when push came to shove, the mimes were right, too. They'd pared things down to the essentials—a jumpsuit, a hat, imaginary flowers and butterflies. It looked like the kind of act the world needed now. Maybe the doom-sayers were right. Maybe the clown days *were* numbered. Maybe they'd played the game with too heavy a hand.

Well, what the hell, clown or mime, hadn't they all sprung from the same crazy pair of ancestors, sitting arm in arm, fishing for the moon in a bucket?

Bozo reached for the bottle of Old Roustabout on the bedside table, drew out the stopper with his teeth, and looked around for his well-thumbprinted glass from the night before. When he couldn't find it, he grunted and spat out the stopper. Then he turned out the light, rolled over in bed, and fell quickly into clown slumber.

# RUTH RENDELL

# A PAIR OF YELLOW LILIES

*Ruth Rendell is one of those rare mystery writers who is equally skilled at both the novel and the short story. Even with her increasing fame and appearances on the best-seller lists, she has never abandoned the short story for long. An anthologist's most difficult task is generally choosing the best selection from two or three excellent stories published each year. I found "A Pair of Yellow Lilies" to be a most satisfying story, especially in the manner of its ending.*

A famous designer, young still, who first became well known when she made a princess's wedding dress, was coming to speak to the women's group of which Bridget Thomas was secretary. She would be the second speaker in the autumn program, which was devoted to success and how women had achieved it. Repeated requests on Bridget's part for a biography from Annie Carter so that she could provide her members with interesting background information had met with no response. Bridget had even begun to wonder if she would remember to come and give her talk in three weeks' time. Meanwhile, obliged to do her own research, she had gone into the public library to look Annie Carter up in *Who's Who*.

Bridget had a precarious job in a small and not very prosperous bookshop. In her mid-thirties, with a rather pretty face that often looked worried and worn, she thought that she might learn something from this current series of talks. Secrets of success might be imparted, blueprints for achievement, even shortcuts to prosperity. She never had enough money, never knew security, could not have dreamed of aspiring to an Annie Carter ready-to-wear even when such a garment had been twice marked down in a sale. Clothes, anyway, were hardly a priority, coming a long way down the list of essentials which was headed by rent, fares, and food, in that order.

191

In the library she was not noticeable. She was not, in any case and anywhere, the kind of woman on whom second glances were bestowed. On this Wednesday evening, when the shop closed at its normal time and the library later than usual, she could be seen by those few who cared to look wearing a long black skirt with a dusty appearance, a T-shirt of a slightly different shade of black—it had been washed fifty times at least—and a waistcoat in dark striped cotton. Her shoes were black-velvet Chinese slippers with instep straps and there was a hole she didn't know about in her turquoise-blue tights, low down on the left calf. Bridget's hair was wispy, long and fair, worn in loops. She was carrying an enormous black-leather bag, capacious and heavy, and full of unnecessary things. Herself the first to admit this, she often said she meant to make changes in the matter of this bag but she never got around to it.

This evening the bag contained a number of crumpled tissues, some pink, some white, a spray bottle of Wild Musk cologne, three ballpoint pens, a pair of nail scissors, a pair of nail clippers, a London tube pass, a British Telecom phone-card, an address book, a mascara wand in a shade called After-Midnight Blue, a checkbook, a notebook, a postcard from a friend on holiday in Brittany, a calculator, a paperback of Vasari's *Lives of the Artists,* which Bridget had always meant to read but was not getting on very fast with, a container of nasal spray, a bunch of keys, a book of matches, a silver ring with a green stone, probably onyx, a pheasant's feather picked up while staying for the weekend in someone's cottage in Somerset, three quarters of a bar of milk chocolate, a pair of sunglasses, and her wallet—which contained the single credit card she possessed, her bank-check card, her library card, her never-needed driving license, and seventy pounds, give or take a little, in five- and ten-pound notes. There was also about four pounds in change.

On the previous evening, Bridget had been to see her aunt. This was the reason for her carrying so much money. Bridget's Aunt Monica was an old woman who had never married and whom her brother, Bridget's father, referred to with brazen insensitivity as "a maiden lady." Bridget thought this outrageous and remonstrated with her father but was unable to bring him to see anything offensive in this expression. Though Monica had never had a husband, she had been successful in other areas of life, and might indeed almost have qualified to join Bridget's list of female achievers fit to speak to her women's group. Inherited-money wisely invested brought her in a substantial income, and this added to the pension derived from having been quite high up the ladder in the Civil Service made her nearly rich.

Bridget did not like taking Monica Thomas's money. Or she told herself she didn't—actually meaning that she liked the money very much but felt humiliated, as a young healthy woman who ought to have been able to keep herself adequately, taking money from an old one who had done so and still did. Monica, not invariably during these visits but often enough, would ask her how she was managing.

"Making ends meet, are you?" was the form this inquiry usually took.

Bridget felt a little tide of excitement rising in her at these words because she knew they signified a coming munificence. She simultaneously felt ashamed at being excited by such a thing. This was the way, she believed, other women might feel at the prospect of lovemaking or discovering themselves pregnant or getting a promotion. She felt excited because her old aunt, her maiden aunt tucked away in a gloomy flat in Fulham, was about to give her fifty pounds.

Characteristically, Monica prepared the ground. "You may as well have it now instead of waiting till I'm gone."

And Bridget would smile and look away—or, if she felt brave, tell her aunt not to talk about dying. Once she had gone so far as to say, "I don't come here for the sake of what you give me, you know," but as she put this into words she knew she did. And Monica, replying tartly, "And I don't see my little gifts as paying you for your visits," must have known that she did and they did, and that the two of them were involved in a commercial transaction, calculated enough, but imbrued with guilt and shame.

Bridget always felt that at her age, thirty-six, and her aunt's, seventy-two, it should be she who gave alms and her aunt who received them. That was the usual way of things. Here the order was reversed, and with a hand that she had to restrain forcibly from trembling with greed and need and excitement she had reached out on the previous evening for the notes that were presented as a sequel to another of Monica's favorite remarks, that she would like to see Bridget better dressed. With only a vague grasp of changes in the cost of living, Monica nevertheless knew that for any major changes in her niece's wardrobe to take place a larger than usual sum would be required and another twenty-five had been added to the customary fifty.

Five pounds or so had been spent during the course of the day. Bridget had plenty to do with the rest, which did not include buying the simple dark coat and skirt and pink twinset Monica had suggested. There was the gas bill, for instance, and the chance at last of settling the credit-card account, on which interest was being paid at twenty-one percent. Not that Bridget had no wistful thoughts of beautiful things she would like to possess and most likely never would. A chair in a shop window in Bond Street, for instance, a chair which stood alone in slender, almost arrogant elegance, with its high-stepping legs and sweetly curved back, she imagined gracing her room as a bringer of daily renewed happiness and pride. Only today a woman had come into the shop to order the new Salman Rushdie and she had been wearing a dress that was unmistakably Annie Carter. Bridget had gazed at that dress as at some unattainable glory, at its bizarreries of zips round the sleeves and triangles excised from armpits, uneven hemline and slashed back, for if the truth were told it was the fantastic she admired in such matters and would not have been seen dead in a pink twinset.

She had gazed and longed, just as now, fetching *Who's Who* back to her seat at the table, she had stared in passing at the back of a glorious jacket. Afterward, she could not have said if it was a man or woman wearing it, a person in jeans was all she could have guessed at. The person in jeans was pressed fairly close up against the science-fiction shelves, so that the back of the jacket, its most beautiful and striking area, was displayed to the best advantage. The jacket was made of blue denim with a design appliqued on it. Bridget knew the work was applique because she had learned something of this technique herself at a handicrafts class, all part of the horizon-widening, life-enhancing program with which she combated loneliness. Patches of satin and silk and brocade had been used in the work, and beads and sequins and gold thread as well. The design was of a flock of brilliant butterflies, purple and turquoise and vermilion and royal blue and fuchsia pink, tumbling and fluttering from the open mouths of a pair of yellow lilies. Bridget had gazed at this fantastic picture in silks and jewels and then looked quickly away, resolving to look no more, she desired so much to possess it herself.

Annie Carter's *Who's Who* entry mentioned a book she had written on fashion in the early eighties. Bridget thought it would be sensible to acquaint herself with it. It would provide her with something to talk about when she and the committee entertained the designer to supper after her talk. Leaving *Who's Who* open on the table and her bag wedged between the table legs and the leg of her chair, Bridget went off to consult the library's computer as to whether the book was in stock.

Afterward she recalled, though dimly, some of the people she had seen as she crossed the floor of the library to where the computer was. An old man in gravy-brown clothes reading a newspaper, two old women in fawn raincoats and pudding-basin hats, a child that ran about in defiance of its mother's threats and pleas. The mother was a woman about Bridget's own age, grossly fat, with fuzzy dark hair and swollen legs. There had been other people less memorable. The computer told her the book was in stock but out on loan. Bridget went back to her table and sat down. She read the sparse *Who's Who* entry once more, noting that Annie Carter's interests were bobsleighing and collecting netsuke, which seemed to make her rather a daunting person, and then she reached down for her bag and the notebook it contained.

The bag was gone.

The feeling Bridget experienced is one everyone has when they lose something important or think they have lost it, the shock of loss. It was a physical sensation, as of something falling through her—turning over in her chest first and then tumbling down inside her body and out through the soles of her feet. She immediately told herself she couldn't have lost the bag, she

couldn't have done, it couldn't have been stolen—who would
have stolen it among that company?—she must have taken it
with her to the computer. Bridget went back to the computer,
she ran back, and the bag wasn't there. She told the two assistant
librarians and then the librarian herself and they all looked
round the library for the bag. It seemed to Bridget that by this
time everyone else who had been in the library had swiftly
disappeared—everyone, that is, but the old man reading the
newspaper.

The librarian was extremely kind. They were about to close
and she said she would go to the police with Bridget, it was on
her way. Bridget continued to feel the shock of loss, sickening
overturnings in her body and sensations of panic and disbelief.
Her head seemed too lightly poised on her neck, almost as if it
floated.

"It can't have happened," she kept saying to the librarian. "I
just don't believe it could have happened in those few seconds
I was away."

"I'm afraid it did," said the woman, who was too kind to say
anything about Bridget's unwisdom in leaving the bag unattended even for a few seconds. "It's nothing to do with me, but
was there much money in it?"

"Quite a lot. Yes, quite a lot." Bridget added humbly, "Well, a
lot for me."

The police could offer very little hope of recovering the
money. The bag, they said, and some of its contents might turn
up. Meanwhile, Bridget had no means of getting into her room,
no means even of phoning the credit-card company to notify
them of the theft. The librarian, whose name was Elizabeth
Derwent, saw to all that. She took Bridget to her own home and
led her to the telephone and then took her to a locksmith. It
was the beginning of what was to be an enduring friendship.
Bridget might have lost so many of the most precious of her
worldly goods, but as she said afterward to her Aunt Monica, at
least she got Elizabeth's friendship out of it.

"It's an ill wind that blows nobody any good," said Monica,
pressing fifty pounds in ten-pound notes into Bridget's hand.

But all this was in the future. That first evening, Bridget had
to come to terms with the loss of seventy pounds, her driving

license, her credit card, her checkbook, the *Lives of the Artists* (she would never read it now), her address book, and the silver ring with the stone which was probably onyx. She mourned, alone there in her room. She fretted miserably, shock and disbelief having been succeeded by the inescapable certainty that someone had deliberately stolen her bag. Several cups of strong hot tea comforted her a little. Bridget had more in common with her aunt than she would have liked to think possible, being very much a latter-day maiden lady in every respect but maidenhood.

At the end of the week, a parcel came. It contained her wallet (empty but for the library card), the silver ring, her address book, her notebook, the nail scissors and the nail clippers, the mascara wand in the shade called After-Midnight Blue, and most of the things she had lost but for the money and the credit card and the checkbook, the driving license, the paperback Vasari, and the bag itself. A letter accompanied the things. It said: "Dear Miss Thomas, This name and address were in the notebook. I hope they are yours and that this will reach you. I found your things inside a plastic bag on top of a litter bin in Kensington Church Street. It was the wallet which made me think they were not things someone had meant to throw away. I am afraid this is absolutely all there was, though I have the feeling there was money in the wallet and other valuable things. Yours sincerely, Patrick Baker."

His address and phone number headed the sheet of paper. Bridget, who was not usually impulsive, was so immediately brimming with amazed happiness and restored faith in human nature that she lifted the phone at once and dialed the number. He answered. It was a pleasant voice, educated, rather slow and deliberate in its enunciation of words, a young man's voice. She poured out her gratitude. How kind he was! What trouble he had been to! Not only to retrieve her things but to take them home, to parcel them up, pay the postage, stand in a queue no doubt at the post office! What could she do for him? How could she show the gratitude she felt?

Come and have a drink with him, he said. Well, of course she would, of course. She promised to have a drink with him and a place was arranged and a time, though she was already getting cold feet. She consulted Elizabeth.

"Having a drink in a pub in Kensington High Street couldn't do any harm," said Elizabeth, smiling.

"It's not really something I do." It wasn't something she had done for years, at any rate. In fact, it was two years since Bridget had even been out with a man, since her sad affair with the married accountant which had dragged on year after year before it finally came to an end. Drinking in pubs had not been a feature of the relationship. Sometimes they had made swift furtive love in the small office where clients' VAT files were kept. "I suppose," she said, "it might make a pleasant change."

The aspect of Patrick Baker which would have made him particularly attractive to most women, if it did not repel Bridget at least put her off. He was too good-looking for her. He was, in fact, radiantly beautiful, like an angel or a young Swedish tennis player. This, of course, did not specially matter that first time. But his looks registered with her as she walked across the little garden at the back of the pub and he rose from the table at which he was sitting. His looks frightened her and made her shy. It would not have been true, though, to say that she could not keep her eyes off him. Looking at him was altogether too much for her, it was almost an embarrassment, and she tried to keep her eyes turned away.

Nor would she have known what to say to him. Fortunately, he was eager to recount in detail his discovery of her property in the litter bin in Kensington Church Street. Bridget was good at listening and she listened. He told her also how he had once lost a briefcase in a tube train and a friend of his had had his wallet stolen on a train going from New York to Philadelphia. Emboldened by these homely and not at all sophisticated anecdotes, Bridget told him about the time her Aunt Monica had burglars and lost an emerald necklace which fortunately was insured. This prompted him to ask more about her aunt and Bridget found herself being quite amusing, recounting Monica's financial adventures. She didn't see why she shouldn't tell him the origins of the stolen money and he seemed interested when she said it came from Monica, who was in the habit of bestowing like sums on her.

"You see, she says I'm to have it one day—she means when she's dead, poor dear—so why not now?"

"Why not indeed?"

"It was just my luck to have my wallet stolen the day after she'd given me all that money."

He asked her to have dinner with him. Bridget said all right, but it mustn't be anywhere expensive or grand. She asked Elizabeth what she should wear. They were in a clothes mood, for it was the evening of the Annie Carter talk to the women's group which Elizabeth had been persuaded to join.

"He doesn't dress at all formally himself," Bridget said. "Rather the reverse." He and she had been out for another drink in the meantime. "He was wearing this kind of safari suit with a purple shirt. But, oh, Elizabeth, he is amazing to look at. Rather too much so, if you know what I mean."

Elizabeth didn't. She said that surely one couldn't be too good-looking? Bridget said she knew she was being silly, but it embarrassed her a bit—well, being seen with him, if Elizabeth knew what she meant. It made her feel awkward.

"I'll lend you my black lace if you like," Elizabeth said. "It would suit you and it's suitable for absolutely everything."

Bridget wouldn't borrow the black lace. She refused to sail in under anyone else's colors. She wouldn't borrow Aunt Monica's emerald necklace, either—the one she had bought to replace the necklace the burglars took. Her black skirt and the velvet top from the secondhand shop in Hammersmith would be quite good enough. If she couldn't have an Annie Carter, she would rather not compromise. Monica, who naturally had never been told anything about the married accountant or his distant predecessor, the married primary-school teacher, spoke as if Patrick Baker were the first man Bridget had ever been alone with, and spoke, too, as if marriage were a far from remote possibility. Bridget listened to all this while thinking how awful it would be if she were to fall in love with Patrick Baker and become addicted to his beauty and suffer when separated from him.

Even as she thought in this way, so prudently and with irony, she could see his face before her, its hawklike lineaments and its softnesses, the wonderful mouth and the large wide-set eyes, the hair that was fair and thick and the skin that was smooth and brown. She saw, too, his muscular figure, slender and graceful yet strong, his long hands and his tapering fingers, and she felt something long-suppressed, a prickle of desire that plucked very lightly at the inside of her and made her gasp a little.

The restaurant where they had their dinner was not grand or expensive, and this was just as well since at the end of the meal Patrick found that he had left his checkbook at home and Bridget was obliged to pay for their dinner out of the money Monica had given her to buy an evening dress. He was very grateful. He kissed her on the pavement outside the restaurant, or, if not quite outside it, under the archway that was the entrance to the mews. They went back to his place in a taxi.

He had quite a nice flat at the top of a house in Bayswater, not exactly overlooking the park but nearly. It was interesting what was happening to Bridget. Most of the time she was able to stand outside herself and view these deliberate acts of hers with detachment. She would have the pleasure of him, he was so beautiful, she would have it and that would be that. Such men were not for her, not at any rate for more than once or twice. But if she could once in a lifetime have one of them for once or twice, why not? Why not?

The life, too, the lifestyle, was not for her. On the whole, she was better off at home with a pot of strong hot tea and her embroidery or the latest paperback on changing attitudes to women in Western society. Nor had she any intention of sharing Aunt Monica's money when the time came. She had recently had to be stern with herself about a tendency, venal and degrading, to dream of that distant prospect when she would live in a World's End studio with a gallery, fit setting for the arrogant Bond Street chair, and dress in a bold, eccentric manner, in flowing skirts and antique pelisses and fine old lace.

Going home with Patrick, she was rather drunk. Not drunk enough not to know what she was doing, but drunk enough not to care. She was drunk enough to shed her inhibitions while being sufficiently sober to know she had inhibitions, to know that they would be waiting to return to her later and to return quite unchanged. She went into Patrick's arms with delight, with the reckless abandon and determination to enjoy herself of someone embarking on a world cruise that must necessarily take place but once. Being in bed with him was not in the least like being in the VAT records office with the married accountant. She had known it would not be and that was why she was there. During the night the central heating went off, and failed, through some inadequacy of a fragile pilot light, to restart itself. It grew cold, but Bridget, in the arms of Patrick Baker, did not feel it.

She was the first to wake up. Bridget was the kind of person who is always the first to wake up. She lay in bed a little way apart from Patrick Baker and thought about what a lovely time she had had the night before and how that was enough and she would not see him again. Seeing him again might be dangerous and she could not afford, with her unmemorable appearance, her precarious job, and low wage, to put herself in peril. Presently she got up and said to Patrick, who had stirred a little and made an attempt in a kindly way to cuddle her, that she would make him a cup of tea.

Patrick put his nose out of the bedclothes and said it was freezing, the central heating had gone wrong, it was always going wrong. "Don't get cold," he said sleepily. "Find something to put on in the cupboard."

Even if they had been in the tropics, Bridget would not have dreamt of walking about a man's flat with no clothes on. She dressed. While the kettle was boiling, she looked with interest around Patrick's living room. There had been no opportunity to take any of it in on the previous evening. He was an untidy man, she noted, and his taste was not distinguished. You could see he bought his pictures ready-framed at Athena Art. He hadn't many books and most of what he had was science fiction, so it was rather a surprise to come upon Vasari's *Lives of the Artists* in paperback between a volume of fighting fantasy and a John Wyndham classic.

Perhaps she did, after all, feel cold. She was aware of a sudden unpleasant chill. It was comforting to feel the warmth of the kettle against her hands. She made the tea and took him a cup, setting it down on the bedside table, for he was fast asleep again. Shivering now, she opened the closet door and looked inside.

He seemed to possess a great many coats and jackets. She pushed the hangers along the rail, sliding tweed to brush against serge and linen against wild silk. His wardrobe was vast and complicated. He must have a great deal to spend on himself. The jacket with the butterflies slid into sudden brilliant view as if pushed there by some stage manager of fate. Everything conspired to make the sight of it dramatic, even the sun which came out and shed an unexpected ray into the open closet. Bridget gazed at the denim jacket as she had gazed with similar lust and wonder once before. She stared at the cascade of butterflies in purple and vermilion and turquoise, royal blue and fuchsia pink that tumbled and fluttered from the open mouths of a pair of yellow lilies.

She hardly hesitated before taking it off its hanger and putting it on. It was glorious. She remembered that this was the word she had thought of the first time she had seen it. How she had longed to possess it and how she had not dared look for long lest the yearning became painful and ridiculous! With her head a little on one side, she stood over Patrick, wondering whether to kiss him goodbye. Perhaps not, perhaps it would be better not. After all, he would hardly notice.

She let herself out of the flat. They would not meet again. A more than fair exchange had been silently negotiated by her. Feeling happy, feeling very light of heart, she ran down the stairs and out into the morning, insulated from the cold by her coat of many colors, her butterflies, her rightful possession.

# HENRY SLESAR
# POSSESSION

*I have been reading Henry Slesar's short stories for more than thirty years, and I was overjoyed to see at last a hardcover collection of his stories,* Death on Television, *published last year by Southern Illinois University Press. Slesar's tales never disappoint the reader and often, as in the case of "Possession," there's an extra little sting in the ending that makes one really stop and think. My only regret is that his long career in television writing has left him with so little time for stories like this.*

The chessboard was all set up by the time Skip arrived at his parents' house in Stormville. As always, his father had seated himself in the Black position, offering him the first-move advantage, a benign concession dating back to his childhood. Skip ignored the little tug of resentment he felt. He was twenty-nine, a police detective, and a better chessplayer.

But not tonight. After dinner, Joe Landis played his customary patzer's game, sly and chancy, and usually no match for Skip's straightforward, muscular style. But tonight a lack of concentration did him in—he fell between the assault of two bishops and resigned. His father didn't hoot or cackle, knowing how heavy a weight lay on those tight blond curls, the burden of grief pulling down those big shoulders. Twenty-nine? His father and mother both saw a suffering twelve-year-old slumped in their overstuffed armchair.

"So, no luck yet?" Joe said, hunting for the pipe he was no longer permitted to smoke. "Still didn't catch that guy, huh?"

"Not yet, Pop."

"So many rotten hoodlums out there, you got too many to choose from. What you ought to do is round up fifty or a hundred of the bastards, stick 'em all in the electric chair. You'll probably get the right one."

203

"It doesn't work that way, Pop." Skip looked up as his mother came in carrying a dessert tray.

"I know, I know," his father sighed. "Hey, you know me, the old liberal from way back. But when I hear about things like what happened to your friend Mitch, I start thinking like the Ayatollah, you know what I mean?"

"Sure, Pop," Skip said, wondering how to tell his mother he didn't want the chocolate pudding she was already crowning with whipped cream from a can. He decided it would be simpler to eat it without argument—the sooner he concluded this duty visit, the sooner he could get back to headquarters and find out what was happening, whether Homicide or the special task force had come up with anything. He could have telephoned, but he didn't want to face the instant disappointment of learning that Mitch Rodriguez' death was still only a question mark in an empty folder, just as it had been for the past three weeks.

The sweet, soft, sentimental taste of the dessert was soothing. He knew why he had been invited, of course, that his parents were aware how much he had been affected by the murder of the man who had been his first partner, his mentor, his best friend. He had brought Mitch home one night, and they had been awed (intimidated?) by the sight of his Hispanic bulk and then enchanted (relieved?) when he played Chopin on the piano and told them about his family, remarkably like their own. Mitch had eased their fears about Skip's safety in the perilous profession he had chosen, and they were grateful.

Six years of friendship later, Mitch was dead, a victim of that profession. Skip's parents had learned about it from the six o'clock news, but he had been there in person, had seen the faceless corpse loaded into the ambulance, had shouted in helpless rage. The sorrow came later. He had wept on the doorstep when he went to tell Mitch's wife Rosa the bad news. When the rage returned, it was like a firestorm, especially when Homicide and all the other Department divisions came up with nothing to explain that sudden explosion of gunshots—no motive, no suspects, nothing but the achingly unsatisfactory conclusion that it had been a random killing by a cop-hating psycho.

"Wash or dry?"

Skip glanced at his mother, who gave him a bent little smile. "I don't let your father help with the dishes anymore," she said. "He's not supposed to be on his feet. At least that's what he tells me. A great alibi, his phlebitis."

When they were alone at the sink, he expected some homey expressions of her maternal concern, but she surprised him by saying: "I know what you think about my friends on South Street, but just maybe one of them could help you."

He answered with a groan, hoping it would be sufficient, but his mother persisted. "I'm not saying it's anything sure, they can't always make contact. But if they could, if one of them could get through to your friend Mitch, who would know better? Who's the best person to ask who did this terrible thing to him? Don't laugh. I can see you're laughing."

Skip wasn't. He was grimacing. But he decided against his normal display of derision whenever his mother introduced the topic of her "friends," the spiritual "advisers"—the "channelers," they called themselves these days—who were always happy to provide their own long-distance service, to arrange for her to talk to her dead father, her brother Bern, her beloved grandmother who croaked out words of endearment from Beyond the Grave in the same hoarse voice as Madame Plotzky or whoever had current possession of the ectoplasm franchise on South Street.

"She's not on South Street," his mother said, as if reading his mind. "The one I'm thinking about lives in the city."

"Who?"

"Her name is Carmen Lopes. She lives on East Sixteenth Street. Mrs. Fitzmaurice was talking to her, and she said she thought she could do something about the case."

"I see," Skip said, spotting a diplomatic escape route. "She's one of these psychic detectives, right? Sorry, Mom. The Department's got a policy about those people."

"I didn't say she was a detective. She's a medium, like Mrs. Fitzmaurice, only sort of extra-sensitive. Sometimes things come to her without anyone asking, if you know what I mean."

"I know somebody's after your pocketbook again, Ma. Why do you want to go wasting Pop's pension on these fakers?"

"It's not me she wants to see," his mother said soberly. "It's you."

The taste of anger was in his mouth, but he swallowed it. "The whole police force doesn't know who shot Mitch. You mean to tell me this woman does?"

"No," his mother said, handing him a wet sugar bowl. "I'm saying *Mitch* does. Would it hurt your pride so much to see this woman? If it means so much to you, does your pride matter?"

The next morning, Ray Eberhart, the best Homicide cop Skip had ever met, sat on the edge of his desk and gave him a hard answer to his question. "No," he said bluntly, "we're not going to crack this one unless we get lucky. Somebody's going to have to walk in here and *tell* us who shot Mitch."

When Ray left, Skip reached for the phonebook. As he dialed the number of Carmen Lopes, he said aloud: "Dumbest thing I ever did."

Carmen Lopes sounded quietly grateful. "Thank you for calling me," she said. "You probably hate the whole idea, but please come to see me. Anytime. I'm in the whole evening."

He arrived at ten minutes of seven. He had to turn down three invitations to supper with people who still treated him like an invalid since Mitch's death. That's what he felt like, actually—someone just out of a sick bed—but now, walking up the worn steps of Carmen Lopes' brownstone on East Sixteenth Street he also felt like a damned fool.

He expected a stuffy apartment with a shawl on the piano and embroidered furniture. Instead, the living room was simply, almost starkly furnished. Carmen Lopes didn't fit any stereotype, either. She was younger than Skip expected her to be—early thirties, maybe—with large dark eyes overwhelming small, vulnerable features. She seemed afraid of him.

"I always know when someone doesn't believe," she said, with an attempted smile. "In your case, I could hear it in your voice over the telephone."

"You're right, Mrs. Lopes, I don't 'believe.' "

"I'm not married. And it's okay about not believing. Sometimes I don't myself. Sometimes what happens to me doesn't seem possible."

"But profitable?"

He said it lightly, but the question seemed to startle her. "I'm not asking for money, you know. Did you think I was?"

"You're in business, aren't you?"

"No," she said. "I work for a broker, on Duane. This is just something I do for friends, or—when it has to be done." She seemed anxious for his approval, but Skip was getting restless.

"Why don't we get right to it, then? Tell me what you think you know about the shooting of Mitchell Rodriguez."

"Why, nothing," she said. "I don't know anything about it. I just have this *feeling*. I had it the night I heard about it on TV. It was very strong." She shut her eyes. "I think he wants to tell me about it."

"Then why hasn't he?"

"Because I haven't been able to reach him. I can't, really, without the presence of somebody *he* wants to reach. Do you understand?"

"And you think that person is me?"

"I saw you on the news, that interview. You had tears in your eyes, I knew you were close to him. So when Mrs. Fitzmaurice said she knew your mother—All I'm asking you to do is try."

"Try what exactly?" Skip said. "A seance?"

"I suppose you can call it that. But don't worry: there won't be other people, we won't sit around a table and hold hands. The way it happens for me, I just sit in the dark and wait. You and me, we would wait together. If your friend wants to reach you, he will. He'll speak through me. That's how it works. Or doesn't work. I just can't tell until we try."

The long speech seemed to exhaust her. She sat down in a straight-backed chair and folded her hands in her lap. "I'd offer you a drink," she said, "but I don't keep spirits in the house." She smiled. "My mother used to say that as a sort of a joke. She *was* in business."

Skip said, "So you inherited this—talent?"

"I've had trance episodes since I was six. The doctors called them 'fugues.' My mother didn't take advantage of me, I'll say that much for her. I always had a fever afterward, sometimes a convulsion—Can we start now, please? Before I lose my nerve?"

Skip was more anxious than she was to get it over with. He

was bothered by something more than his capitulation, a sense that this woman might be sincere. He might not even have the satisfaction of exposing a fraud, of purging some of his anger. Skip needed to be angry at somebody, and Carmen Lopes with her venal exploitation of Mitch's death would have done just fine.

She asked him to sit in a boxy chair of imitation leather, and then rose to turn off the light. The darkness was so complete that Skip didn't see her return to the straight-backed chair, but she was there, all right; he heard her measured breathing. It was the only sound in the room, except for the almost imperceptible tick of a clock somewhere in another part of the apartment. Skip had done enough night duty to train his eyes to rapid adaptation and he was soon perceiving her faint outline, her body so rigid it seemed to be a fixed part of the chair's silhouette.

They sat silently for what seemed like an interminable length of time, although Skip was sure it wasn't more than three or four minutes. He was trying to decide on a deadline when Carmen groaned.

"What is it?" Skip said. "Are you okay?"

She groaned again and Skip was annoyed to feel the ripple of an icy sensation on his spine. It was all in the staging, of course. Theatrics. He wasn't immune to the primeval effects of darkness on the imagination, but he resented having them artificially stirred. When Carmen caught a sob in her throat, he almost stood up with the intention of finding the light switch, but he stopped when he heard the voice, *her* voice, of course, but modified, altered, halfway between a whisper and—what? He wasn't sure. It was so low-pitched it should have been inaudible, and yet it wasn't. He could hear her distinctly. She was speaking his name—but that was different, too.

*"Skipper. Skipper—"*

Only his parents called him Skipper, the result of his winning a model-boat race at the age of ten, and Mitch had picked it up. And somehow so had Carmen Lopes, using her ghostly half whisper of a voice that did bear a faint resemblance to Mitch's.

The blood rushed to Skip's head. Satisfying anger burned in

his throat. He wanted to pull her out of that chair and shout his fury, but something held him back and forced him to listen.

"Skipper," the voice said. "Ask her. Ask *her.*"

"Ask her *what?*"

There was no reply.

"Miss Lopes," Skip said loudly, "what am I supposed to ask you?"

"Ask *her,*" the voice said, now hoarse with urgency. "Rosa. *Rosa.*"

"Rosa!" Skip repeated, startled to hear the name in this dark room. He hardly knew his partner's wife—Mitch had rarely talked about his home life, keeping it separate and distinct. "What does Rosa have to do with it?" he said. "What am I supposed to ask her?"

There was a pause that wasn't a complete silence, and the voice said: "Why I'm dead."

Then the woman was sobbing, sobbing in her own voice, heartbreak in the sound. Acting on instinct, Skip hit the light switch.

Carmen Lopes was no longer rigid. Her body had folded into itself, her head almost in her lap, her hands covering her face. Skip didn't know what to do. She had said something about feverish reactions to her trances, even convulsions. Was she ill? Was this some form of occult grief? Or simply part of the con? Whatever its cause, the tears were real; they were so profuse that they flowed out from between her fingers. He took a hesitant step toward her, but then she looked up, her coal-dark eyes even larger through the magnifying lens of moisture.

"What did I say?" she pleaded. "Please tell me! What did I say about that man?"

"You didn't mention him," Skip said. "You mentioned his wife. You said I should ask her something, but I don't know what."

She simply stared back. Skip realized she had nothing more to say to him. There was something naked about her now and observing her like this was kind of an embarrassment. It was time to leave.

There were two messages on his answering machine. One was from his mother, asking him to do what he had already done. The other was from Enid, the actress-waitress he was seeing. She left a number where she could be reached. Instead, he dialed the number of Rosa Rodriguez and asked if he could come over. She seemed surprised by the request, as if his one condolence call had been sufficient, but she said to come ahead.

The Rodriguez apartment was in one of the better housing projects. It had a view of the river and good security, mainly because of high occupancy of police officers, but it was showing signs of decay. The same could be said of Rosa Rodriguez. When Skip had first met her, she was a bubbly young woman with the body of a flamenco dancer. Now she was thick at the waist and the lines in her face had nothing to do with laughter.

The visit was even more uncomfortable than his first. At least then there had been a clear errand, and emotion to write the scenario. Now they moved about each other uncertainly, Skip grateful for the drink and the chair she offered. He answered her first question even before it was formed.

"Nothing yet," he said. "We're still waiting for a break. That's what usually happens, somebody gets drunk in a bar and starts bragging, somebody hears him. You know about the reward?"

"No," Rosa said.

"That newspaper publisher. He's offering twenty-five thousand for information leading to conviction. We had two dozen calls the first day, none of them worth a damn."

"I read where they might call it off, give it up."

"Don't believe it. No homicide case is ever closed. Especially when it's a cop. But one thing is true, they're not dragging in people like they did at first."

"Yes—even Luis," Rosa said. Skip looked at her blankly. "My brother Luis. They hold him for three weeks now, for nothing. Maybe you could do something for him."

Skip hadn't even known there was a brother.

"What was the charge?" he asked.

"Possession."

Thoughts of the occult. But of course she meant possession of narcotics.

"It was all a mistake," Rosa said. "I think maybe it was planted on him. Not by the cops," she added hastily. "Somebody he knows—a jealous girl friend, I think." She tried a smile. "Luis is a devil with girls—from one to the other, like a butterfly. Will you see what you can do, Skip?"

"Sure, Rosa, of course," he said. "His full name is what?"

"Luis Madrid," she said.

"Mitch never mentioned a brother-in-law. Did they get along okay?"

"Oh, yes," Rosa said. "I mean, they didn't see each other much, but then *I* didn't see much of Mitch, did I? You cops." She meant it to sound ruefully affectionate, but it came out flat.

When he left, she walked him to the door and said: "Tell me what you think, Skip, what you really believe. About the chances of finding the one who did it?"

He looked at her directly and said: "The truth? Not too good. If we were going to get a break, we would have gotten it by now. That's what I think, but I could be wrong."

In the street, he was troubled. She had taken his bad news too well. She didn't *rage.* If Mitch's best friend felt rage, why didn't his wife?

At the precinct, he spoke to a narcotics officer named Spier who came up with Luis Madrid with no trouble. He had been picked up at a crack house on the night of a planned police raid. There went the jealous girl-friend story.

There was one fact that caught Skip's attention. The arrest was made on the night Mitch was shot. As if Rosa didn't have enough dumped on her head that night. Yet she had spoken of Luis with loving indulgence.

Skip went out with Enid that evening. She took him to a cramped little theater in the Village to see an uplifting verse drama. Enid was always trying to improve his cultural outlook, but the play made no sense to him. He tuned it out, thinking other thoughts, trying to answer other questions than those being asked by the playwright. Suddenly one appeared that hit him hard.

Why hadn't *Rosa* mentioned the date her brother was busted? It should have been engraved on her mind, just as it was on Mitch's tombstone. Why didn't she say anything to Skip about the grim coincidence?

Enid was pleased with Skip's deeply thoughtful expression when they left the theater, certain he had been moved by art.

In the morning, he saw Luis Madrid in the visiting room of the holding center, offering his credentials as a friend of his brother-in-law. Luis still looked suspicious, even when Skip said, "You won't have a hard time. It's a first-time offense—the worst you'll get is a slap on the wrist."

"I already got three weeks in here," Luis said bitterly. "Who'll give me back my three weeks?" He was handsome, vain, older than his sister maybe by ten years. If he let his hair go grey, he could have passed for her father. It was true about his police record—his yellow sheet was blank—but Luis Madrid had been in the country less than a year, who knew what he was doing back home?

When Skip asked why he was picked up, Luis shrugged. He wasn't a user, he said, he was too careful about his body. He worked out. He had a good job with a roofing-and-insulation company. That night he had just gotten a little drunk with friends—he was along for the companionship.

Which didn't track with the arrest report, which stated that none of the customers in the crack house knew each other. But it wasn't Luis Madrid's words that haunted Skip for the rest of the day. It was Carmen Lopes'. Or rather, the chilling half whisper that came out of her throat. Ask *her* why I'm dead.

At five o'clock, Skip learned that Luis would be released. He strolled over to the housing project to tell Rosa the good news, but she wasn't home. He was about to leave when he heard the music in the apartment next door and remembered a primary rule of investigation: always talk to the nearest neighbor. He rang the doorbell, and a woman in her late fifties, wearing thick-lensed glasses prescribed for cataract patients, stared out. She wasn't alarmed by the police badge he flashed and let him in, happy for the social opportunity. Her name was Mrs. Fuchs and she had only three cats for company.

"Sure, I'm friendly with Mrs. Rodriguez. She's a nice quiet woman. Not that things have been so quiet over there *lately.*" She cocked her head and gave him a wise smile.

"What do you mean by that, Mrs. Fuchs?"

"Well, you know—a lot of shouting and fighting. All in Spanish, so don't ask me what they were fighting about."

"Do you mean Mrs. Rodriguez and her husband?"

"No, not him. He hasn't been around for practically six months. Isn't it terrible what happened?"

"Yes," Skip said. "So if it wasn't her husband, Mrs. Fuchs, who was she quarreling with?"

"She tells people he's her brother." One of the cats was on the sofa cushion beside her. Their expressions were identical.

"If you mean Luis Madrid," Skip frowned, "he *is* her brother." She blinked behind the thick lenses, obviously disappointed in a private theory.

But when Skip left, he had his own theory, and it made him hurt all over.

He went to a cafeteria across the street and tried to choke down some beef stew, but his appetite was gone. He used the pay phone to call Rosa, and was finally rewarded by her voice on the other end. He told her where he was, and asked her to sit still.

She must have taken him literally. When he arrived, she called out that the door was open. She was sitting in a chair at the kitchen table, a glass of tea cooling in front of her.

He told her all about Luis, but she seemed to know all about it, and didn't react. Then he asked her about the night of the shooting. "Didn't you think it was strange that your brother should have been arrested the same time your husband was killed?"

"I didn't know about it until later," Rosa said.

"Weren't you surprised about Luis? Your brother doesn't use drugs, does he?"

"No, never. But he's new to this country—he doesn't know what it's like around here, this neighborhood."

"He knew one thing, didn't he? That Mitch had moved out." She didn't answer. "I didn't know that myself until tonight. Mitch didn't talk much about his home life. Why did he move out, Rosa?"

She picked up the glass and sipped her tea, and Skip realized he was going to have to answer his own questions.

"I guess I should have noticed something myself," he said. "Mitch had somebody else, didn't he? Another woman?"

"I told him to move out," Rosa said flatly. "I gave him a choice, her or me. He took her."

"Was that when Luis showed up here? When he heard about it?" She didn't say no. "You wrote Luis a letter, and he showed up here, all upset about what was happening to his kid sister. He's your only family, isn't he? A brother and father both. He came here to straighten things out for you, didn't he, Rosa?"

"I told him not to," Rosa said. "He doesn't understand things, the way they are here."

"He tried to make Mitch drop this other woman, but Mitch wouldn't listen to him. So one night, he threatened him. That's probably all he meant to do. Only you don't go waving a gun in the face of a man like Mitch, he'll take it from you. That's what Mitch tried to do, and that's how he got killed. And Luis got scared, and ran into a house, and let himself get arrested as an alibi."

The door opened. Luis Madrid was in the kitchen before he realized his sister wasn't alone. Then he seemed to realize what was happening almost at once and turned to reverse direction. When Skip's hand dove for his service revolver, Luis grinned and said, "Hey, no sweat!" But then he was pulling open a kitchen drawer and Skip shouted at him to freeze. It proved a useful confrontation. The gun was in the drawer. Luis hadn't disposed of the weapon that killed Mitch Rodriguez—he didn't know the way things were done in this country.

She said she would be home all evening, and she was. When Skip arrived, Carmen Lopes was in the living room watching television. She turned it off when he entered.

"I thought you only looked at crystal balls," Skip said.

"Is it really true, what you said on the phone? Someone's been arrested?"

"Yes," Skip said. "Turns out it wasn't just some street psycho who killed Mitch. It was a domestic quarrel. But of course you knew that, didn't you? Your spooks told you."

"I don't remember saying anything like that."

"Don't be modest." He sat down without an invitation. "If it wasn't for what you said about Mitch's wife, I never would have followed up the lead. I mean, there wouldn't have been any reason. I knew Rosa was at home the night Mitch died. It never would have occurred to me that she and Mitch were having problems, that there was another woman."

"If I helped you in some way, I'm glad," Carmen said. But she didn't look any less mournful.

"Sure you helped me. You *wanted* to help the police from the beginning. Only it would have been very hard to come to us with your suspicion that Rosa Rodriguez had something to do with her husband's death—She didn't, by the way, not directly. It was her brother."

"Thank you for coming here," Carmen said. "I'm glad it's over. Now I'm a little tired."

"I want to know if you feel better about getting what you wanted. You had to put on an act, but you succeeded."

"It wasn't an act!"

"You just didn't want to tell me the truth—that you were Mitch's lady friend."

"That has nothing to do with it!"

"That's why you did such a good job on Mitch's voice. You really did sound like him, Carmen, but then you'd heard his voice often enough."

She fixed her dark eyes on his. "I didn't fake anything. What you heard, you heard. Everything I told you about myself is true. From the age of six, it's been true. What I felt for Mitch, what I thought about his death, that doesn't matter. What matters is, there are times when the dead talk through me."

Skip's vision blurred, and he realized his anger was returning. Even though it was all over, he felt anger at this woman and her smug mystical faith.

"All right," he said. "All right, I'm willing to believe it. I'm even willing to let you try again—if you would."

She was surprised. "Try again? To reach Mitch?"

"No," Skip said. "Mitch can rest in peace. I want to reach someone else—someone I've always wanted to talk to again. Someone I loved very much."

"Who?"

"My father."

Carmen stared at him. He put on a solemn expression. He almost managed to bring a film of tears to his eyes. He was impressed with his own performance, and she was, too.

"I don't know if I can."

"You said the—departed had to *want* to reach you. I think my father would. Very much. Could you at least try? Don't you think you owe me that much, Carmen?"

She hesitated, then walked to the light switch.

They sat in darkness for almost five minutes. Again he heard her breathing, again he was aware of the ticking of the clock.

Then Carmen groaned, and in the cover of the darkness Skip couldn't help a cynical smile.

It was a full minute later before the voice emerged from her throat—even more of a low-pitched whisper than the first time but surprisingly clear and audible and just as impassioned as it spoke his name, the name that Mitch must have mentioned to her. *"Skipper—Skipper—"*

"Is that you, Pop?" Skip asked in an appropriately hushed tone. "Is that you?"

"Skipper," the voice said with almost unbearable sadness, "take care of your mother. Take care of yourself."

"Yes, Pop," Skip said. "You can rest easy. I'll take care of Mom. You can count on me."

It had been a long time since he had actually looked forward to visiting the house in Stormville. He knew his parents would be surprised. They would assume he had come to share his triumph with them. It would be an added pleasure to be able to tell them the story of Carmen Lopes and her latest seance.

The house was almost dark when he arrived. His parents seemed to retire earlier and earlier.

When his mother came to the door, he expected her to be in her nightdress, but she was fully clothed. She came into his arms and embraced him in tears.

"I guess you heard the news," he said. "We've got the guy, finally. It's all over and done with."

She pulled away from him and searched his eyes. "That's why you came out?" she said. "Not because you heard?"

"Heard what?"

"I left a message on your machine to call me—so I could tell you. Skipper, your father passed away this morning in his sleep. So quiet I never knew." She opened her arms, and he went into that warm comforting circle—but felt cold, very very cold.

# DONALD E. WESTLAKE

# TOO MANY CROOKS

*It is a rare year indeed when the MWA Edgar Award for the year's outstanding short story goes to a humorous tale. In fact it could be argued that it's never happened before. But if there is any modern crime writer who can produce a genuinely funny Edgar winner, you know his name has to be Donald E. Westlake. Here are Dortmunder and friends, encountering a real surprise inside a bank vault.*

"Did you hear something?" Dortmunder whispered.

"The wind," Kelp said.

Dortmunder twisted around in his seated position and deliberately shone the flashlight in the kneeling Kelp's eyes. "What wind? We're in a tunnel."

"There's underground rivers," Kelp said, squinting, "so maybe there's underground winds. Are you through the wall there?"

"Two more whacks," Dortmunder told him. Relenting, he aimed the flashlight past Kelp back down the empty tunnel, a meandering, messy gullet, most of it less than three feet in diameter, wriggling its way through rocks and rubble and ancient middens, traversing 40 tough feet from the rear of the basement of the out-of-business shoe store to the wall of the bank on the corner. According to the maps Dortmunder had gotten from the water department by claiming to be with the sewer department, and the maps he'd gotten from the sewer department by claiming to be with the water department, just the other side of this wall was the bank's main vault. Two more whacks and this large, irregular square of concrete that Dortmunder and Kelp had been scoring and scratching at for some time now would at last fall away onto the floor inside, and there would be the vault.

Dortmunder gave it a whack.

Dortmunder gave it another whack.

The block of concrete fell onto the floor of the vault. "Oh, thank God," somebody said.

What? Reluctant but unable to stop himself, Dortmunder dropped sledge and flashlight and leaned his head through the hole in the wall and looked around.

It was the vault, all right. And it was full of people.

A man in a suit stuck his hand out and grabbed Dortmunder's and shook it while pulling him through the hole and on into the vault. "Great work, Officer," he said. "The robbers are outside."

Dortmunder had thought he and Kelp were the robbers. "They are?"

A round-faced woman in pants and a Buster Brown collar said, "Five of them. With machine guns."

"Machine guns," Dortmunder said.

A delivery kid wearing a mustache and an apron and carrying a flat cardboard carton containing four coffees, two decafs and a tea said, "We all hostages, mon. I gonna get fired."

"How many of you are there?" the man in the suit asked, looking past Dortmunder at Kelp's nervously smiling face.

"Just the two," Dortmunder said, and watched helplessly as willing hands dragged Kelp through the hole and set him on his feet in the vault. It was really very full of hostages.

"I'm Kearney," the man in the suit said. "I'm the bank manager, and I can't tell you how glad I am to see you."

Which was the first time any bank manager had said *that* to Dortmunder, who said, "Uh-huh, uh-huh," and nodded, and then said, "I'm, uh, Officer Diddums, and this is Officer, uh, Kelly."

Kearney, the bank manager, frowned. "Diddums, did you say?"

Dortmunder was furious with himself. Why did I call myself Diddums? Well, I didn't know I was going to need an alias inside a bank vault, did I? Aloud, he said, "Uh-huh. Diddums. It's Welsh."

"Ah," said Kearney. Then he frowned again and said, "You people aren't even armed."

"Well, no," Dortmunder said. "We're the, uh, the hostage-rescue team; we don't want any shots fired, increase the risk for you, uh, civilians."

"Very shrewd," Kearney agreed.

Kelp, his eyes kind of glassy and his smile kind of fixed, said, "Well, folks, maybe we should leave here now, single file, just make your way in an orderly fashion through—"

"They're coming!" hissed a stylish woman over by the vault door.

Everybody moved. It was amazing; everybody shifted at once. Some people moved to hide the new hole in the wall, some people moved to get farther away from the vault door and some people moved to get behind Dortmunder, who suddenly found himself the nearest person in the vault to that big, round, heavy metal door, which was easing massively and silently open.

It stopped halfway, and three men came in. They wore black ski masks and black leather jackets and black work pants and black shoes. They carried Uzi submachine guns at high port. Their eyes looked cold and hard, and their hands fidgeted on the metal of the guns, and their feet danced nervously, even when they were standing still. They looked as though anything at all might make them overreact.

"Shut up!" one of them yelled, though nobody'd been talking. He glared around at his guests and said, "Gotta have somebody to stand out front, see can the cops be trusted." His eye, as Dortmunder had known it would, lit on Dortmunder. "You," he said.

"Uh-huh," Dortmunder said.

"What's your name?"

Everybody in the vault had already heard him say it, so what choice did he have? "Diddums," Dortmunder said.

The robber glared at Dortmunder through his ski mask. "Diddums?"

"It's Welsh," Dortmunder explained.

"Ah," the robber said, and nodded. He gestured with the Uzi. "Outside, Diddums."

Dortmunder stepped forward, glancing back over his shoulder at all the people looking at him, knowing every goddamn one of them was glad he wasn't him—even Kelp, back there pretending to be four feet tall—and then Dortmunder stepped through the vault door, surrounded by all those nervous maniacs with machine guns, and went with them down a corridor flanked by desks and through a doorway to the main part of the bank, which was a mess.

The time at the moment, as the clock high on the wide wall confirmed, was 5:15 in the afternoon. Everybody who worked at the bank should have gone home by now; that was the theory Dortmunder had been operating from. What must have happened was, just before closing time at three o'clock (Dortmunder and Kelp being already then in the tunnel, working hard, knowing nothing of events on the surface of the planet), these gaudy showboats had come into the bank waving their machine guns around.

And not just waving them, either. Lines of ragged punctures had been drawn across the walls and the Lucite upper panel of the tellers' counter, like connect-the-dot puzzles. Wastebaskets and a potted Ficus had been overturned, but fortunately, there were no bodies lying around; none Dortmunder could see, anyway. The big plate-glass front windows had been shot out, and two more of the black-clad robbers were crouched down, one behind the OUR LOW LOAN RATES poster and the other behind the OUR HIGH IRA RATES poster, staring out at the street, from which came the sound of somebody talking loudly but indistinctly through a bullhorn.

So what must have happened, they'd come in just before three, waving their guns, figuring a quick in and out, and some brown-nose employee looking for advancement triggered the alarm, and now they had a stalemate hostage situation on their hands; and, of course, everybody in the world by now has seen *Dog Day Afternoon* and therefore knows that if the police get the drop on a robber in circumstances such as these circumstances right here, they'll immediately shoot him dead, so now hostage negotiation is trickier than ever. This isn't what I had in mind when I came to the bank, Dortmunder thought.

The boss robber prodded him along with the barrel of his Uzi, saying, "What's your first name, Diddums?"

Please don't say Dan, Dortmunder begged himself. Please, please, somehow, anyhow, manage not to say Dan. His mouth opened. "John," he heard himself say, his brain having turned desperately in this emergency to that last resort, the truth, and he got weak-kneed with relief.

"OK, John, don't faint on me," the robber said. "This is very simple what you got to do here. The cops say they want to talk, just talk, nobody gets hurt. Fine. So you're gonna step out in front of the bank and see do the cops shoot you."

"Ah," Dortmunder said.

"No time like the present, huh, John?" the robber said, and poked him with the Uzi again.

"That kind of hurts," Dortmunder said.

"I apologize," the robber said, hard-eyed. "Out."

One of the other robbers, eyes red with strain inside the black ski mask, leaned close to Dortmunder and yelled, "You wanna shot in the foot first? You wanna *crawl* out there?"

"I'm going," Dortmunder told him. "See? Here I go."

The first robber, the comparatively calm one, said, "You go as far as the sidewalk, that's all. You take one step off the curb, we blow your head off."

"Got it," Dortmunder assured him, and crunched across broken glass to the sagging-open door and looked out. Across the street was parked a line of buses, police cars, police trucks, all in blue and white with red gumdrops on top, and behind them moved a seething mass of armed cops. "Uh," Dortmunder said. Turning back to the comparatively calm robber, he said, "You wouldn't happen to have a white flag or anything like that, would you?"

The robber pressed the point of the Uzi to Dortmunder's side. "Out," he said.

"Right," Dortmunder said. He faced front, put his hands way up in the air and stepped outside.

What a *lot* of attention he got. From behind all those blue-and-whites on the other side of the street, tense faces stared. On the rooftops of the red-brick tenements, in this neighborhood deep in the residential heart of Queens, sharpshooters began to familiarize themselves through their telescopic sights with the contours of Dortmunder's furrowed brow. To left and right, the ends of the block were sealed off with buses parked nose to tail pipe, past which ambulances and jumpy white-coated medics could be seen. Everywhere, rifles and pistols jittered in nervous fingers. Adrenaline ran in the gutters.

"I'm not with *them!*" Dortmunder shouted, edging across the sidewalk, arms upraised, hoping this announcement wouldn't upset the other bunch of armed hysterics behind him. For all he knew, they had a problem with rejection.

However, nothing happened behind him, and what happened out front was that a bullhorn appeared, resting on a police-car roof, and roared at him, *"You a hostage?"*

"I sure am!" yelled Dortmunder.

*"What's your name?"*

Oh, not again, thought Dortmunder, but there was nothing for it. "Diddums," he said.

*"What?"*

*"Diddums!"*

A brief pause: *"Diddums?"*

*"It's Welsh!"*

"Ah."

There was a little pause while whoever was operating the bullhorn conferred with his compatriots, and then the bullhorn said, *"What's the situation in there?"*

What kind of question was that? "Well, uh," Dortmunder said, and remembered to speak more loudly, and called, "kind of tense, actually."

*"Any of the hostages been harmed?"*

"Uh-uh. No. Definitely not. This is a . . . this is a . . . nonviolent confrontation." Dortmunder fervently hoped to establish that idea in everybody's mind, particularly if he were going to be out here in the middle much longer.

*"Any change in the situation?"*

Change? "Well," Dortmunder answered, "I haven't been in there that long, but it seems like—"

*"Not that long? What's the matter with you, Diddums? You've been in that bank over two hours now!"*

"Oh, yeah!" Forgetting, Dortmunder lowered his arms and stepped forward to the curb. "That's right!" he called. "Two hours! *More* than two hours! Been in there a long time!"

*"Step out here away from the bank!"*

Dortmunder looked down and saw his toes hanging ten over

the edge of the curb. Stepping back at a brisk pace, he called, "I'm not supposed to do that!"

*"Listen, Diddums, I've got a lot of tense men and women over here. I'm telling you, step away from the bank!"*

"The fellas inside," Dortmunder explained, "they don't want me to step off the curb. They said they'd, uh, well, they just don't want me to do it."

"Psst! Hey, Diddums!"

Dortmunder paid no attention to the voice calling from behind him. He was concentrating too hard on what was happening right now out front. Also, he wasn't that used to the new name yet.

"Diddums!"

*"Maybe you better put your hands up again."*

"Oh, yeah!" Dortmunder's arms shot up like pistons blowing through an engine block. "There they are!"

"Diddums, goddamn it, do I have to *shoot* you to get you to pay attention?"

Arms dropping, Dortmunder spun around. "Sorry! I wasn't— I was—Here I am!"

*"Get those goddamn hands up!"*

Dortmunder turned sideways, arms up so high his sides hurt. Peering sidelong to his right, he called to the crowd across the street, "Sirs, they're talking to me inside now." Then he peered sidelong to his left, saw the comparatively calm robber crouched beside the broken doorframe and looking less calm than before, and he said, "Here I am."

"We're gonna give them our demands now," the robber said. "Through you."

"That's fine," Dortmunder said. "That's great. Only, you know, how come you don't do it on the phone? I mean, the way it's normally—"

The red-eyed robber, heedless of exposure to the sharpshooters across the street, shouldered furiously past the comparatively calm robber, who tried to restrain him as he yelled at Dortmunder, "You're rubbing it in, are ya? OK, I made a mistake! I got excited and I shot up the switchboard! You want me to get excited again?"

"No, no!" Dortmunder cried, trying to hold his hands straight up in the air and defensively in front of his body at the same time. "I forgot! I just forgot!"

The other robbers all clustered around to grab the red-eyed robber, who seemed to be trying to point his Uzi in Dortmunder's direction as he yelled, "I did it in front of everybody! I humiliated myself in front of everybody! And now you're making fun of me!"

"I *forgot!* I'm sorry!"

"You can't forget that! Nobody's ever gonna forget that!"

The three remaining robbers dragged the red-eyed robber back away from the doorway, talking to him, trying to soothe him, leaving Dortmunder and the comparatively calm robber to continue their conversation. "I'm sorry," Dortmunder said. "I just forgot. I've been kind of distracted lately. Recently."

"You're playing with fire here, Diddums," the robber said. "Now tell them they're gonna get our demands."

Dortmunder nodded, and turned his head the other way, and yelled, "They're gonna tell you their demands now. I mean, *I'm* gonna tell you their demands. *Their* demands. Not *my* demands. *Their* de—"

*"We're willing to listen, Diddums, only so long as none of the hostages get hurt."*

"That's good!" Dortmunder agreed, and turned his head the other way to tell the robber, "That's reasonable, you know, that's sensible, that's a very good thing they're saying."

"Shut up," the robber said.

"Right," Dortmunder said.

The robber said, "First, we want the riflemen off the roofs."

"Oh, so do I," Dortmunder told him, and turned to shout, "They want the riflemen off the roofs!"

*"What else?"*

"What else?"

"And we want them to unblock that end of the street, the— what is it?—the north end."

Dortmunder frowned straight ahead at the buses blocking the intersection. "Isn't that east?" he asked.

"Whatever it is," the robber said, getting impatient. "That end down there to the left."

"OK." Dortmunder turned his head and yelled, "They want

you to unblock the east end of the street!" Since his hands were way up in the sky somewhere, he pointed with his chin.

*"Isn't that north?"*

"I knew it was," the robber said.

"Yeah, I guess so," Dortmunder called. "That end down there to the left."

*"The right, you mean."*

"Yeah, that's right. Your right, my left. *Their* left."

*"What else?"*

Dortmunder sighed, and turned his head. "What else?"

The robber glared at him. "I can *hear* the bullhorn, Diddums. I can *hear* him say 'What else?' You don't have to repeat everything he says. No more translations."

"Right," Dortmunder said. "Gotcha. No more translations."

"We'll want a car," the robber told him. "A station wagon. We're gonna take three hostages with us, so we want a big station wagon. And nobody follows us."

"Gee," Dortmunder said dubiously, "are you sure?"

The robber stared. "Am I *sure?*"

"Well, you know what they'll do," Dortmunder told him, lowering his voice so the other team across the street couldn't hear him. "What they do in these situations, they fix a little radio transmitter under the car, so then they don't have to *follow* you, exactly, but they know where you are."

Impatient again, the robber said, "So you'll tell them not to do that. No radio transmitters, or we kill the hostages."

"Well, I suppose," Dortmunder said doubtfully.

"What's wrong *now?*" the robber demanded. "You're too goddamn *picky*, Diddums; you're just the messenger here. You think you know my job better than I do?"

I know I do, Dortmunder thought, but it didn't seem a judicious thing to say aloud, so instead, he explained, "I just want things to go smooth, that's all. I just don't want bloodshed. And I was thinking, the New York City police, you know, well, they've got helicopters."

"Damn," the robber said. He crouched low to the littered floor, behind the broken doorframe, and brooded about his situation. Then he looked up at Dortmunder and said, "OK, Diddums, you're so smart. What *should* we do?"

Dortmunder blinked. "You want *me* to figure out your getaway?"

"Put yourself in our position," the robber suggested. "Think about it."

Dortmunder nodded. Hands in the air, he gazed at the blocked intersection and put himself in the robbers' position. "Hoo, boy," he said. "You're in a real mess."

"We *know* that, Diddums."

"Well," Dortmunder said, "I tell you what maybe you could do. You make them give you one of those buses they've got down there blocking the street. They give you one of those buses right now, then you know they haven't had time to put anything cute in it, like time-release tear-gas grenades or anyth—"

"Oh, my God," the robber said. His black ski mask seemed to have paled slightly.

"Then you take *all* the hostages," Dortmunder told him. "Everybody goes in the bus, and one of you people drives, and you go somewhere real crowded, like Times Square, say, and then you stop and make all the hostages get out and run."

"Yeah?" the robber said. "What good does that do us?"

"Well," Dortmunder said, "you drop the ski masks and the leather jackets and the guns, and *you* run, too. Twenty, thirty people all running away from the bus in different directions, in the middle of Times Square in rush hour, everybody losing themselves in the crowd. It might work."

"Jeez, it might," the robber said. "OK, go ahead and—What?"

"What?" Dortmunder echoed. He strained to look leftward, past the vertical column of his left arm. The boss robber was in excited conversation with one of his pals; not the red-eyed maniac, a different one. The boss robber shook his head and said, "Damn!" Then he looked up at Dortmunder. "Come back in here, Diddums," he said.

Dortmunder said, "But don't you want me to—"

"Come back in here!"

"Oh," Dortmunder said. "Uh, I better tell them over there that I'm gonna move."

"Make it fast," the robber told him. "Don't mess with me, Diddums. I'm in a bad mood right now."

"OK." Turning his head the other way, hating it that his back was toward this badmooded robber for even a second, Dortmunder called, "They want me to go back into the bank now. Just for a minute." Hands still up, he edged sideways across the sidewalk and through the gaping doorway, where the robbers laid hands on him and flung him back deeper into the bank.

He nearly lost his balance but saved himself against the sideways-lying pot of the tipped-over Ficus. When he turned around, all five of the robbers were lined up looking at him, their expressions intent, focused, almost hungry, like a row of cats looking in a fish store window. "Uh," Dortmunder said.

"He's it now," one of the robbers said.

Another robber said, "But *they* don't know it."

A third robber said, "They will soon."

"They'll know it when nobody gets on the bus," the boss robber said, and shook his head at Dortmunder. "Sorry, Diddums. Your idea doesn't work anymore."

Dortmunder had to keep reminding himself that he wasn't actually *part* of this string. "How come?" he asked.

Disgusted, one of the other robbers said, "The rest of the hostages got away, that's how come."

Wide-eyed, Dortmunder spoke without thinking: "The tunnel!"

All of a sudden, it got very quiet in the bank. The robbers were now looking at him like cats looking at a fish with no window in the way. "The tunnel?" repeated the boss robber slowly. "You *know* about the tunnel?"

"Well, kind of," Dortmunder admitted. "I mean, the guys digging it, they got there just before you came and took me away."

"And you never mentioned it."

"Well," Dortmunder said, very uncomfortable, "I didn't feel like I should."

The red-eyed maniac lunged forward, waving that submachine gun again, yelling, "*You're* the guy with the tunnel! It's your tunnel!" And he pointed the shaking barrel of the Uzi at Dortmunder's nose.

"Easy, easy!" the boss robber yelled. "This is our only hostage; don't use him up!"

The red-eyed maniac reluctantly lowered the Uzi, but he turned to the others and announced, "*Nobody*'s gonna forget when I shot up the switchboard. Nobody's *ever* gonna forget that. He wasn't *here!*"

All of the robbers thought that over. Meantime, Dortmunder was thinking about his own position. He might be a hostage, but he wasn't your normal hostage, because he was also a guy who had just dug a tunnel to a bank vault, and there were maybe 30 eyeball witnesses who could identify him. So it wasn't enough to get away from these bank robbers; he was also going to have to get away from the police. Several thousand police.

So did that mean he was locked to these second-rate smash-and-grabbers? Was his own future really dependent on *their* getting out of this hole? Bad news, if true. Left to their own devices, these people couldn't escape from a merry-go-round.

Dortmunder sighed. "OK," he said. "The first thing we have to do is—"

"We?" the boss robber said. "Since when are you in this?"

"Since you dragged me in," Dortmunder told him. "And the first thing we have to do is—"

The red-eyed maniac lunged at him again with the Uzi, shouting, "Don't you tell us what to do! *We* know what to do!"

"I'm your only hostage," Dortmunder reminded him. "Don't use me up. Also, now that I've seen you people in action, I'm your only hope of getting out of here. So this time, listen to me. The first thing we have to do is close and lock the vault door."

One of the robbers gave a scornful laugh. "The hostages are *gone,*" he said. "Didn't you hear that part? Lock the vault door after the hostages are gone. Isn't that some kind of old saying?" And he laughed and laughed.

Dortmunder looked at him. "It's a two-way tunnel," he said quietly.

The robbers stared at him. Then they all turned and ran toward the back of the bank. They *all* did.

They're too excitable for this line of work, Dortmunder thought as he walked briskly toward the front of the bank. *Clang* went the vault door, far behind him, and Dortmunder stepped through the broken doorway and out again to the sidewalk, remembering to stick his arms straight up in the air as he did.

"Hi!" he yelled, sticking his face well out, displaying it for all the sharpshooters to get a really *good* look at. "Hi, it's me again! Diddums! Welsh!"

"Diddums!" screamed an enraged voice from deep within the bank. "Come back here!"

Oh, no. Ignoring that, moving steadily but without panic, arms up, face forward, eyes wide, Dortmunder angled leftward across the sidewalk, shouting, "I'm coming out again! And I'm *escaping!*" And he dropped his arms, tucked his elbows in and ran hell for leather toward those blocking buses.

Gunfire encouraged him: sudden burst behind him of *ddrrritt, ddrrritt,* and then *kopp-kopp-kopp,* and then a whole symphony of *fooms* and *thug-thugs* and *padapows.* Dortmunder's toes, turning into high-tension steel springs, kept him bounding through the air like the Wright brothers' first airplane, swooping and plunging down the middle of the street, that wall of buses getting closer and closer.

"Here! In here!" Uniformed cops appeared on both sidewalks, waving to him, offering sanctuary in the forms of open doorways and police vehicles to crouch behind, but Dortmunder was *escaping.* From everything.

The buses. He launched himself through the air, hit the blacktop hard and rolled under the nearest bus. Roll, roll, roll, hitting his head and elbows and knees and ears and nose and various other parts of his body against any number of hard, dirty objects, and then he was past the bus and on his feet, staggering, staring at a lot of goggle-eyed medics hanging around beside their ambulances, who just stood there and gawked back.

Dortmunder turned left. *Medics* weren't going to chase him; their franchise didn't include healthy bodies running down the street. The cops couldn't chase him until they'd moved their buses out of the way. Dortmunder took off like the last of the dodoes, flapping his arms, wishing he knew how to fly.

The out-of-business shoe store, the other terminus of the tunnel, passed on his left. The getaway car they'd parked in front of it was long gone, of course. Dortmunder kept thudding on, on, on.

Three blocks later, a gypsy cab committed a crime by picking him up even though he hadn't phoned the dispatcher first; in the city of New York, only licensed medallion taxis are permitted to pick up customers who hail them on the street. Dortmunder, panting like a Saint Bernard on the lumpy back seat, decided not to turn the guy in.

His faithful companion May came out of the living room when Dortmunder opened the front door of his apartment and stepped into his hall. "*There* you are!" she said. "Thank goodness. It's all over the radio *and* the television."

"I may never leave the house again," Dortmunder told her. "If Andy Kelp ever calls, says he's got this great job, easy, piece of cake, I'll just tell him I've retired."

"Andy's here," May said. "In the living room. You want a beer?"

"Yes," Dortmunder said simply.

May went away to the kitchen and Dortmunder limped into the living room, where Kelp was seated on the sofa holding a can of beer and looking happy. On the coffee table in front of him was a mountain of money.

Dortmunder stared. "What's *that?*"

Kelp grinned and shook his head. "It's been too long since we scored, John," he said. "You don't even recognize the stuff anymore. This is money."

"But—From the vault? How?"

"After you were taken away by those other guys—they were caught, by the way," Kelp interrupted himself, "without loss of life—anyway, I told everybody in the vault there, the way to keep the money safe from the robbers was we'd all carry it out with us. So we did. And then I decided what we should do is put it all in the trunk of my unmarked police car in front of the shoe store, so I could drive it to the precinct for safekeeping while they all went home to rest from their ordeal."

Dortmunder looked at his friend. He said, "You got the hostages to carry the money from the vault."

"And put it in our car," Kelp said. "Yeah, that's what I did."

May came in and handed Dortmunder a beer. He drank deep, and Kelp said, "They're looking for you, of course. Under that other name."

May said, "That's the one thing I don't understand. Diddums?"

"It's Welsh," Dortmunder told her. Then he smiled upon the mountain of money on the coffee table. "It's not a bad name," he decided. "I may keep it."

# THE YEARBOOK OF THE MYSTERY AND SUSPENSE STORY

## THE YEAR'S BEST
## MYSTERY & SUSPENSE NOVELS

Lawrence Block, *Out on the Cutting Edge* (Morrow)

Mary Higgins Clark, *While My Pretty One Sleeps* (Simon and Schuster)

Michael Collins, *Castrato* (Donald I. Fine)

Patricia Daniels Cornwell, *Postmortem* (Scribners)

Len Deighton, *Spy Line* (Knopf)

Michael Dibdin, *Ratking* (Bantam)

E. L. Doctorow, *Billy Bathgate* (Random House)

Umberto Eco, *Foucault's Pendulum* (Harcourt Brace Jovanovich)

Frederick Forsyth, *The Negotiator* (Bantam)

Elizabeth George, *Payment in Blood* (Bantam)

Sue Grafton, *"F" Is for Fugitive* (Henry Holt)

John le Carré, *The Russia House* (Knopf)

Elmore Leonard, *Killshot* (Arbor House/Morrow)

Ed McBain, *Vespers* (Morrow)

Marcia Muller, *The Shape of Dread* (Mysterious Press)

Barbara Paul, *Good King Sauerkraut* (Scribners)

Ruth Rendell, *The Bridesmaid* (Mysterious Press)

Anita Shreve, *Eden Close* (Harcourt Brace Jovanovich)

Martin Cruz Smith, *Polar Star* (Random House)

Thomas Tryon, *The Night of the Moonbow* (Knopf)

# BIBLIOGRAPHY

## *I. Collections*

1. Allingham, Margery. *The Return of Mr. Campion*. London: Hodder & Stoughton. Four uncollected Campion stories plus two author's essays on her character, together with seven other stories, two published for the first time. Edited and introduced by J. E. Morpurgo.
2. Asimov, Isaac. *Puzzles of the Black Widowers*. New York: Doubleday. Nine reprints, mainly from *EQMM,* plus three new stories.
3. Barnard, Robert. *Death of a Salesperson and Other Untimely Exits*. New York: Scribners. Sixteen stories, four previously unpublished.
4. Brown, Fredric. *Whispering Death*. Missoula, MT: Dennis McMillan Publications. Nine stories from the pulps in the 15th volume of this series.
5. Burgess, Anthony. *The Devil's Mode*. New York: Random House. Nine stories, a few criminous, including a Sherlockian tale.
6. Clark, Mary Higgins. *The Anastasia Syndrome and Other Stories*. New York: Simon and Schuster. The title novella, a new suspense fantasy, and four novelettes, mainly from *Woman's Day*.
7. Crumley, James. *Whores*. Missoula, MT: Dennis McMillan Publications. Nine stories, mainly noncriminous, but including an interview about Crumley's crime novels and an excerpt from his crime novel in progress.
8. Dale, Celia. *A Personal Call and Other Stories*. London: Constable. Eighteen stories, one new, five from the *Winter's Crimes* series. some fantasy. (1986)
9. Greco, Frank. *The Investigative Eye of Albert Ward*. Bryn Mawr, PA: Dorrance. Four new stories. (1987)
10. Keating, H. R. F. *Inspector Ghote, His Life and Crimes*. London: Hutchinson. Fourteen stories, 1969–1988, with a long introduction by the author.

11. Lane, Willoughby. *The Exploits of Billy the Page*. New York: Magico. Six stories about a youthful friend of Sherlock Holmes. (1986)

12. Litzinger, Herman Anthony. *Traveling with Sherlock Holmes and Dr. Watson*. Bryn Mawr, PA: Dorrance. Ten new Sherlockian stories. (1988)

13. Marsh, Ngaio. *The Collected Short Fiction of Ngaio Marsh*. New York: International Polygonics. Seven stories, three about Roderick Alleyn, plus two brief essays and a television play. Edited and introduced by Douglas G. Greene.

14. Matsumoto, Seicho. *The Voice and Other Stories*. New York: Kodansha. Six stories and novelettes translated from the Japanese. First published in Japan 1959–1965.

15. McInerny, Ralph. *Four on the Floor*. New York: St. Martin's. Four novelettes, three new and one from *AHMM,* about Father Dowling.

16. Mortimer, John. *Rumpole and the Age of Miracles*. New York: Penguin Books. Seven new stories.

17. Murray, Will. *Spicy Zeppelin Stories*. Chicago, IL: Tattered Pages Press. Six satires on various pulp styles of the 1930s, some criminous.

18. Porges, Arthur. *Three Porges Parodies and a Pastiche*. New York: Magico. Sherlockian parodies about sleuth Stately Homes, together with a Holmes pastiche, edited by Michael Kean. (1988)

19. Powell, Talmage. *Written for Hitchcock*. Nashville, TN: Rutledge Hill Press. Twenty-five stories from *AHMM,* 1958–1981.

20. Ray, Satyajit. *The Adventures of Feluda*. New York: Penguin Books. Four detective novellas by the well-known film director, originally published, 1971–1981, in a magazine for young people in India. (1988)

21. Ritchie, Jack. *Little Boxes of Bewilderment: Suspense Comedies*. New York: St. Martin's. Thirty-one stories from various sources, edited and introduced by Francis M. Nevins, Jr., who also includes a complete Ritchie checklist.

22. Skvorecky, Josef. *Sins for Father Knox*. New York: Norton. Ten connected stories about Lt. Boruvka and singer-sleuth

Eve Adam, each of which breaks one of Father Ronald Knox's ten commandments for mystery writers.

23. Slesar, Henry. *Death on Television: The Best of Henry Slesar's Alfred Hitchcock Stories*. Carbondale, IL: Southern Illinois University Press. Nineteen stories dramatized on Hitchcock's TV series, 1957–1964. Edited by Francis M. Nevins, Jr., & Martin H. Greenberg. Introduction by the author.

24. Westlake, Donald E. *Tomorrow's Crimes*. New York: Mysterious Press. A 1967 novel, *Anarchaos*, and nine fantasy stories, 1961–1984.

25. Yates, Dornford. *The Best of Berry*. London: Dent. Fifteen stories, 1919–1935, about the mainly criminous adventures of Berry & Co., an upper-class British family. Selected and introduced by Jack Adrian.

## II. Anthologies

1. Asimov, Isaac; Martin H. Greenberg & Carol-Lynn Rossel Waugh, eds. *Senior Sleuths*. Boston: G. K. Hall. Fifteen stories of older detectives.

2. Asimov, Isaac; Martin H. Greenberg & Charles G. Waugh, eds. *Tales of the Occult*. Buffalo, NY: Prometheus Books. Twenty-two stories, mainly fantasy but a few criminous.

3. Ayres, Harriet, ed. *Murder and Company*. London: Pandora. Eleven stories by women writers, eight new, including six winners of a British contest.

4. Gorman, Ed & Martin H. Greenberg, eds. *Stalkers*. Arlington Heights, IL: Dark Harvest. Nineteen new horror and mystery stories, some fantasy.

5. Green, Jan, ed. *Reader, I Murdered Him*. New York: St. Martin's. Sixteen stories, all but two new, by women writers.

6. Greenberg, Martin H., ed. *Deadly Doings*. New York: Ivy/Ballantine. Thirteen stories, two new, in the sixth volume of a continuing anthology series. See also #27 below.

7. ———. *Foundation's Friends*. New York: Tor Books. Seventeen new pastiches, mainly science fiction but a few

criminous, in which other authors use the characters and themes of Isaac Asimov's fiction.

8. _____. *The Further Adventures of Batman*. New York: Bantam. Fourteen new stories by mystery and fantasy writers.

9. _____. *The Further Adventures of the Joker*. New York: Bantam. Twenty new stories by mystery and fantasy writers.

10. _____ & Rosalind M. Greenberg, eds. *Phantoms*. New York: DAW Books. Thirteen new stories, some criminous, inspired by *The Phantom of the Opera*. Introduction by Isaac Asimov.

11. Hale, Hilary, ed. *Winter's Crimes 21*. London: Macmillan. Twenty-one new stories by British writers, some previously published in *EQMM*.

12. Harris, Herbert, ed. *John Creasey's Crime Collection 1989*. New York: Gollancz/David & Charles. Fifteen stories, four new, in the annual anthology from Britain's Crime Writers Association.

13. Hoch, Edward D., ed. *The Year's Best Mystery and Suspense Stories 1989*. New York: Walker. Twelve of the best stories from 1988, with annual bibliographic data.

14. _____ & Martin H. Greenberg, eds. *Murder Most Sacred: Great Catholic Tales of Mystery and Suspense*. New York: Dembner Books. Eleven stories from various sources, with a checklist of novels and stories on Catholic themes.

15. Jakubowski, Maxim, ed. *New Crimes*. London: Robinson Publishing. Twenty-one stories, fourteen new, plus an interview with Patricia Highsmith. First of an annual series. U.S. edition: Carroll & Graf.

16. Jordan, Cathleen, ed. *Alfred Hitchcock's Murder & Other Mishaps*. New York: Davis Publications. Twenty-one stories from *AHMM*, 1957–1982.

17. Kaye, Marvin, ed. *Witches & Warlocks: Tales of Black Magic, Old and New*. Garden City, NY: Guild America Books. Forty-one stories, mainly fantasy but a few criminous.

18. Lewis, Jon E. *Red Handed: An Anthology of Radical Crime Stories*. London: Allison & Busby. Ten stories, two new.

19. Lovesey, Peter, ed. *The Black Cabinet: Stories Based on*

*Real Crimes*. New York: Carroll & Graf. Fourteen stories from various sources.

20. MacLeod, Charlotte, ed. *Mistletoe Mysteries*. New York: Mysterious Press. Fifteen new stories with Christmas settings.

21. Mason, Tom, ed. *Spicy Detective Stories*. Newbury Park, CA: Eternity Publishing. Seven stories and a comic strip from the pulp magazine of the same title, 1935–1937.

22. (McCormick, Kenneth D.) *Great American Mystery Stories of the Twentieth Century*. Franklin Center, PA: Franklin Library. Twenty-three stories from various sources. A volume in the Franklin Library of Mystery Masterpieces. No editor given, but the suggestions of Kenneth D. McCormick are acknowledged.

23. McCullough, David Willis, ed. *City Sleuths and Tough Guys*. Boston: Houghton Mifflin. Twenty-nine selections including stories and novelettes, excerpts from novels, an essay by Raymond Chandler, and his screenplay for *Double Indemnity*.

24. Nava, Michael, ed. *Finale*. Boston: Alyson Publications. Eight crime and mystery stories, all but one new, by gay and lesbian writers.

25. Paretsky, Sara, ed. *Beastly Tales*. New York: Wynwood Press. Thirteen reprints and two new stories involving animals, some fantasy, in the annual anthology from Mystery Writers of America.

26. (Pike, B. A.) *Murder Takes a Holiday*. London: Michael O'Mara Books. Sixteen stories about murder in vacation settings. No editor given, but the help of B. A. Pike is acknowledged.

27. Pronzini, Bill & Martin H. Greenberg, eds. *Felonious Assaults*. New York: Ivy/Ballantine. Fourteen stories, one new, in the fifth volume of a continuing anthology series. See also #6 above.

28. _____. *New Frontiers, Volume I*. New York: Tor Books. Sixteen new western stories, two criminous, plus a poem.

29. Randisi, Robert J. & Ruth Ashby, eds. *The Black Moon*. New York: Lynx Books. Five connected novelettes by private eye writers, all new.

30. Roosevelt, Elliot, ed. *Perfect Crimes: My Favorite Mystery Stories*. New York: St. Martin's. Eleven stories, mainly classics.
31. Sellers, Peter, ed. *Cold Blood II*. Oakville, Ontario, Canada: Mosaic Press. Thirteen new stories by Canadian writers.
32. Smith, Marie, ed. *Ms. Murder*. New York: Citadel Press. Seventeen classic and modern stories by women writers, featuring women sleuths.
33. Sullivan, Eleanor, ed. *Ellery Queen's 11 Deadly Sins*. New York: Davis Publications. Twenty-one stories, mainly from EQMM.
34. _____ & Chris Dorbandt, eds. *Murder in New England*. Secaucus, NJ: Castle Books. Nineteen stories, mainly from EQMM.
35. _____. *Tales of Espionage*. Secaucus, NJ: Castle Books. Thirty-one stories from *EQMM*, 1969–1983, in four separate series: Robert Edward Eckels's CIA tales, Brian Garfield's Charlie Dark adventures, and Edward D. Hoch's stories about Rand of Concealed Communications and Sebastian Blue of Interpol.
36. Wallace, Marilyn, ed. *Sisters in Crime*. New York: Berkley. Twenty-two stories, all but three new, by American women writers. First of a planned series.
37. Waugh, Carol-Lynn Rossel; Martin Greenberg & Isaac Asimov, eds. *Purr-fect Crime*. New York, Lynx Books. Fourteen stories involving cats. Introduction by Asimov.
38. Waugh, Charles G.; Frank D. McSherry Jr. & Martin H. Greenberg, eds. *Murder and Mystery in Maine*. New York: Dembner Books. Fourteen stories from various sources.
39. Wolfe, Sebastian, ed. *The Misadventures of Sherlock Holmes*. London: Xanadu. Fourteen parodies and pastiches, one new. No connection with the 1944 Ellery Queen anthology of the same title.
40. Zahava, Irene, ed. *The Second WomanSleuth Anthology*. Freedom, CA: Crossing Press. Twelve new stories by women writers, plus one reprint from *AHMM*.

## III. Nonfiction

1. Barzun, Jacques & Wendell Hertig Taylor. *A Catalogue of Crime*. New York: Harper & Row. A revised and enlarged

edition of the Edgar-winning reader's guide first published in 1971, with critical comments on 5,045 novels, short stories, anthologies, plays, biographies, true crime books, and related items.

2. Benstock, Bernard & Thomas F. Staley, eds. *British Mystery Writers, 1920–1939*. Detroit: Gale Research. Critical-biographical essays, with bibliographies, of forty-five important writers who began their careers during this period. Volume 77 of the *Dictionary of Literary Biography*, following the editor's previous title (volume 70, 1988): *British Mystery Writers, 1860–1919*.

3. Binyon, T. J. *'Murder Will Out': The Detective in Fiction*. Oxford & New York: Oxford University Press. A study of fictional detectives from Poe to the present.

4. Bonn, Thomas L. *Heavy Traffic & High Culture*. Carbondale, IL: Southern Illinois University Press. A history of the paperback publisher, New American Library, during its first seventeen years, 1945–1961. Includes accounts of its dealings with Mickey Spillane and other mystery writers.

5. Breen, Jon L. & Martin Harry Greenberg, eds. *Murder Off the Rack: Critical Studies of Ten Paperback Masters*. Metuchen, NJ: Scarecrow Press. Ten essays by current mystery writers on paperback writers of the past and present.

6. Bruccoli, Matthew J. & Richard Layman, eds. *Hardboiled Mystery Writers*. Detroit: Gale Research. Documents, reviews, and articles about the life and work of Raymond Chandler, Dashiell Hammett, and Ross Macdonald, in volume 6 of the *Dictionary of Literary Biography* Documentary Series.

7. Cooper, John & B. A. Pike. *Detective Fiction: The Collector's Guide*. Somerset, England: Barn Owl Books. Checklists of 105 of the most collected mystery writers, with details of first editions, series characters, uncollected short stories, etc. (U.S. distribution: Spoon River Press, P.O. Box 3676, Peoria, IL 61614)

8. Crowther, Bruce. *Film Noir: Reflections in a Dark Mirror*. New York: Continuum. A study of the film genre popular during the 1940s and 1950s, with numerous illustrations from mystery and suspense films.

9. Dawidziak, Mark. *The Columbo Phile: A Casebook*. New York: Mysterious Press. An illustrated history of the popular TV series, with plot synopses of all forty-five shows aired 1971–1978.

10. Dove, George N. *Suspense in the Formula Story*. Bowling Green, OH: Bowling Green State University Popular Press. Methods of interpreting the mystery-suspense story, with a study of ten popular novels.

11. Geherin, David. *Elmore Leonard*. New York: Continuum. A study of Leonard's novels through 1988, with a biographical chapter and a bibliography.

12. Keating, H. R. F. *The Bedside Companion to Crime*. New York: Mysterious Press. An informal study of various aspects of crime fiction.

13. Lehman, David. *The Perfect Murder: A Study in Detection*. New York: Free Press/Macmillian. The various forms the detective story has taken since Poe.

14. Magill, Frank N., ed. *Critical Survey of Mystery and Detective Fiction*. Pasadena, CA: Salem Press. A four-volume study of 275 authors, containing biographical and bibliographical information, as well as an analysis of their work.

15. Maida, Patricia D. *Mother of Detective Fiction: The Life & Works of Anna Katharine Green*. Bowling Green, OH: Bowling Green State University Popular Press. A survey of Green's novels and stories, with a brief biography and a bibliography.

16. Martin, Richard. *Ink in Her Blood: The Life and Crime Fiction of Margery Allingham*. Ann Arbor, MI: UMI Research Press. A critical biography of Albert Campion's creator. (1988)

17. Meyers, Ric. *Murder on the Air*. New York: Mysterious Press. A survey of fifteen great television mystery series, from *Martin Kane, Private Eye* to *Murder, She Wrote*.

18. OCork, Shannon. *How to Write Mysteries*. Cincinnati: Writer's Digest Books. Tips for the beginning writer.

19. Sherry, Norman. *The Life of Graham Greene. Volume I: 1904–1939*. New York: Viking. Mammoth, detailed biography of the British novelist and suspense writer, showing the influence of his life on his work.

20. Shreffler, Philip A., ed. *Sherlock Holmes By Gas-Lamp: Highlights From the First Four Decades of The Baker Street Journal*. New York: Fordham University Press. Sixty-eight brief Sherlockian essays, 1946–1986.

21. Simon, Reeva S. *The Middle East in Crime Fiction: Mysteries, Spy Novels and Thrillers From 1916 to the 1980s*. New York: Lilian Barber Press. A study of the Middle East as a setting for crime fiction, with an annotated bibliography of some 600 titles.

22. Skenazy, Paul. *James M. Cain*. New York: Continuum. Critical study of Cain's twenty novels, with chapters on his life, screenwriting career, critical reception, etc. Includes chronology, bibliography, and filmography.

23. Skinner, Robert E. *Two Guns From Harlem: The Detective Fiction of Chester Himes*. Bowling Green, OH: Bowling Green State University Popular Press. A survey of Himes's eight Harlem novels about Coffin Ed Johnson and Grave Digger Jones.

24. Spencer, William David. *Mysterium and Mystery: The Clerical Crime Novel*. Ann Arbor, MI: UMI Research Press. A study of novels and short stories featuring rabbis, priests, nuns, monks, ministers, and missionaries as detectives.

25. Strosser, Edward, ed. *The Armchair Detective Book of Lists*. New York: The Armchair Detective. Complete listings of MWA Edgars and other awards given by writers' organizations, plus "best mystery" lists from Ellery Queen, Julian Symons, H. R. F. Keating, Robin W. Winks, and others.

26. Viney, Charles. *Sherlock Holmes in London*. Boston: Houghton Mifflin. A photographic record of London, 1879–1914, with text linking the pictures to Conan Doyle's stories.

27. Webb, Nancy & Jean Francis, eds. *Plots and Pans: Recipes and Antidotes from The Mystery Writers of America*. New York: Wynwood Press. Hundreds of recipes and some brief anecdotes about food from members of MWA.

# AWARDS

## *Mystery Writers of America "Edgar" Awards*

Best Novel: James Lee Burke, *Black Cherry Blues* (Little Brown)
Best First Novel: Susan Wolfe, *The Last Billable Hour* (St. Martin's)
Best Original Paperback: Keith Peterson, *The Rain* (Bantam)
Best Fact Crime: Jack Olsen, *Doc: The Rape of the Town of Lovel* (Atheneum)
Best critical/biographical work: Norman Sherry, *The Life of Graham Greene, Volume I: 1904–1939* (Viking)
Best Young Adult Novel: Alane Ferguson, *Show Me the Evidence* (Bradbury)
Best Short Story: Donald E. Westlake, "Too Many Crooks" (*Playboy,* August)
Best Episode in a TV Series: David J. Burke & Alfonce Ruggiero, Jr., "White Noise" (*Wiseguy,* CBS)
Best Television Feature: John Sayles, "Shannon's Deal" (NBC)
Best Motion Picture: Daniel Waters, *Heathers* (New World)
Best Play: Larry Gelbart, *City of Angels*
Grandmaster: Helen McCloy
Ellery Queen Award: Joel Davis
Special Raven: Carol Brener
Reader of the Year: Sarah Booth Conroy
Robert L. Fish Memorial Award: Connie Holt, "Hawks" (*Alfred Hitchcock's Mystery Magazine,* June)

## *Crime Writers Association* (Britain)

Gold Dagger: Colin Dexter, *The Wench Is Dead* (Macmillan)
Silver Dagger: Desmond Lowden, *Shadow Run* (Deutsch)
Gold Dagger for Nonfiction: Robert Lindsey, *A Gathering of Saints* (Simon and Schuster)
John Creasey Memorial Award for First Novel: Annette Roome, *A Real Shot in the Arm* (Hodder)
Last Laugh Award for Humorous Crime Novel: Mike Ripley, *Angel Touch* (Collins)
Diamond Dagger: Julian Symons

*Ellery Queen's Mystery Magazine Readers Award*

James Powell, "A Dirge for Clowntown" (*EQMM,* November)

*Private Eye Writers of America "Shamus" Awards* (for 1988)

Best Novel: John Lutz, *Kiss* (Henry Holt)
Best First Novel: Gar Haywood, *Fear of the Dark* (St. Martin's)
Best Paperback Novel: Rob Cantnor, *Dirty Work* (Bantam)
Best Short Story: Loren Estleman, "The Crooked Way" (*A Matter of Crime #3*)

*Bouchercon "Anthony" Awards* (for 1988)

Best Novel: Thomas Harris, *The Silence of the Lambs* (St. Martin's)
Best First Novel: Elizabeth George, *A Great Deliverance* (Bantam)
Best Paperback Original: Carolyn Hart, *Something Wicked* (Bantam)
Lifetime Achievement: Dorothy Salisbury Davis
Distinguished Contribution to the Field: Joan Kahn

*Malice Domestic "Agatha" Awards* (for 1988)

Best Novel: Carolyn Hart, *Something Wicked* (Bantam)
Best First Novel: Elizabeth George, *A Great Deliverance* (Bantam)
Best Short Story: Robert Barnard, "More Final Than Divorce" (*EQMM,* October 1988)

*Mystery Readers International "Macavity" Awards* (for 1988)

Best Novel: Tony Hillerman, *A Thief of Time* (Harper & Row)
Best First Novel: Caroline Graham, *The Killing at Badger's Drift* (Adler & Adler)
Best Short Story: Doug Allyn, "Deja Vu" (*AHMM,* June 1988)
Best Nonfiction or Critical Work: Victoria Nichols & Susan Thompson, *Silk Stalkings: When Women Write of Murder* (Black Lizard)

*Crime Writers of Canada "Arthur Ellis" Awards* (for 1988)

Best Novel: Chris Scott, *Jack* (Macmillan of Canada)
Best First Novel: John Brady, *A Stone of the Heart* (Collins)

Best Short Story: Jas. R. Petrin, "Killer in the House" (*AHMM,*
   Mid-December 1988)
Best Nonfiction Work: Mick Lowe, *Conspiracy of Brothers* (Mac-
   millan of Canada)

# NECROLOGY

1. Edward Abbey (1927–1989). Mainstream writer who authored a single crime novel, *The Monkey Wrench Gang* (1975).
2. Dulan Barber (1940–1988). British author and editor of more than thirty books including at least nine crime novels under the pseudonym of "David Fletcher."
3. Raleigh Bond (1935?–1989). Stage and screen actor who published some stories in *EQMM,* beginning in December 1962.
4. John William Corrington (1932–1988). Mainstream novelist who coauthored with his wife Joyce, three New Orleans detective novels starting with *So Small a Carnival* (1986).
5. Ralph Dennis (1931–1989). Author of thirteen paperback novels about an Atlanta detective named Hardman.
6. Daphne du Maurier (1907–1989). Best-selling author of a half-dozen crime novels including the modern classic *Rebecca* (1938), as well as shorter suspense stories such as "The Birds" and "Don't Look Now." Winner of the Grand Master Award from Mystery Writers of America.
7. James M. Fox (1907–1989). Best-known pseudonym of Johannes Matthijs Willem Knipscheer, Dutch-American writer who also published as "Grant Holmes." Author of some twenty-two crime and mystery novels, notably *The Lady Regrets* (1947).
8. Glyn Hardwicke (1921–1989). British solicitor, author of a single crime novel, *Acting on Information Received* (1986).
9. Hans Helmut Kirst (1914–1989). Well-known German writer, more than fifteen of whose novels contain elements of crime and detection, notably *The Night of the Generals* (1963).
10. Lucille C. Lewis (?–1989). Short-story writer.
11. Arnold Marmor (1927?–1988). Short-story writer who authored some paperback mysteries under his own name and

as "Nick Carter." His first hardcover mystery was *The Secret Past* (1985).

12. Mary McCarthy (1912–1989). Famed mainstream writer who published a single crime novel, *Cannibals and Missionaries* (1979).

13. Anne Morice (1918–1989). British author of more than twenty novels about actress sleuth Tessa Crichton Price. Also published nonmysteries as "Felicity Shaw."

14. Frank O'Rourke (1916–1989). Well-known western writer who published seven mystery novels under his own name and one as "Frank O'Malley."

15. Judson Philips (1903–1989). Author, under his own name and as "Hugh Pentecost," of more than one hundred novels and at least 125 short stories featuring numerous series characters. Past president of Mystery Writers of America and winner of its Grand Master Award.

16. Zola Helen Ross (1912?–1989). Historical novelist and juvenile author who published three adult mysteries in the 1940s as Z. H. Ross, and others in the 1950s as "Helen Arre" and "Bert Iles."

17. Dennis Schuetz (1946?–1989). Coauthor with Michael McDowell of four gay detective novels about Boston sleuths Valentine and Lovelace, starting with *Vermilion* (1980), all published under the pseudonym of "Nathan Aldyne." Two nonseries paperback mysteries appeared as by "Axel Young."

18. Georges Simenon (1903–1989). World-renowned Belgian author of several hundred books including 132 suspense novels and some eighty short detective novels about Inspector Jules Maigret. Past president of Mystery Writers of American and winner of its Grand Master Award.

19. William F. Temple (1914–1989). British science fiction writer who authored two crime novels, *The Dangerous Edge* (1951) and *Shoot at the Moon* (1966).

20. Robert Penn Warren (1905–1989). Pulitzer Prize-winning novelist and poet, whose novels *All the King's Men* (1946) and *Meet Me in the Green Glen* (1971) contain strong crime elements.

21. Jonathan Webster (1948?–1989). Short-story writer who published a single story in *EQMM,* August 1989.
22. Harry Whittington (1915–1989). Prolific author of more than 150 suspense and western novels, mainly paperback originals, some under the name of "Whit Harrison."

# HONOR ROLL

Abbreviations:
*AHMM—Alfred Hitchcock's Mystery Magazine*
*EQMM—Ellery Queen's Mystery Magazine*
(*Starred stories are included in this volume. All dates are 1989.*)

Adcock, Thomas, "Shoot Me, I'm Already Dead," *EQMM*, January
*Adrian, Jack, "The Phantom Pistol," *Felonious Assaults*
Allyn, Doug, "The Last Reunion," *EQMM*, June
*_____, "Star Pupil," *EQMM*, October
_____, "Cannibal," *AHMM*, November
Atoda, Takashi, "Napoleon Crazy," *EQMM*, March
Barancik, Steve, "My First Murder," *AHMM*, January
Barnard, Robert, "Post Mortem," *EQMM*, May
_____, "A Business Partnership," *Death of a Salesperson*
Block, Lawrence, "Cleveland in My Dreams," *EQMM*, February
Cail, Carol, "Out of Her Misery," *EQMM*, April
Clark, Mary Higgins, "Death on the Cape," *Woman's Day*, July 18
Crenshaw, Bill, "August Body," *AHMM*, May
de la Torre, Lillian, "The Earl's Nightingale," *EQMM*, May
Doorley, Lawrence, "Not a Pretty Story," *AHMM*, June
*DuBois, Brendan, "Fire Burning Bright," *AHMM*, Winter Double Issue
Edlow, Jonathan A., "Time and Materials," *AHMM*, August
Elkins, Aaron, "Dutch Treat," *Mistletoe Mysteries*
Freitas, J. V., "Duffle Bag," *EQMM*, June
*Fraser, Antonia, "The Moon Was to Blame," *EQMM*, December
Friedman, Mickey, "Stormy Weather," *Sisters in Crime*
Gallagher, Stephen, "The Wishing Ball," *John Creasey's Crime Collection 1989*
Gavrell, Kenneth, "A Better Chess Player," *AHMM*, November
Gilbert, Michael, "The Jackal and the Tiger," *EQMM*, February
Godfrey, Peter, "The Stairs of Sand," *EQMM*, January
*Graviros, Ruth, "Ted Bundy's Father," *EQMM*, November
Grossman, Ellie, ". . . Birthday to You," *AHMM*, March

Halsted, Robert, "The Girl and the Gator," *AHMM,* December

Hansen, Joseph, "Molly's Aim," *EQMM,* June

Healy, Jeramiah, "Bertie's Mom," *EQMM,* September

Hoch, Edward D., "The Circus Murders," *EQMM,* August

———, "The Gypsy Bear," *EQMM,* November

———, "The Problem of the Dying Patient," *EQMM,* December

———, "The Theft of the Christmas Stocking," *EQMM,* Mid-December

———, "The Stalker of Souls," *Stalkers*

*Holt, Connie, "Hawks," *AHMM,* June

Holton, William P., "Sworn Testimony," *Woman's World,* June 6

Howard, Clark, "Crowded Lives," *EQMM,* October

Johnston, Linda O., "The Perfect Plot," *EQMM,* October

Keating, H. R. F., "A Snaking Suspicion," *EQMM,* Mid-December

Lovesey, Peter, "A Case of Butterflies," *EQMM,* December

*———, "The Haunted Crescent," *Mistletoe Mysteries*

McCrumb, Sharyn, "A Wee Doc and Doris," *Mistletoe Mysteries*

Mitchell, Sharon, "Good Neighbors," *AHMM,* June

Monfredo, Mariam Grace, "The Vigil Table," *EQMM,* February

Moyes, Patricia, "The Extra Mile," *EQMM,* March

*Muller, Marcia, "Silent Night," *Mistletoe Mysteries*

Mullins, Terry, "Late Developments," *EQMM,* April

Murray, Millie, "A Blessing in Disguise," *Reader, I Murdered Him*

*Natsuki, Shizuko, "The Love Motel," *EQMM,* July

Obwemayr, Erich, "A Matter of Brazilian Import," *AHMM,* May

Olson, Donald, "A Letter from the North," *EQMM,* July

———, "Deceiving Appearances," *AHMM,* September

———, "Bearing Witness," *EQMM,* December

Parker, Karen, "Summer Notes," *AHMM,* May

*Peters, Elizabeth, "The Locked Tomb Mystery," *Sisters in Crime*

Pickard, Nancy, "Afraid All the Time," *Sisters in Crime*

Powell, James, "A New Leaf," *EQMM,* January

*———, "A Dirge for Clowntown," *EQMM,* November

Pronzini, Bill, "Wooden Indian," *AHMM,* March

Raymond, Hope, "Neighbors," *AHMM,* July

*Rendell, Ruth, "A Pair of Yellow Lilies," *EQMM,* April

———, "The Copper Peacock," *EQMM,* June

Robinson, Peter, "Fan Mail," *Cold Blood II*

Satterthwait, Walter, "Make No Mistake," *AHMM,* June

———, "The Gold of Mayani," *AHMM,* Winter Double Issue

Schofield, Dorothy Hunt, "One Day in August," *EQMM,* April

*Slesar, Henry, "Possession," *EQMM,* April

Staat, Sherri C., "One-Way Streets," *AHMM,* April

Stanesby, Anne, "Non-Custodial Sentence," *Reader, I Murdered Him*

Stevens, B. K., "True Confession," *AHMM,* May

Stodghill, Dick, "A Deceitful Way of Dying," *AHMM,* September

Thomson, June, "A Walk to the Paradise Garden," *EQMM,* Mid-December

Tippee, Bob, "Stuff," *AHMM,* October

Toole, Wyc, "The Chinese Guilt Trip," *AHMM,* February

Walton, Bryce, "Nature of the Beast," *New Frontiers, Volume I*

Wasylyk, Stephen, "Homecoming," *AHMM,* January

———, "Common Ground for Murder," *AHMM,* February

———, "Bargain Getaway," *AHMM,* May

———, "For Loyal Service," *AHMM,* August

———, "The Suit Box," *AHMM,* October

*Westlake, Donald E., "Too Many Crooks," *Playboy,* August

Whitehead, J. W., "The Usual," *EQMM,* April

Woodward, Ann F., "An Inconsiderable Person," *AHMM,* December

If you have enjoyed this book and would like to receive details of other Walker Mystery-Suspense novels, please write for your free catalog:

Walker and Company
720 Fifth Avenue
New York NY 10010